DON'T TRUST HER

ROWEN CHAMBERS

Don't Trust Her

By Rowen Chambers

Published by Waltham Publishing, LLC

Cover Designed by Marisa Black of Cover Me Darling

1

"Schedule the meeting for tomorrow," I say to my assistant, Emma, when she answers my call. "I have a doctor's appointment this afternoon."

"Really?" she says with excitement. "Does that mean—"

"No," I say, cutting her off. "It's with the fertility specialist."

"Oh," she says, sounding disappointed. "Sorry. It's just that you haven't said anything for a while so I thought you might be..." Her voice trails off.

"There's no need to be sorry. I can see why you thought that. Unfortunately, it isn't true."

"Well, I'm sure it'll happen," she says, trying to sound hopeful. "You just need more time."

More time? Drew and I have been trying for almost three years. I've taken supplements and followed special diets. I've meditated to reduce my stress. I've even made manifestation boards covered with photos of babies and cribs and cute little onesies. And I still don't have a baby.

"Will you be back this afternoon?" Emma asks. "Or should I block out your calendar?"

"Block it out. I have some errands to run after my appointment."

I don't, but I'd rather tell her that than admit the truth, which is that I'll be too emotionally drained to go back to the office. Seeing a fertility specialist is a big step for me—one I didn't want to have to take.

I end the call with Emma and go back to eating my lunch. Today it's a kale salad with grilled salmon, walnuts, blueberries, and avocados — all foods that are supposed to boost fertility. I've been eating this way for years, and honestly, I'm sick of it. I'd love a greasy cheeseburger and fries, but I worry that eating even one unhealthy meal will ruin my chances of getting pregnant, especially since I'm 35 now, an age when fertility really starts to decline.

Two women come into the cafe and go up to the counter to order. They're around my age and each holding a baby. Why are they able to have a baby and I can't? It's so unfair.

My phone rings and I see it's the fertility clinic calling. "Hello, this is Sara."

"Hi, Sara. It's Haley, from Dr. Caldwell's office. He isn't feeling well and has to cancel your appointment today. I'm calling to reschedule. Does three weeks from today work?"

"He doesn't have anything sooner?" I ask.

"I'm afraid not, but I can call you if something opens up."

My shoulders slump and I let out a sigh. Maybe I'm being dramatic, but I feel like this cancelled appointment is a sign telling me not to do this.

Something about it doesn't feel right. I felt that way when I made the appointment. I think that means I'm not ready to do it.

"I'm not going to reschedule," I say to Haley as the two women with babies sit at the table next to mine. One of the women notices me staring, and I quickly look away.

"If you wait, it'll be months before you can get in," Haley says.

"I realize that, but I'm, um…" I pause, wondering if I should just make the appointment. I could always cancel it.

"Sara?" Haley says. "Are you still there?"

"Yes, sorry. I'll call you when I'm ready to reschedule."

"Okay," she says like it's no big deal. She has no idea what a huge decision I just made. And I didn't even talk to Drew about it!

How will he react when he finds out? All I've talked about since we got married is wanting a baby. We've tried for years to make it happen. And now I'm just giving up?

But I'm not really giving up. I'm just choosing to delay fertility treatments. We can still keep trying for a baby the traditional way.

"Sorry about that," someone says. "He's in the stage of wanting to throw things."

I look over and see the woman at the table next to mine smiling at me, her baby on her lap.

"Excuse me?" I say, not sure what she's talking about.

"His pacifier." She points to it, and I see it next to

my salad bowl. "He threw it and it landed on your table. I'm really sorry."

"It's fine." I pick it up and hand it to her, my eyes going to her baby. "He's adorable."

"Thank you," she says, bouncing him on her leg as he fusses. "Do you have any?"

I shake my head. "No."

She looks away, like she's lost interest in me now that she knows I'm not a mother. She focuses back on her friend, and the two of them get into a discussion about diaper rash creams.

I'm not done with my salad, but my appetite is gone. I take what's left of my lunch and dispose of it in the trash, then go up to the guy behind the counter.

"Could I get a refill, please?" I say, holding out my cup.

He nods and goes off to get it.

"But you're just going to throw it out," a woman says, coming up beside me. "Why not give it away?"

She's talking to one of the servers, a young man holding a plate with a sandwich on it. She watches him as he goes behind the counter.

"I'm not allowed to give food away," he says, dumping the sandwich in the trash. "It's a health code violation."

The woman looks at me. "Is that true, or is he making it up?"

"Oh, um, I don't know," I say, not wanting to get in the middle of this.

She lets out a frustrated sigh, her head dropping as her hand goes to her stomach. That's when I notice she's pregnant. Very pregnant. She looks like she could have the baby any day now.

"Congratulations," I say, then realize it's never good to say that until you've confirmed the person is actually pregnant, but in this case, it's obvious she's not just carrying extra weight. It's all in front, like a round basketball sticking out of her otherwise small body.

"Thanks," she mutters, rubbing her stomach.

"When are you due?"

"In a few weeks. Middle of February." She looks up at me and I notice her face is dirty. She isn't wearing makeup and her thick blond hair looks like it hasn't been brushed in a while. And the brown tweed coat she's wearing is stained and missing several buttons. Given how she looks, I'm wondering if she might be homeless.

What if she is? Is that why she was asking for the sandwich the server threw away?

"Forgive me if I'm overstepping," I say, "but is there anything I could get you? Maybe something to eat?"

She shrugs and looks away. "Don't worry about it. I'll figure something out."

It's obvious she needs help but is afraid to ask. Or maybe she's embarrassed to.

"No, really." I smile at her. "I'd be happy to buy you lunch. In fact, I do this all the time."

Actually, I don't. I never have, but this poor woman needs to eat.

She crinkles up her nose. "You buy lunch for strangers?"

"Yes, it's part of my commitment to do at least one nice thing a day for someone."

I haven't actually committed to that, but I've thought about it.

"I'm Sara," I say, reaching out to shake her hand.

"Molly," she says, eyeing me with suspicion. "This isn't some kind of scam, is it?"

"Of course not. I simply want to buy you lunch." I motion to the order board hanging on the wall. "Order whatever you'd like."

"Okay." She smiles and her eyes light up. She has beautiful bright blue eyes. She's really pretty and would be even prettier if she cleaned herself up.

The guy behind the counter takes her order. As I pay, Molly takes the metal stand with the order number on it and finds a table. Since my appointment was cancelled, I decide to join her.

Maybe this was fate. Maybe my appointment was cancelled so I'd be led to help this woman. Or it's possible she's a con artist who pretends to be homeless so people will pay for her meals.

But I don't think that's the case. Molly seems like a nice young woman who genuinely needs help. And I think we met so I could be the one to help her.

2

As I WALK over to her table, I notice Molly glancing at the people around us. She looks uncomfortable, like she thinks people are staring at her, judging her for her appearance. Some of them probably are, but they shouldn't. Who knows what this poor girl has been through?

"Mind if I join you?" I ask, sitting across from her.

"Go ahead." She glances at my blouse. "Don't you have to go to work?"

"I took the afternoon off. I had an appointment, but it was cancelled." And I didn't reschedule. How am I going to explain that to Drew? We were on a waiting list for months to get into that fertility clinic, and I just turned down our appointment.

"Where do you work?" Molly asks.

"Just down the street. I write articles for a website. We cover women's health, fashion, career issues." I smile. "We have several good articles about pregnancy."

"It's a little late for that," she says with a laugh.

"Yes, I suppose you're right. So, is this your first?"

She nods. "I wasn't sure I wanted kids." She looks at her stomach. "This wasn't planned."

"Oh," I say, feeling a surge of anger that she got pregnant without even trying while I've been trying for years. But that isn't her fault. And she's younger than me. She has a better chance of conceiving.

"I'm excited about it now," she says, "but I wasn't at first. I even considered giving it up."

"What about the father?" I ask. "Would he have been okay giving the baby up?"

"There isn't a father. I mean, obviously there's a father, but he's not around anymore."

"I'm sorry to hear that. So you're doing this all on your own?"

"You say that like you don't think I can," she says, eyeing me across the table.

"I'm not saying that at all. I was just wondering if you had anyone to help. Like maybe your mother? Or a sister? Some friends?"

She shakes her head. "I don't have sisters. And all my friends ditched me when I couldn't go out with them anymore because I had to take care of my mom."

"So you have your mother to help. That's good. I'm sure she's—"

"My mother's dead," Molly blurts out. "She died about a month ago from cancer. I was taking care of her. I couldn't work because she needed me there all the time."

"I'm very sorry about your mother. I can't imagine having to watch my mother go through something like that."

"Yeah, it was bad. And then after she died, I tried to

get a job but..." She points to her stomach. "They saw this and wouldn't even give me an interview."

"What type of work do you do?"

She shrugs. "Anything. I was doing temp jobs before I quit to take care of my mom. Mostly administrative assistant stuff. Working at offices." She glances behind me. "Over here."

The server stops at our table and drops off the sandwich and chips Molly ordered.

"Thanks for lunch," she says before stuffing the sandwich in her mouth. "This is really good."

The way she's devouring it makes me think she hasn't eaten for a while.

"Do you live around here?" I ask.

She doesn't answer. She either didn't hear me or doesn't want to tell me.

"Molly?" I say as she gulps down some water.

Her eyes dart to the table next to us. An older couple was there, but they left. "You think they're coming back?"

"No. Why do you ask?"

She reaches over to the table, grabs a half-eaten brownie, and sets it on her plate.

"Molly, don't eat that!" I say, sounding like my mother. "It could be contaminated."

"With what? Those people didn't look sick."

"It doesn't matter." I snatch the brownie from her plate and wrap it in a napkin. "If you want a brownie, I'll order you one."

"Just give me that one," she says. "That lady barely touched it."

"Yes, but you're pregnant. You can't risk harming

your child with whatever germs that woman might've had."

Molly rolls her eyes. "It's not going to hurt the baby. Believe me, I've eaten way worse things and nothing's happened."

"What do you mean? What have you eaten?"

She sighs and sets down her sandwich. "If I tell you this, I don't want you feeling sorry for me. It's only temporary. Until I can figure something out."

"What is it?" I ask, but I'm guessing it's what I already assumed.

"I'm kind of..." She leans toward me and lowers her voice. "Without a place to live. I tried the women's shelter, but they didn't have any room."

"But you're pregnant," I say, shocked that a shelter would turn away a woman about to give birth. "Couldn't they make an exception?"

She stuffs the rest of her sandwich in her mouth, not answering me.

"Where does that leave you?" I ask. "Please don't tell me you're living in an alley somewhere."

She grabs her napkin and wipes her hands. "I've been staying in the park. I feel safer there than on the streets."

This woman is nine months pregnant and she's sleeping outside on the ground? In the middle of winter? My heart breaks when I think about that. It's absolutely horrible. Why hasn't anyone helped her?

"How long have you been doing this?" I ask.

"Only a few weeks. I got evicted from my mom's apartment when I couldn't keep paying rent."

"I can't believe they evicted you in your condition." I huff. "People have no decency these days."

"To be fair, I hadn't paid rent in three months. My mom didn't have any money, and I wasn't working." She gulps down the rest of her water, then slides her chair back. She grabs the table for support as she pushes up to standing. "I should get going, but thanks again for lunch."

"Molly, wait!" I say as she starts to leave.

She turns back. "Yeah?"

I shouldn't do this, not without talking to Drew. But I can't let this poor woman go back to living in the park. It isn't safe, and it definitely isn't sanitary. And it's winter. She could freeze to death!

I need to help her, at least until I can find her a safe place to live. There has to be a shelter that would take her. Until then, she can stay with us.

Drew won't like it. He doesn't even like it when our relatives stay with us. But once I explain Molly's situation, I'm sure he'll be okay with it. He's a compassionate man. He wouldn't want this woman living outside in the cold.

"Were you going to say something?" Molly asks, and I realize I've been too busy contemplating this in my head to answer her.

I get up and go over to her. "I'd like you to stay with me. I live a few blocks from here. It's an apartment, but it's very large and has a spare bedroom that's not being used."

"Sara, no," Molly says, shaking her head. "I couldn't do that. You don't even know me."

"Are you saying I should be concerned?" I say it jokingly. I'm sure she's harmless, and yet there's something about her that's making me a little uneasy. But I often feel that way around homeless people, which

I know is wrong. It's not like Molly chose this. She was forced to live this way, and the only way she'll get back on her feet is if someone helps her.

"Don't worry. I'm harmless," Molly says with a smile, but it's not the same smile I saw before. It looks more like a smirk.

I'm sure I'm misinterpreting it. I'm nervous about doing this, so I'm seeing things to make me doubt my decision. But I know it's the right one. I'm sure of it.

"Are you okay to walk a few blocks?" I ask Molly. "If not, I could—"

"I can walk," she says as we make our way to the door. "I just can't go very fast."

"I'll let you set the pace." We go out to the sidewalk. "Do you have anything you need to go get? Some clothes or personal items?"

"I have some bags of clothes at the park. I hid them behind a bush so people wouldn't steal them."

"We can go get them later."

"We don't have to," she says. "Most of them don't fit anymore now that I'm huge."

"You're not huge," I say, smiling at her. "If I saw you from the back, I wouldn't even know you're pregnant."

"Hey, um…don't you need to ask your husband about this?"

I look at her. "How do you know I'm married?"

"Your ring." She points to it. "I noticed it when we were at the table."

"Oh, yes, I've been married for several years now. It's just my husband and me. We don't have any children."

"Don't you want to ask him about this? What if he says no?"

"He won't say no. Drew's a very kind man. He would never turn away someone who needs help."

I don't actually know that. In all the years we've been together, Drew's never helped anyone or volunteered for anything. But that doesn't mean he wouldn't. This is our opportunity to give back, to do something good for someone in need.

I still have reservations about this, but it's the right thing to do. That's the one thing I'm sure of.

3

"THE GUEST ROOM is down the hall on the right," I say as I lead Molly into the apartment. "Before we head down there, can I get you anything to drink?"

"No, thanks." She slowly turns around, taking in the large open room. "This place is really nice. What do you guys pay for rent?"

"More than we should," I say with a laugh, dodging her question. I'm not someone who openly shares information about my finances.

Drew's the reason we're able to afford this luxurious apartment in the heart of downtown Boston. As a partner at a large regional accounting firm, Drew makes more than enough to cover our expenses. It's nice not having to worry about money, but I wish he didn't work so much. His job is very demanding. He stays late most nights and sometimes goes into the office on weekends.

"I've always wanted a fireplace," Molly says, walking over to it. "Do you use it much?"

"Yes, especially this time of year. Let me show you to your room."

She follows me down the hall to the room directly across from the one Drew and I share. Drew will say he's not comfortable having a stranger sleeping in our guest room, but he'll have to get over it. It's only temporary, and he works so much he won't be here to see her.

"What do you think?" I ask as Molly and I go into the guest room.

"It's great!" She smiles. "Way better than a park bench."

"That's where you were sleeping? On a bench?" I can't imagine how painful it would be to sleep on a hard bench, especially when you're pregnant. Her back must be killing her.

"It was warmer than sleeping on the ground, especially when it snowed."

"And you've been doing this for how long?"

"A few weeks."

How could a shelter turn this woman away? Certainly, they could've made room for her or found her an alternate place to go.

Molly walks over to the window. "You have a great view of the city from here. Is that why you got this place? Because of the view?"

"It was more about it being close to our offices. I'm close enough that I can walk to work when the weather's nice. Drew's office is a few miles away, but it's a much shorter commute than if we lived in the suburbs. But we plan to move there once we have—" I stop and clear my throat.

"Have what?" Molly walks back to me.

"Nothing." I clear my throat again. "Never mind."

"Did you mean kids? Are you guys trying to have a baby?"

"Yes, but we haven't been successful, at least not yet. Anyway, let me show you the bathroom." I hurry over to it, wanting to get off the topic of my fertility struggles.

"You have a bathtub," Molly says with a dreamy sigh. "I've missed taking baths."

"Go ahead and take one. Or take a shower if you'd like. It's stocked with soap and shampoo, but if you'd like something different, I have more to choose from." I open the linen closet and show her the collection of products I've neatly organized in shallow bamboo boxes, an idea I got from a professional organizer I interviewed for an article I wrote last year.

"Wow, it's like being at a hotel," Molly says, gazing at all the products. "It's so nice of you to do this, Sara." Her gaze moves back to me. "I can't tell you how much I appreciate it." She puts her hand over her belly. "This little guy does too."

"You're having a boy?" I ask, imagining the sweet little infant she'll soon hold in her arms. My heart aches, knowing I may never have that.

"Yeah, and he never stops kicking." She laughs. "I think he's going to be a soccer player. You want to feel it?" Before I can answer, she takes my hand and puts it over her belly.

"It's very strong." I pull my hand away, wishing she hadn't done that. I'm trying to keep my emotions out of this, but having her here is going to be extremely difficult for me. Every time I see her hand go to her belly, I think about what that would be like. How it would feel if it were me.

"Are you okay?" Molly asks with concern.

"I'm fine. Why do you ask?"

"You seem upset. Was it something I said?"

I force out a smile. "Of course not. I'm just tired. I didn't sleep well last night."

"Speaking of sleep, would you mind if I took a nap?"

"I think that's a wonderful idea. I'll be in the living room if you need me."

I leave the guest room and hear the shower running. I should give her some clothes. She can't put the ones she was wearing back on. They're filthy.

Going into my room, I head to the closet and look through my things. Nothing I own would fit her, given that she's pregnant and several inches shorter than me. I go to Drew's side of the closet and grab one of his T-shirts, then I go to our dresser and find a pair of elastic-waisted shorts. I got them for Drew to wear to the gym, but he never did. I don't think he's ever worn them.

"Molly?" I knock on the guest room door, then notice the shower's still running. I'll just leave the clothes on the bed so she'll see them when she gets out of the bathroom.

I open the door and go into the room, stopping when I hear Molly talking. Who is she talking to? Is she on the phone? Does she even have a phone? I don't know how she could if she doesn't even have money for food.

Molly starts laughing. Why is she laughing? What's so funny? I hope she's not laughing at me or something I did. I'm sure that's not it. She's probably just remembering something she found humorous.

I'm about to leave when I notice the laughter stop and hear Molly talking again. "I told you so. I was right. I told you." She pauses. "I won't do that. I promise." She pauses. "Yes. Always. I promise."

Who is she talking to? Herself? If so, she's not making any sense.

I wonder if Molly has mental health issues. She seemed perfectly fine at the cafe, but we were only there for a short time, and she spent most of that time eating.

Maybe this was a mistake. I brought a stranger into my home who could have issues I don't know about. What if she's dangerous?

"I know, baby," I hear her say. "Don't you worry. It's all going to be okay. I promise."

She's talking to the baby. That must've been who she was talking to before. It had to be. What she said still didn't make sense, but it's possible I only heard part of it with the shower running.

The water shuts off and I hurry out of the room and close the door. I hear my phone ringing and realize I left it in the kitchen. By the time I get to it, it's gone to voicemail. It was Drew calling, but he didn't leave a message.

A text pops up that reads, *I'm heading to the appointment. I got caught up in a meeting so I'll be a few minutes late.*

The appointment! I forgot to tell Drew it was cancelled.

Our appointment was cancelled, I text Drew. *You can go back to the office.*

My phone rings. It's Drew calling.

"Hey, honey," I answer. "Sorry, I should've told you sooner about the appointment."

"It's fine. I'd just left the office when I got your message. Did they reschedule?"

"Let's talk when you get home," I say. This is not something I want to discuss over the phone.

"Why?" Drew says in a suspicious tone, like he knows something's up. "What happened?"

"Nothing. I'm just in the middle of something and need to go. We'll talk tonight. You'll be home for dinner, right?"

"Sara," Molly says, much louder than necessary given that she's walking straight toward me. She's wrapped in a towel, with another one around her head. "Sorry," she whispers. "I didn't know you were on the phone."

"Who was that?" Drew asks.

This is definitely something I need to tell him in person.

"It's the TV," I say. "I'll turn down the volume."

"You're at home?" Drew asks.

"Yes, I decided to take the afternoon off and get some things done."

"What's going on with you?" Drew asks. "You're acting strange."

I nervously laugh. "I'm not acting strange. I'm just busy and don't have time to talk. I'll see you tonight."

"Yeah, okay. I should be home around six."

He *should* be, but most nights it's closer to seven before he walks in the door. It's something we often argue about, especially when I take the time to make dinner and then end up eating it by myself. But tonight, I'm actually hoping Drew is late. The longer I can put off telling him my news, the better.

4

"DID YOU NEED SOMETHING?" I say, walking over to Molly.

"I was wondering if you had any antacids. I have really bad heartburn."

"Yes, I'll go get you some." I go to my bathroom, get the antacids, and return to the living room.

Molly is standing behind the couch, running her hand along the back of it and smiling to herself. I find it odd, but maybe she's just thinking of something that made her smile.

"Here you go," I say, handing her the bottle of antacids.

She shakes a few out and pops them in her mouth.

"Are you sure you should take that many?" I ask.

She shrugs. "The baby's pretty much grown. Anything I do now isn't going to hurt him."

That isn't actually true, but I'm not going to tell her that. I have a feeling she wouldn't listen if I did.

"Did you see the clothes I left out?" I say.

"Those were for me? They look like men's clothes."

"They are. They belong to my husband. I couldn't find anything of mine that would fit you."

She laughs. "You mean because I'm so fat?"

"No, of course not. I meant that I'm taller than you and—"

"I was just joking. Are you sure your husband won't mind me wearing his clothes?"

"What I gave you he never wears, and it's only for today. We can go out tomorrow and get you some new things."

"Sara, I couldn't let you do that."

"I want to. You can't keep wearing the clothes you had on. They're worn out and stained. And you definitely need a new coat. A warmer one. We'll go out tomorrow and find you a few basic items to get you through the next few weeks until you have the baby."

"Don't you have to work tomorrow?"

Tomorrow's Wednesday, and I told Emma to schedule a meeting in the morning. If I go to the office, Molly will be here by herself. Can I trust her? What if she steals all our valuables and takes off? I shouldn't think the worst of her, but part of me wonders if I got scammed. Molly seems genuine, but an experienced scam artist can make themselves appear like a good, honest person.

"I'll go get dressed," Molly says, heading to her room.

I sit on the couch, my chest tightening up as I wonder if I've made a terrible mistake. Am I really going to let a stranger be alone in my apartment all day? A woman who's desperate for money and might have mental health issues?

Molly appears again, dressed in Drew's T-shirt and

shorts. They fit her around the middle but are far too long. The shirt goes past her knees and the shorts nearly reach her ankles.

"What do you think?" She spins around. "Just like a runway model, right?"

I smile. "I'm sorry I didn't have anything better. Maybe we should go out now and get you something."

"I'm fine with this," she says, joining me on the couch. "I'm just happy to have clean clothes again. I've been wearing those old ones for weeks."

"Didn't you say you had clothes at the park?"

"Yeah, but most of them didn't fit so I kept wearing the same ones."

It's awful she's been living that way. How could she be there for weeks and nobody offered to help her?

"I really like your place," she says, glancing around the room. "It's upscale but still feels cozy."

"Thank you," I say. "I'm not much of a decorator. I get most of my ideas from articles online."

Molly puts her feet up on the coffee table. "If you want to go out and do something, you can. You don't have to stay here and entertain me."

"There's nothing I need to do," I tell her, even though I can think of at least ten errands I need to run. But I don't feel comfortable leaving her here unsupervised.

She yawns and rubs her eyes.

"You look tired," I tell her. "Why don't you go rest?"

"I tried, but I couldn't sleep." She takes her feet off the coffee table and turns to me. "So what did your husband say? When you told him I'm here?"

"I didn't tell him. I thought it would be best to wait until he gets home."

"Why? Do you think he'll be mad?"

"No, but he'll be surprised. I've never done anything like this, and Drew doesn't like having guests. He doesn't even like it when his parents stay here."

"Then maybe I should leave before he gets home."

"You're not leaving. Drew will be fine. He'll just need to get used to the idea."

"Are you sure? I don't want to cause problems between the two of you." She looks at me with concern, like she truly is worried her stay will cause Drew and me to fight.

"It won't be a problem," I say. "But I do have a favor to ask."

"Sure. What do you need?"

"I'd like you to wait in your room when Drew gets home. I want to talk to him before I introduce you to him."

"I can do that. Or I could just stay in my room all night and leave you guys alone."

"No, I want you to meet him. I just need to talk to him before you do."

"What's he like?"

"My husband? He's very smart. And serious, although he loosens up after a few drinks." I smile. "That's how we met. I went to a bar after work and Drew was there with some friends. He'd had too much to drink, which I'm convinced is the only reason he came over to talk to me. That's not something he would do if he were sober. He disagrees, but I can't imagine him having the courage to do it if he hadn't been drinking. Anyway, he asked me to have dinner with him and here we are, married for five years."

"So your husband is one of those shy, quiet guys."

"I suppose you could say that, although he's not shy at work. He can't be. Part of his job is bringing in new clients."

"What does he do?"

"He's a partner at an accounting firm." I realize I'm telling her a lot about myself and finding out nothing about her. I need to redirect the conversation. "Tell me about you. Are you originally from Boston?"

"Yeah, but I took off after high school and followed this guy to New York. We broke up after a year, and I ended up in Connecticut working as a nanny."

"So you have experience with children," I say. "That will come in handy. How old were they?"

"Oh, um..." She looks up at the ceiling. "One was like six and the other was three."

She doesn't seem very certain of their ages. Maybe it was a while ago and she's having trouble remembering, although it couldn't have been that long. She's not very old.

"Do you mind if I ask your age?" I say. "I don't mean to be nosy. It's just that you look much younger than you probably are."

She tilts her head to the side. "How old do you think I am?"

"Twenty-five?"

"Close. I'm twenty-six. What about you? I'd guess thirty."

I smile. "That's very flattering. I'm actually thirty-five. I'll be thirty-six next month."

"What about your husband? Are you two the same age?"

"He's ten years older than me. He was well-established in his career when we met, which I found appealing. I didn't want a man who was still trying to prove himself and making work his top priority." And yet Drew's job takes priority over everything else, even though he's the boss and doesn't need to work so hard. He keeps saying he'll spend more time with me, but it never happens. "So how long were you a nanny?"

"About a year. I moved around after that, took whatever job I could get, and then my mom got sick and I came home to take care of her."

"I'm very sorry about your mother. It must've been so hard to watch her go through all that and then lose her."

"Yeah, it was tough." Molly runs her hand over her stomach. "But now I have this little guy. I just wish my mom had lived long enough to meet him."

"You don't have anyone else? No other family?"

"I have an uncle and some cousins, but we're not close. They live in Arizona. I only met them once and it was when I was really young. I don't even remember them."

The poor woman has no family. No friends. She has no support system to help her raise this child, yet she doesn't seem concerned. I'd be feeling overwhelmed if I were her.

"And the baby's father," I say. "You said he took off?"

"Basically, yeah."

"Does he know about the baby?"

"No. It wasn't like we were dating. It was more of a... I don't know how you'd describe it. Let's just say we didn't spend our time getting to know each other."

I'm assuming she means the relationship was only physical, but she could still tell him about the baby. He's the father. He needs to offer her support, even if it's just financial.

"This man should be paying child support," I say. "You need to tell him about the baby so he knows he's responsible for helping you with the expenses."

"Yeah, I don't see that happening."

"Why is that?"

She looks at me. "He doesn't want his wife finding out."

"This man is married?" I ask, furious with a man I don't even know. He cheated on his wife and got another woman pregnant? And then he just gets to continue on without any consequences? Molly's been sleeping on a park bench while this man has been going home to a warm bed every night. With his wife!

"I didn't know it at first," Molly says. "I found out later, after his wife called when we were together. I only saw him a few more times after that."

"Molly, you can't let him get away with this. You have to tell him about the baby, and you need to demand he help pay for the child's expenses. If he won't, you'll need to get a lawyer involved."

"Yeah, like I have money to hire a lawyer," she says, rolling her eyes.

"Maybe you wouldn't need one. Maybe if you told this man about the baby, he'd do the right thing without having to involve the legal system."

"He wouldn't. I told you, he doesn't want his wife finding out."

"It doesn't matter what he wants," I say, my anger building. "There's a child involved. This man needs to step up and take responsibility for what's happened."

Molly faces forward and rests her feet on the coffee table. "What would *you* do?"

"I'd find this man and—"

"No. If you were the wife. Would you want him to pay for his kid? Even if it wasn't yours?"

"Of course! It's not the child's fault this happened."

Molly glances at me. "Let's talk about something else. I can see I'm upsetting you."

"It's not you. It's the situation."

"It is what it is." She looks down at her belly. "I don't want to talk about it anymore."

She needs to deal with this. She needs to tell this man he's going to be a father. He may not want to be involved in the child's life, but he should at least help Molly with the expenses. I realize it could harm his marriage, but he should've considered that before having an affair.

Why did Molly get involved with him? She said she didn't know he was married at first, but once she found out, why did she keep seeing him? She's an attractive young woman. She could've easily found someone else. I still have compassion for her and for her situation, but I think less of her knowing she continued sleeping with this man after finding out he was married.

I wouldn't have thought she would do something like that, which just shows how little I know about the woman now living in my home.

5

"Sara?" Drew calls out as he comes into the apartment just after six. "Where are you?"

I race down the hall to the living room. "Hi, honey. I was just putting some clothes away in the bedroom."

He comes up to me and gives me a kiss. "I'm right on time tonight. Aren't you proud of me?"

Why should I be proud of him for that? He should be home when he says he will, without needing special recognition for doing so. As I'm thinking that, I realize I'm taking my anger at that man out on Drew. It's been hours since Molly told me about the father of her child, and I'm still upset. But that's not an excuse to be harsh to my husband.

"I've got some good news to share." Drew smiles and brings me into his arms.

"I can't wait to hear about it. But first, I have to tell you something."

"I'd really like to go first, if you don't mind."

My stomach's been in knots waiting for him to get

home so I could tell him what happened today. I'd rather not wait, but I'm not going to argue with him about it.

"Go ahead," I say.

"You know that new client I was trying to get? The owner of that large hotel chain?"

"Yes," I say, wanting him to hurry up.

"He called today and said he's going to sign with us. And since I'm the one who brought him in, I'll be getting a huge bonus!"

"That's wonderful. Congratulations."

Drew pulls back, looking at me with concern. "What's wrong? Why aren't you more excited about this?"

"Sorry, I just have a lot on my mind." I smile. "I'm happy for you, honey. It's great you got a new client."

"I've been thinking about what to do with the money," he says with excitement, "and I've decided to get a new car. I was looking online today and saw a few options I want to test drive."

It's great he's getting a bonus, but I'm a little annoyed he's made a plan for the money without even checking with me. He already has a nice car, and it's only a year old.

"What about a house?" I say. "We could add this bonus money to the money we've already saved and—"

"I don't want to use it for the house. I want to use it for something fun. Something I really want, like a shiny red sports car." His face lights up as if he's already imagining himself driving it.

"Could we go sit down?" I say, my pulse racing as I prepare to tell him my news. I shouldn't be nervous about this. He's my husband. I should be able to tell him anything and not worry about his reaction. "I need to talk to you."

"Let me get a drink first," he says. "It's been a long day."

I watch as he goes to the kitchen and pours himself some whiskey. He swigs it, then refills the glass.

"Honey, would you please come join me?" I say, sitting on the couch.

"What is it?" He swirls the whiskey around in his glass. "Just tell me."

His mood has changed drastically from when he walked in the door. He seems annoyed with me, maybe even a little angry. Is it because I didn't go along with his decision to get a sports car? He couldn't possibly think I'd be excited about that. He knows I want a house. We both do, and this money could help us buy one now instead of having to wait. But it sounds like he's already decided he's getting the car.

"I'd really like you to come over here," I say. "I don't want to have to yell across the room."

He takes another drink, then walks over to the couch, setting his glass on the table as he sits down. "What is it? What do you need to tell me?"

"Two things. First, I decided not to reschedule our appointment at the clinic." I wait for him to say something, but he doesn't, so I continue. "I know I was the one pushing to do fertility treatments, but when they tried to reschedule the appointment, I couldn't do it. I don't know why. I think maybe I need a break from trying to have a baby. I think we both do."

He nods. "I agree."

"You do?" I say, shocked, because that was not the

reaction I was expecting. I thought he'd be upset, or at least surprised.

"It was getting to be too much," he says, leaning back on the couch. "Our entire lives were about having a baby, and honestly, I was tired of it."

"Are you saying you no longer want a baby?" I ask, my heart breaking at the thought of that.

"I'm saying we need to stop focusing on it. It was hurting our marriage. Neither of us wanted to say it, but you know it's true."

Hurting our marriage? He really thought that? And he's just telling me this now?

"I didn't know you felt that way," I say, my eyes going to his. "I thought it was bringing us closer. I know it's been difficult, but it's the difficult times that make a relationship stronger. If you felt it was harming our marriage, why didn't you tell me before now?"

"Because I was trying to be supportive, but come on, Sara, you really think I wasn't sick of it? It's all we talked about."

"If you didn't want us to keep trying," I say in a harsh tone, "you should've told me."

"Honey, don't be mad at me. I'm on your side. I think it's good you quit."

"I didn't quit. I'm just taking a break."

"And I support you in that." He puts his arm around me. "We should go out and do something tonight. Did you already make dinner?"

"Yes, it's in the oven."

"Then we'll go out after dinner. There's a band playing at the bar down the street. We could go get a drink. Listen to some music."

I look down, my pulse going faster. "We can't tonight. Maybe some other time."

"Why not tonight?"

I pull away from him and move down a little on the couch, turning to face him. "Drew, I need to tell you something."

"I thought you already did."

"This is something else." I pause. "Something you might be upset about, but keep in mind, it's only temporary."

Drew angles his body toward me, his arm extending along the back of the couch. "I'm listening."

I sit up straighter and take a breath. "I was having lunch at the cafe and I, um... I ran into someone."

"Who was it?"

"You don't know her. I didn't either until today. I noticed her at the counter and asked her to join me for lunch."

That's not exactly what happened, but it's close enough.

Drew's brows rise. "You asked a stranger to join you for lunch?"

"Yes, and I bought her a sandwich. It was obvious she didn't have the money to buy herself a meal. I overheard her asking the server if she could have the food he was about to throw out. He wouldn't let her have it, and I couldn't let this poor young woman go hungry, so I offered to buy her a meal."

"And you thought I'd be upset? Because you bought this woman lunch? Honey, I think it's great that you did that. I probably would've done the same thing."

I smile, feeling more relaxed as I realize how silly it

was for me to worry about Drew's reaction to this. He's a kind and compassionate man. If he'd seen Molly begging that server for food, he would've bought her a meal just like I did. He wouldn't have invited her to live with us, but once he meets her and sees the condition she's in, I can't imagine he'd tell her to leave.

"Was that it?" he says, reaching over to get his glass. "Was that what you wanted to tell me?"

"No. There's more."

He swigs what's left of his whiskey and sets the glass down. "Go ahead."

"While she was having lunch, we were talking and I found out she got evicted from her apartment a few weeks ago and has been living in the park."

"Why didn't she go to a shelter?"

"She did, but they didn't have room for her." I turn to Drew and grip his hand. "Honey, I couldn't just let her leave, knowing she had nowhere to go. She can't be sleeping outside in the cold. And she's all alone. Her mother recently died, and she has no one else. No family. No friends."

"Sara, what did you do? Just tell me."

He already knows. I can tell by the look he's giving me, but he doesn't seem mad, so that's good.

"I invited her to stay with us," I say, rushing the words out. "But it's only temporary. I know you don't like having guests, but I wouldn't be able to sleep at night if I'd let her go back to living on the streets. Do you know how dangerous that is for a woman?"

A sound comes from down the hall, and Drew whips his head that way. "Is that her? Is she here right now?"

"Yes." I squeeze Drew's hand. "Honey, please be

okay with this. I really want to help this woman. She has no money. No place to live. And the clothes she was wearing were filthy. I think she'd been wearing them for days, maybe a week."

Drew lets out a sigh. "How long? Are we talking a night? Two nights? How long would she be staying with us?"

"I don't know. I haven't gotten that far. This all happened so fast, I haven't thought about what to do next. I might need to take tomorrow off from work. I'm not sure I want her being here alone."

"Why?" Drew says, his brows drawing together. "Do you think she'd steal from us?"

"No, of course not. But I'd like to get to know her better before she's here all day by herself."

Drew shakes his head. "Sara, I don't know about this. I know you want to help her, but there's got to be another way. Did you try calling some other shelters?"

"I haven't had time, but she said the one she went to told her all the places in town are full. Would you at least meet her before you make a decision?"

"Fine," he groans.

I jump up from the couch. "I'll go get her."

When I go to her room, I find Molly resting on the bed.

"You can come out now," I say. "He knows about you and wants to meet you."

"Is he mad?" she asks, pushing herself up from the bed.

"No, but he hasn't officially agreed to let you stay here." I give her a reassuring smile. "I'm sure he will once he gets to know you."

We go down the hall to the living room with me

leading the way. I stop next to the couch. Drew's looking at his phone.

"Honey," I say, getting his attention. "I want to introduce you to our guest."

He sets his phone down and stands up.

I move aside. "Drew, this is Molly. And Molly, this is my husband—"

"Andy?" Molly says.

Drew stares at her, the color draining from his face. He doesn't say hi or shake her hand. He just stands there, like he's frozen in place.

What's going on with him? And why did Molly call him Andy?

I move over next to Drew, nudging him. "Honey, say something."

"I should go," Molly says, her voice quivering. "Sara, I'm so sorry."

"Sorry?" I ask, confused. "About what?"

Drew finally speaks, his eyes still locked on Molly. "What are you doing here?"

"I just told you why she's here," I say. "She had nowhere to—"

"That's not what he means," Molly says, tearing up. "I'm sorry, Sara. I had no idea."

"What are you talking about?" My eyes bounce between Drew and Molly. "No idea about what?"

"Are you going to tell her?" Molly asks Drew.

"Tell me what?" I say, my chest tightening. I don't know what's going on here, but it's making me very nervous. One of them needs to hurry up and explain what's happening.

"The man I told you about," Molly says. "The one who took off?"

"Don't," Drew growls, glaring at Molly.

"Don't what?" I look at Drew, then back at Molly. "Would one of you tell me what's going on?"

"The guy I told you about." Molly raises her arm and points at Drew. "It's him."

6

"You're obviously confused," I say to Molly, thinking she's making some kind of joke, although I don't know why she'd think that's funny. "Perhaps he looks like that man, but—"

"No, it's him," Molly says, her eyes still on my husband. "He's the guy I met at the bar. Tell her, Andy."

I turn to Drew, my heart pounding. "Drew, say something. Tell her she's wrong."

"I can't," he mutters.

"What do you mean you can't?" I say, my stomach knotting up. "You've never even met this woman." I pause. "Have you?"

He lets out a heavy sigh. "It was a long time ago, and it didn't mean anything."

"Wait—what?" I rear back. "What are you saying? That you and her..." I can't even finish that sentence. I'm sickened to even think it might be true.

Drew had an affair? With Molly? And now she's pregnant? Drew's the married man Molly was telling me about? The father of her child?

My mind is racing as I try to comprehend how this is even possible. I have so many questions, but the biggest one is why I didn't know about this. How could I see Drew every day and not even suspect he might be having an affair?

"I'll get out of here," Molly says, turning away.

"Molly, no," I say. "Wait in the guest room. I need to talk to Drew."

She nods, then hurries down the hall.

Drew turns to me. "Sara, I can explain."

"Explain what? Why you cheated on me? Why you lied to me for months? Why you let your pregnant girlfriend live on the streets?"

"She is not my girlfriend," he snaps. "And I didn't know she was pregnant until just now. I haven't seen her in months!"

"Is that another one of your lies?" I scoff. "Because I really can't tell." I walk away from him, then turn back. "I thought I knew you, but I clearly have no idea who I'm married to. I never in a million years thought you would do something like this!"

When I say it, I realize how naïve I sound. Drew's a very handsome man, and he's always staying late at the office. I should've been at least a little suspicious he might be having an affair.

"Sara, I—"

"When did it start?" I say, interrupting him. "When did you meet her?"

He hesitates, then says, "It was last year. In the spring. I stopped at a bar after work. The one in that hotel near my office. She sat next to me, and we started talking. We'd both had too much to drink and... we ended up getting a room."

Last spring, when this apparently happened, I was really depressed, thinking I'd never be a mother. I had no energy and would often go to bed soon after I got home from work. Drew would stay up and watch TV, or sometimes he'd go back to the office. That's what he told me, but was he really with her?

"How long did it go on?" I ask.

"It only happened a few times," he says, running his hand through his hair. "I saw her for maybe a week or two? I don't know. I can't remember."

"How could you not remember how long you had an affair?" I shout, furious that he's still lying to me.

"Because I've been trying to forget it!" he yells, tossing his hands up. "You really think I want to remember this? It was a mistake, Sara! A stupid mistake that never should've happened!"

"But it did," I say, glaring at him. "And now she's pregnant! She's having your child, Drew!"

"We don't know that it's mine. Who knows how many guys she was with? She was ready to get a room five minutes after meeting me. You really think someone like that wasn't with other men?"

"When did this happen?" I demand. "What month? And don't say you don't remember!"

He pauses. "It was last May."

May. And she's due in February, a few weeks from now. The timing works out, but that doesn't mean Drew is the father. Like he said, it's possible she'd been with other men, although Molly didn't make it sound like that was the case. She seemed certain there was only one man who could be the father.

"When in May?" I ask. "When did it start?"

Drew rubs his jaw. "It was around the middle of the

month. It went on for maybe a couple of weeks and then I never saw her again."

The baby is Drew's. It has to be. I'd need a calendar to actually count the weeks, but a quick calculation in my head tells me the timing lines up.

"Did you use anything?" I feel sick just asking the question. I don't want to think about this. I don't want to even imagine my husband being with her, but I need to know if there's a chance he might not be the father.

"No," he mutters.

I stare at him, unable to believe he'd be that careless. My husband is one of the most meticulous people I know. He's not someone who's forgetful or careless, so how is it possible he'd forget to wear a condom?

"I was drunk," he says, as if he knew what I was thinking. "And it's not like I carry condoms around. I know it was careless, but at the time, I wasn't thinking. It all happened so fast."

"Drew, you could've given me something! Did you even consider that?"

He doesn't answer, his gaze lowering to the floor.

"What about the other times?" I say through gritted teeth. "Were you drunk then too?"

He slowly nods. "After it happened, I felt like shit for what I'd done, so I drank, hoping it'd make me forget. Molly showed up and..." Drew's eyes rise to mine. "I can't explain it. After the first time, I swore I'd never do it again."

"And yet you did. You kept going back there. Back to that hotel. To be with Molly."

"No." He shakes his head. "That wasn't the plan. I wasn't going there to see her. She just—"

"Stop lying!" I yell, unable to hold back my rage.

"Stop telling me it was a mistake! That you didn't mean to do it. That you just happened to run into Molly over and over again. Just admit that you had an affair! Admit that you purposely went to that bar to see Molly!"

The room becomes silent, the only noise being the sound of my breaths, which are shallow and fast. My chest is so tight it hurts, or maybe the pain is coming from my heart, from the betrayal it feels after finding out the man I love was seeing another woman.

"Say something," I snap, glaring at Drew. "You don't get to be silent. I deserve to know what happened. The truth, not some version of it."

"Sara, what I told you is the truth. I honestly didn't think I'd see her again. I realize it was stupid to go back to that bar, but I thought she was gone. She told me she didn't live here. She said she was only in town to see her mother."

It's similar to what Molly told me, although she made it sound like she'd moved back here a while ago. Or maybe I just assumed that.

"And she just happened to show up again?" I huff. "At the same time you were there? You really think that was just a coincidence?"

"I didn't plan it. I swear. But I'd had too much to drink, and when I saw her again, I wasn't thinking, at least not with my head."

"Obviously," I mutter, rolling my eyes. "How many times did this happen? How many times did you just happen to run into her?" I say sarcastically.

"I don't know, Sara. I really don't. I've been trying to forget it ever happened. But like I said, it didn't last long. It went on for maybe a week or two, and then I ended it."

"Why'd you do it?" I ask, my anger now mixed with sadness. "Why did you want her when you have me? Your wife?"

He shrugs and averts his gaze. "I don't know. It was stupid. And wrong. Which is why I never did it again."

"There's a reason you did this," I say, keeping my eyes on him. "It wasn't just because you were drunk. There was some other reason." I pause, tears stinging my eyes. "What was it, Drew? Tell me."

He finally looks at me. "I was angry. I know that's not a good excuse, but—"

"Angry at what?"

"You." He sighs. "We'd been fighting about having your parents here for Memorial Day. I told you I wanted it to be just the two of us, and you said you were inviting them anyway."

"But I didn't. I decided not to after our fight."

I'm still upset with Drew about that. My parents are in their seventies. I worry they won't be around much longer, which is why I want to spend time with them. They live several hours away, so we usually only see them at holidays, which has always upset Drew. He wants holidays to be only the two of us and says we can see our parents some other time of the year. It's a constant argument and makes me dread holidays.

"You went along with it, yes, but you held it against me," Drew says. "You barely spoke to me, and when you did, we ended up fighting. I went to the bar that week because I didn't want to go home and argue with you again. I'd only been there a few minutes when Molly showed up. She was easy to talk to and took my mind off what was happening at home."

"Did you tell her you were married?"

"I didn't tell her, but she had to have known." He holds up his left hand. "I never took off my ring. She had to have seen it."

So Molly knew he was married when she met him. And she still slept with him.

"And you were the one who ended it?" I ask.

"Yes," Drew says. "I told her I never wanted to see her again. And I haven't. Not until tonight."

I'm not sure I believe him, not after finding out he's been lying to me for months. What else hasn't he told me? Can I trust that anything he's said is true?

What does this mean for our marriage? I'd planned to be with Drew forever. To have his children. Grow old with him. But that was before he betrayed me.

"I can't believe you did this to me," I mutter, looking down. "To us."

"Sara, it was a mistake." He moves closer and holds my hand. "A horrible mistake that I deeply regret. If I could go back in time and fix this, I would. I don't know what was wrong with me. What I was thinking." He squeezes my hand. "I love you. I never wanted to hurt you."

I hear a door open and footsteps coming down the hall. Molly appears, dressed in the clothes she had on when she got here, her ratty coat barely closing over her large belly. Her eyes look red and puffy, like she's been crying. As angry as I am with her for being with my husband, I also feel bad for her.

"I'm gonna go," Molly says, not looking at Drew and me as she races to the door.

"Molly, wait!" I say.

"Let her go." Drew grabs my arm as I try to go past him. "She can't stay here, Sara."

I whip back to him and lower my voice. "We can't let her sleep on the street. It's freezing out there. And she's carrying your child!"

"We don't know that it's mine," he says, his gaze going to Molly. "And until we do, I don't want her anywhere near us."

He says it as if he thinks she's dangerous, which is ridiculous. She's pregnant, and other than her huge stomach, she's a very small woman. What does he think she's going to do to us?

Molly stops at the door and turns back, her eyes on Drew. "I wasn't with anyone else. Just you. The baby is yours."

"You think I'm just going to take your word on that?" he snaps. He lets go of me and storms over to Molly. "If you came here to get money, I'm not—"

"Drew, stop it!" I say, racing up behind him. "She didn't come here wanting money. I invited her."

"Which is exactly what she wanted," Drew says. "You really think she just happened to show up at the place where you have lunch every day? You really think that was a coincidence?"

"It was," Molly mutters. "I honestly didn't know."

Molly's eyes are glistening with tears and her breaths are shaky as she stares down at the floor.

"You need to leave," Drew says to her. "You can't stay here."

She nods, not looking at us, and opens the door.

"Drew, she has nowhere to go," I say, urging him to give this more thought. Even if the baby isn't his, she's still a woman in need of help.

She's halfway out the door when Drew takes out his

wallet and pulls some money out. "Here." He shoves the money at her. "Get a hotel for the night."

She glances up at him. "Thanks."

"We should get your number," I say to Molly. "In case—"

"We don't need it," Drew interrupts. "She knows where we live."

He's being extremely cold to this woman. I know he's angry, but Molly could be the mother of his child. Even if he doesn't like her, he should still be nice to her.

"I don't have a phone anyway, so..." Molly's voice trails off and she goes out to the hall. She stops and looks past Drew to me. "Thank you again, Sara, for all that you did for me. I'm really sorry." She looks down at her stomach. "For everything."

She walks off, going down the hall. Drew shuts the door and locks it. Then he turns to me, his eyes narrowed. "Stay away from her. Do you understand me? You are not to speak to her again."

What is he talking about? If he's the father of her baby, of course we're going to speak to her again. She's going to be part of our lives, whether we like it or not.

Maybe Drew's in shock. Maybe he needs more time to process this. I certainly do. Within a matter of minutes, my entire world has shattered. I learned my husband not only had an affair, but may soon be a father. It's what he's always wanted, but it was supposed to be with me. Not some other woman.

7

"Drew, she needs our help," I say, following behind him as he goes to the kitchen.

"I gave her money for a hotel. What the hell else do you expect me to do?" He grabs the bottle of whiskey and pours some in a glass.

"If she really is having your baby, you can't just ignore her. You need to be involved."

"It's not mine," he says, gripping the glass so hard I'm afraid he might break it.

"How do you know it's not yours? You need to take a test to make sure."

"I don't need a test." He gulps the whiskey, then slams the glass down. "It's not mine. It can't be."

"Why couldn't it?"

He takes another swig of whiskey. "If it were that easy, you and I would've had a child years ago."

His words sting, but I know they weren't meant to hurt me. He's just angry and trying to make sense of this.

"I'm sorry, Sara. I shouldn't have said that." He

takes another drink. "My point is that it was only a few times. How could she get pregnant that fast?"

"It only takes one time," I mutter.

He shakes his head. "It can't be mine. It's gotta be someone else's. The woman practically threw herself at me. If she was that way with me, chances are she was that way with other men too."

"She threw herself at you?" I ask. "That's not how you described it before. You made it sound like she just sat next to you."

"I was trying to be nice and not make her sound like some woman who throws herself at men out of some desperate need for attention. But that's exactly the feeling I got from her."

Molly didn't seem that way at all, at least not in the short time I spent with her. It's possible she acts differently when she's been drinking. It's also possible Drew is only saying this to place all the blame on Molly instead of himself.

"Regardless of what happened," I say, "you need to address this. You need to know if the baby is yours."

Drew finishes what's left of his whiskey and sets down the glass. "I can't talk about this." He heads over to the closet and takes out his coat.

"What are you doing?"

"I'm going out."

"Now? Drew, you can't just leave." I race over to him. "We need to discuss this."

He shrugs on his coat and turns to me. "What's there to discuss? It's over. It never should've happened."

"But it did," I say, shocked that he thinks we can just move on from this. "You had an affair. And you lied to me. How am I supposed to trust you after that?"

He lets out a heavy sigh. "Sara, that woman means nothing to me. What I had with her wasn't an affair. It was a few nights of me being stupid. Telling you about it would've hurt our marriage. I wanted to move on from it. Pretend it never happened."

"That's not how it works." I swallow, feeling the burn in my throat as I choke back tears. "You don't get to pretend this didn't happen. You don't get off that easily. You betrayed me, Drew. You betrayed our marriage. Betrayed my trust."

"And I'm sorry for that." He holds my face between his hands and looks into my eyes. "If I could go back in time and fix this, I would. Hurting you is the last thing I ever wanted. I love you, Sara. You're everything to me. My whole life."

"If that were true, you wouldn't have done this." I shove his hands off of me and take a step back. "Maybe you're right. Maybe you should go."

"What are you saying?" he asks, his eyes darting around my face. "That you want me to move out?"

"I don't know." I turn away, not wanting to see the hurt on his face. I refuse to feel sorry for him. No matter what excuse he had for doing this, it doesn't change the fact that he did it and lied to me about it. "I need time to think about this."

I hear him walking to the door, his steps heavy but quick on the wood floor, echoing in the otherwise silent room. The door opens, then shuts. He's gone.

I collapse to my knees, my tears finally breaking free. How could Drew do this to me? And to our marriage? I thought we were okay. I'd even say our marriage was good. Sure, we have issues, but what couple doesn't? It's normal to argue now and then, but an argument shouldn't lead to an affair. I remember the fight we had that Drew claims led him to be with Molly. It was nothing more than a disagreement. Neither of us even raised our voices. If that's all it takes for him to justify an affair, then how could I possibly believe this won't happen again?

Maybe it already has. Maybe Drew's been cheating on me for our entire marriage. How do I know he's telling the truth when he says it only happened with Molly? What if it wasn't just her? What if there were others?

A loud knock on the door startles me from my thoughts. I stand up and clear my throat. "Who is it?"

"Judith Reed," she calls out. "I live in the building. I need to speak with you."

Her name doesn't sound familiar, but that's not surprising. I haven't met most of the people in the building. Everyone keeps to themselves. They don't even look at you when you pass them in the hall.

"Just a minute," I call out, wiping the tears from my face as I head to the door. I open it just a crack and see an older woman standing there. I recall seeing her in the lobby, but we've never spoken before. "Can I help you?" I ask.

"Yes, I was on my way into the building when a young woman approached me asking for money. As you know, it's rare for beggars to be loitering in this area so I asked her what she was doing here. She said she was visiting someone in the building. I asked her who and she gave me your name. I thought I should check her story before I called the police."

Is she talking about Molly? She has to be, but why is

Molly outside asking for money when Drew just gave her some?

"Was the woman pregnant?" I ask.

"Yes. Very. I'd say she was due to have the baby any day now." Judith stands up straighter. "So you know this woman? The one loitering outside our building?"

"Yes, but not well. I just met her today."

"Was she telling the truth?" Judith asks. "Did you invite her here?"

"I did." I pause, not sure how to explain this. I really shouldn't have to. I don't even know this woman, but from our brief encounter, she seems like a busybody who thinks she's in charge of protecting the building. "I spent the afternoon with her. I didn't realize she was still here."

"Well, she is," Judith says in a haughty tone. "And I am not comfortable having some woman begging for money outside our building. If you don't deal with her, I'll have no choice but to call the police."

I nod. "I'll go speak with her. Thank you for letting me know."

Judith turns and walks off. I shut the door and get my coat from the closet. I quickly put it on and grab my keys from the counter.

When I get outside, I look for Molly but don't see her. Maybe she left. Maybe Judith scared her off. I walk down the sidewalk, shivering as the bitterly cold wind whips around me. I hope Molly found a hotel for the night. She shouldn't be out in this weather.

"Excuse me," I hear someone say.

I stop and notice a woman walking toward me from the alley. "Molly?"

"Sara," she says, coming out to the sidewalk where I can see her. "I didn't know it was you."

"What are you doing out here? You were supposed to get a hotel."

She shakes her head. "It costs too much. Everything around here is at least $300 a night." She pulls something out of her pocket. It's the money Drew gave her. I didn't see how much it was, but it looks like it's only a few twenty-dollar bills. I assumed he gave her more than that. I wasn't even thinking about what a hotel would cost, but Molly is right. In this part of town, a room would be several hundred dollars a night, and the hotel would require a credit card to check in.

Molly couldn't get a hotel room even if we'd given her more money. I didn't consider that when Drew sent her away. I was too shocked and upset after finding out he'd had an affair.

"I'll go back to the park," Molly says, stuffing the cash back into her pocket. "I'll use the money to get a taxi. Would you mind calling one? I haven't seen any go by."

I shouldn't do this. Drew will be furious with me, but why do I care? He created this problem and left me to deal with it, so I'll do what I feel is best.

"You'll stay with us tonight," I say. "In the morning, we'll figure out what to do."

"Sara, I can't," she says, shaking her head. "You heard Andy. He doesn't want me staying with you. And he's right. I shouldn't be here. I've caused enough problems between you two. I don't want to—"

"It's just for a night," I say, taking her arm. "Come on. You can't be out here in this weather." I lead her back down the sidewalk.

"But what about Andy?"

I don't like that she calls him that. It's what his mother calls him, and I'm not a huge fan of Drew's mother. She's very old-fashioned and thinks I should stay home and devote my life to caring for her son. Whenever she visits, she sees it as an opportunity to teach me things, like how to properly do laundry or cook her son's favorite meals. I used to find it infuriating, but now I just smile and pretend I'm listening. Drew thinks it's funny, but I wish he'd stand up for me and tell his mother to back off.

"Drew will just have to deal with it," I say, wondering where he went or if he'll come home tonight. Maybe he'll decide to get a hotel. I wouldn't mind if he did. I need time to cool off before we talk again.

"It feels good to be inside," Molly says, shivering as we stand in the lobby. "That wind is brutal."

"Yes, I think a storm might be coming." I go to the elevator and push the button.

An older couple joins us, looking at Molly with suspicion when they see her filthy, ragged coat. They're probably wondering what she's doing here. The people in this building are all professionals who make good money and dress well. Someone who looks like Molly stands out. I need to take her shopping for a new coat and some clothes that fit her.

I can't believe I'm doing this. I can't believe I'm helping the woman who had an affair with my husband.

8

"Where's Andy?" Molly asks when we're back in the apartment.

"He went out," I say, taking her coat. "And please don't call him that. His name is Drew."

"Sorry," she mutters, watching as I hang our coats in the closet. "I only know him as Andy. That's what he said his name was when we met."

"Yes, well, it's not his name, or not the name he goes by." I walk past Molly to the kitchen, eyeing the whiskey bottle and thinking of pouring myself some. I could really use a drink right now, but decide to have a cup of tea, knowing it will calm my nerves better than alcohol.

"You're angry," Molly says. She joins me in the kitchen, standing several feet away as I fill the teakettle at the sink.

"Of course I'm angry," I say, shutting off the faucet. "My husband lied to me."

"I meant you're angry at *me*," Molly says. "For being with him. And because of this." I glance at her and see her hand moving over her stomach.

I put the kettle on the stove, not responding to her comment. There's no need to. She knows I'm angry with her. I'm more than angry. I'm furious. But there's nothing I can do. She's having Drew's baby whether I like it or not.

"Would you like some tea?" I ask, getting a mug from the cupboard.

"No, thanks," she mutters.

The oven timer dings, startling me so much I almost drop my mug. I set it down on the counter and hurry over to the oven. I grab some potholders and carefully take the casserole out. It's a spaghetti casserole, Drew's favorite. I made it because I knew he'd be upset that I'd invited a stranger to stay with us. I was hoping his favorite food would make him feel better about the situation. Of course, that was before I knew about his history with Molly.

"I completely forgot about this," I say, setting the casserole dish on the counter. "I'm not hungry, but if you'd like some, you're welcome to help yourself."

She nods. "Do you have a plate?"

I take one from the cupboard and hand it to her, then get a serving spoon from the drawer. The teakettle whistles, and I race to the stove to take it off the burner.

"When is Andy—I mean, Drew—getting home?" Molly asks.

"I don't know," I say, pouring hot water into my mug. I set the kettle on the stove and turn back to see Molly sitting at the table next to the kitchen. I had it already set with placemats and napkins for the dinner I'd planned for the three of us.

"Where'd he go?" Molly asks, talking with her

mouth full. She's already eaten half of what she served herself. She must've been starving.

"I don't know," I say, leaning back against the counter, my mug held between my hands. "He didn't say."

"Is he coming back?"

I look over at her. "Why are you asking?"

"Because I feel like this is all my fault. Like me showing up here caused him to leave."

"He just needs time to clear his head." I sip my tea, hoping the warmth of it will soothe my nerves.

"Did he say anything to you?" Molly asks. "After I left?" She pauses. "About me?"

"Not really. We didn't talk much. He left soon after you did."

She moves the spaghetti around her plate with her fork, not looking at me. "If you want to talk about it, we can. Or maybe you'd rather not know."

I do, and I don't. I'm torn between wanting to know all the details of their affair and wanting to know nothing about it. But I *am* curious if Molly's version of what happened matches up with what Drew said.

Going over to the table, I sit down across from her. "I do have a few questions."

She sets her fork down. "What do you want to know?"

"When did it start?" I clear my throat and sit up straighter. "When did you meet him?"

"Last May. Like the middle of the month. He was at this fancy hotel, sitting at the bar."

So far, her story aligns with what Drew said. It was the middle of May when Drew and I had that fight about my parents coming for Memorial Day. I can't believe that's why he cheated, assuming he's telling the truth and that really was the reason.

"Why were you at the hotel?" I ask.

"To apply for a job. There was an opening to work at the front desk."

"You were living here back then?"

"Yeah, I moved here last March."

Drew said she was in town visiting her mother the week they met, but Molly claims she already lived here. One of them is lying.

"I thought I could work the night shift and take care of my mom during the day," Molly says. "But I didn't get the job. The guy who interviewed me said I was too emotional because I started crying when I told him my mom was dying of cancer." She shrugs. "I guess it made him uncomfortable."

"That's awful. That shouldn't be a reason not to hire someone."

"Thinking about it now, I shouldn't have told him about my mom. I only did because I wanted him to know I'd have to leave work if something happened and she needed me." Molly picks up her fork. "Anyway, I was upset that he didn't hire me so I went to the bar to get a drink. Then I saw the prices and realized I couldn't afford anything, not even a beer. I was about to leave when Andy—I mean, Drew—offered to buy me a drink."

Why would Drew offer to buy her a drink? That's something men do to show a woman they're interested. Is that why he was there that night? To find a woman?

He made it sound like Molly had approached him and aggressively pursued him. He said she threw herself at him.

"So Drew approached you?" I ask. "It wasn't the other way around?"

"No," she says with a short laugh. "That was the last thing on my mind. I was thinking about how I was going to pay rent when I didn't have a job. My mom had a little money saved up, but not enough to last more than a few months."

"What happened after he bought you a drink?"

"We talked." She moves her fork around her plate, watching its movement and avoiding my gaze. "He kept asking me questions." She finally looks at me. "It was nice. People don't usually show that much interest in me."

That doesn't sound like my husband. Drew would rather talk about himself than ask questions of others. That was one of the things that bothered me when we were dating. On our very first date, he asked me all about myself, but as time went on, he asked less and less, and soon all we talked about was him and the topics that interested him.

"How long did you talk?" I ask.

"I think it was a couple of hours." She looks over at the counter. "Could I have more casserole? It's really good."

"Have all that you'd like." I get up and bring the casserole dish to the table.

"Thanks," she says, helping herself to more. "You're a really good cook."

"I'm still learning, but I've definitely improved over the years. Drew's mother gave me this recipe. It's his favorite so she insisted I make it for him."

"Do his parents live around here?"

"No, they live in South Carolina. They're retired." I

watch as Molly devours more of the casserole. It reminds me of how quickly she ate that sandwich at lunch. I do feel bad for her. She's probably eaten more today than she has all week.

"The night you met Drew," I say, continuing with my questions. "Would you say he'd had too much to drink?"

She stops eating and looks up at the ceiling, like she's thinking back to that night. "I wouldn't say he was drunk, if that's what you're asking."

That's exactly what I'm asking, and her answer means Drew was lying.

"And after you two talked, that's when you..." I don't know what words to use to describe what they did. I know what I'm thinking, but I don't want to say it.

"We what?" she asks.

Does she really not know? I think it's obvious what I'm asking.

"Decided to get a room," I say, feeling my anger flare up. I've been trying to suppress it and focus on what led to them being together that night, but we're now at the part of the story that makes images form in my head. Images of the two of them together.

"He already had the room," Molly casually says as she scoops up some spaghetti. "He invited me up there to talk some more, but then, well, you know what happened."

"Drew had already reserved a room?" I say, my heart beating faster. "Are you sure he didn't get it while you were at the bar? Maybe you were in the restroom and he—"

"No, he already had it. His stuff was there."

"What stuff?" I ask. "What did he have?"

"A suitcase. A small one, like a carry-on. And there was one of those toiletry bags in the bathroom."

Why would Drew have a room at a hotel and bring a suitcase? Was he planning to leave me?

"Did he explain why he had a room there?" I ask, noticing my voice trembling. My mind is spinning, wondering what's real and what's not. I feel like I don't even know this man she's talking about. He doesn't sound anything like my husband.

"He said he was in town for a conference," Molly says. "Some kind of accounting thing."

So he didn't go to that hotel just to get a drink. He got a room and made up a story to go with it. He was at the bar to find a woman. A woman to lure to his room and sleep with.

I think I'm going to be sick. It was bad enough when I thought he got drunk and slept with another woman, but it's even worse knowing he planned it. That he went there with the intention of cheating on me.

9

"I'M STUFFED," Molly says, leaning back in her chair, her hand over her belly. "And this little guy is really kicking. I don't think I'll be getting much sleep tonight."

I jump up from the table and grab her empty plate. I couldn't sit there a second longer and hear about Drew's lies or the child he made with this woman. I want to scream at the top of my lungs. I want to toss this plate against the wall and smash it. I want to strangle Drew and watch as his face turns purple.

"Do you need help cleaning up?" Molly asks. I look over and see her grabbing the table for support as she stands up.

"No, I can do it. Why don't you try to get some rest? I know it's still early, but I'm sure you're exhausted."

"Yeah, okay." She gives me a sad smile. "Thanks again for doing all this. You're a really nice person, Sara. Drew is lucky to have you."

He is, but I don't know if he'll have me for much longer. How can I forgive him for this? It wasn't just some drunken mistake. He planned it! Was he really that desperate to be with someone else? Some random stranger?

"Wait," I say as Molly heads to her room.

She turns back. "Yeah?"

I walk over to her. "When did it end? When was the last time you saw Drew?"

"The last week of May. The doctor said that's probably the week I got pregnant."

"How many times were you two..." I pause to consider how to say this. "Together that week?"

"I don't remember. Maybe three or four? He kept asking me to come see him because he was flying home on Friday." She shrugs. "Or that's what he told me. I didn't know he lived in town."

"But you knew he had a wife," I say, folding my arms over my chest. "You didn't have a problem with that?"

"He said he was separated and in the process of getting divorced." She frowns. "I'm really sorry. I thought he was telling the truth. I didn't know he was lying until I tried to find him and couldn't. That's when I realized he'd made everything up."

"How did you try to find him?"

"First, I called the phone number he gave me, but it was no longer in service. Then, I searched for him online. I couldn't find anyone with his name in Baltimore, so I searched the whole state of Maryland and still couldn't find him. That's when I assumed he'd given me a fake name and a fake story about who he was."

The more she tells me, the more concerned I'm getting about Drew. Who did I marry? Because the person she's describing doesn't at all sound like the man I've been living with for the past five years.

"He said he was from Baltimore?" I ask, not sure why he would pick that particular city. He has no connection to it. I don't think he's ever been there, although it's possible he has and never told me.

"Yeah, he said he grew up there."

"What name did he give you?" I ask.

"Andy Platzberg." Molly sighs. "That's not his last name, is it?"

"No, his last name is Tallow. And only his mother calls him Andy."

"He said he's an accountant."

"That's actually true. He's a partner at his accounting firm. But he wasn't at a conference last May. That hotel where you met him is close to his office. He sometimes stops there after work for a drink, usually with coworkers."

That's what Drew told me, but I'm wondering if it's even close to the truth. What if he's been meeting women there for years? Lying to them about who he is? Inviting them up to his room?

My heart's beating erratically and I feel like the room is spinning. I need to sit down. I stumble on my way to the table and feel Molly grip my arm.

"Are you okay?" she asks with concern.

I shake my head. "I'm not feeling well."

"Can I get you something? Maybe you need to eat."

"No. My stomach couldn't handle it. Maybe a glass of water would help."

She opens the cupboards until she finds the one that has the drinking glasses. She takes one out and fills it up at the sink. "Here," she says, handing me the glass.

"Thank you." I take a sip, but can barely choke it down.

"I'll stay here with you until I know you're okay." She pulls out a chair.

"No, I'm fine. You go ahead and rest."

"Are you sure?"

I nod. "Yes. I don't feel like talking anymore."

She comes over to me and puts her hand on my shoulder. "I'm sorry if I upset you. I was just trying to answer your questions."

My body stiffens at the feel of her touching me. She seems sincere, but there's something about her that bothers me, and it's not just because she slept with my husband. It's something else. Something I felt even before I knew about her involvement with Drew.

"Please, Molly," I say. "I'd like to be alone right now."

"Okay." She gives me a slight smile, then leaves. I hear the door to her room softly close and am left with only the sound of the brutal wind howling outside the windows.

I wonder where Drew went. Is he out walking the streets? Did he go to a bar? To his office? To a hotel? It bothers me not knowing where he is and if he's okay.

I shouldn't care, but I do. He's my husband. Until just an hour ago, I'd planned to be with him forever. I take out my phone to call him, then stop myself. I'm not ready to talk to him. I'll text him instead.

Where are you? I hit send and wait for his response.

My phone rings, and I see Drew's name on the screen.

"Hello, Drew," I say in a tone that sounds like I'm

talking to a stranger. That's how he feels to me now. Like someone I don't even know.

"Hey," he says, his voice quiet and deep. "I got your text. I'm at a sports bar. I needed to get out of the cold. The wind is really picking up."

Why is he talking about the weather instead of our marriage and what he did? Does he think this is just like any other fight where he can go away for an hour and come back and everything will return to normal?

"Molly's here," I blurt out.

"At the apartment?" He sounds alarmed and a little angry. "Why? I told her to get a hotel."

"With the eighty dollars you gave her?" I say sarcastically. "Do you have any idea what hotels cost these days?" I let out a harsh laugh. "You should, given that you stay at them so often."

"What are you talking about? I haven't—"

"I don't want to discuss this right now," I say, not wanting to hear more of his lies. "I think it'd be best if you didn't come home tonight."

"Sara, come on. I know you're upset with me, but I'm still coming home. I'll sleep on the couch if that makes you feel better."

"You're not getting it, Drew. I don't want you here." A tear slides down my cheek. "I don't want you to come home."

"Honey, I know I messed up, but we can work this out. I'll leave right now. I'll head home and we can talk."

"Drew, you're not listening," I say, raising my voice. "I don't want to talk. I don't even want to see you right now."

The phone is silent, then I hear him let out a sigh.

"Fine. I won't come home. Goodbye, Sara." He ends the call.

His abruptness and frigid tone feel like a dagger being shoved through my heart. After what he did, he should be treating me with kindness and understanding. He should be thinking about how his actions have affected me. The damage he caused to our relationship. But instead he turns it around, tries to make me the bad guy.

I don't know what to do about this. About Drew. About Molly. About the baby they're about to have.

Never in a million years did I think something like this would happen. Now that it has, I don't know how, or if, we can ever get past it.

10

In the morning, I wake up on the couch wearing the same clothes as last night. I don't even remember falling asleep.

"You're up," Molly says, appearing beside me, a big grin on her face. Her hair is wet and she's wearing one of my robes. The yellow terry cloth one Drew's mother gave me for my birthday last year. "You want some coffee? I'd be happy to make it even though I can't have any." She sighs. "I really miss coffee."

"Why are you wearing that?" I ask.

"The robe?" She looks down at it. "I needed something to put on after my shower." She scrunches her face up. "Are you mad? I know I shouldn't have taken it, but you were asleep and I didn't want to wake you up. I'll go take it off." She undoes the tie.

"No, it's fine," I say, getting up. "It's from Drew's mother. I never liked it. You can have it. I just wish you'd asked me instead of going through my closet."

"Sorry," she mutters, chewing on her lip. "I won't do it again."

dripping down the sides and onto the stovetop. It's going to burn and cause a stain that I'll have to clean up. I hate cleaning the stovetop, which is why I'm extremely cautious whenever I cook.

Molly cracks another egg, so hard that it splatters all over the stove. "Oops," she says with a laugh. "Can you grab me another?"

"Let me do it," I say, my patience with her gone. "You go sit down."

I grab the paper towels from under the sink and quickly get to work cleaning the area around the skillet.

Molly watches me from the table. "Guess I made a mess."

"It's fine," I say, moving the skillet to another burner. "But in the future, please don't use the kitchen."

"Why?"

"Because you're our guest." And you should ask before assuming you can do whatever you'd like in someone's home. That's what I want to say, but instead I continue to clean up her mess. "If you'd like something, I'll make it. You just need to ask."

"Sara, I really don't mind doing it myself."

"Yes, but I do." I give her a strained smile. "As I said, I'm a bit of a neat freak, and I'd rather not have to clean up messes from spilled food."

"Then you better not have a kid," she says jokingly. "All kids do is make messes."

"Not all children are like that. You can train them to clean up after themselves." The stove is clean now so I move the skillet to its original spot and turn on the heat.

"Your parents must've been really strict," Molly says. "My mom let me be as messy as I wanted. I'm gonna raise my kid like that too."

Until now, I hadn't even considered how she'd raise her child. What if she's one of those mothers who sets no limits and doesn't have any rules? And then her son comes here and destroys everything? Drew wouldn't let that happen. He likes order and a clean home. He wouldn't allow his child to run loose and do whatever he pleased. Would he?

"It's probably none of my business," Molly says, "but can I ask what happened to Drew? I'm guessing he didn't come home last night."

She's right. It's none of her business, but I'm sure she's already figured it out.

"He decided to stay somewhere else." I put the eggs on a plate and bring them over to Molly. "I hope you like scrambled."

"I do. Thanks. Are you having anything?"

"No, I'm not hungry." I get a fork and a napkin and set them on the table next to the plate.

"Would you sit with me?" Molly asks. "I don't like eating alone."

She's single and homeless. She should be used to eating alone.

I reluctantly sit across from her, feeling unsettled and like I need to get out of here. I should be at work right now, not watching Drew's lover eat breakfast. A breakfast I made.

"Did Drew not stay here because of me?" Molly asks.

"That was part of it, yes."

"What was the other part?"

I sit back and straighten my shoulders. "I decided I didn't want him here after finding out he betrayed me and lied to me about it for months."

"He lied to me too," Molly says, poking her fork around in her eggs. "But I'm sure it's way worse being his wife. I wouldn't have even cared that he lied if I wasn't carrying his kid."

"What would you have done if you'd found him last summer? After you'd learned you were pregnant?"

She shrugs. "I would've told him about the baby. Asked if he wanted to be involved."

"What about now?" I eye her across the table. "What are you expecting of Drew? What do you want from him?"

11

Before Molly can answer, I hear the front door open. I turn back and see Drew coming into the apartment. He looks horrible, like he had too much to drink last night and didn't sleep. His eyes are droopy, his skin is pale, and his clothes are a wrinkled mess. He drops his coat on the chair next to the couch and walks over to the table where I'm sitting with Molly.

"Good morning," he says to Molly in a businesslike tone. "I hope you slept well."

"I did. Thanks." She gives me a brief smile, then goes back to eating her eggs.

"Good morning, sweetheart," Drew says as he leans down to give me a kiss. He straightens up and gently rubs my shoulder. "Could I make you some coffee?"

What is he doing? Why is he acting as though nothing's wrong? Is this some kind of performance for Molly's sake? Does he think she doesn't know that we're fighting?

"I'll make it myself," I say, pulling away from him and getting up. "You should get ready for work."

He follows me to the coffee machine, stopping behind me and wrapping his arms around my waist. My body stiffens at his touch. I wish he'd stop with the loving husband act. He can't possibly think I've forgiven him after just a few hours. I don't know if I can *ever* forgive him.

"I missed you last night," he whispers in my ear, pressing himself against me and kissing the side of my neck.

Seriously, what is he doing? Has he lost his mind? Did he forget that I know about his affair? His pregnant lover is sitting just a few feet away!

"Stop it," I whisper, turning to face him. I glance over at Molly, who seems oblivious to our interaction, her attention on her breakfast. Or maybe she's just pretending not to notice this ridiculous spectacle Drew is putting on. I would if I were her. It's awkward and uncomfortable. I can't believe Drew is acting this way.

"Let's go to the bedroom," Drew says to me. "We need to talk."

"Fine," I say through gritted teeth. "I'll be back in a minute," I say to Molly. "Leave your dishes in the sink. I'll take care of them."

"Okay," she says, watching as Drew and I leave.

We go into the bedroom and Drew shuts the door.

"What the hell were you doing?" I say, standing in front of him, my hands on my hips. "You think you can just come home and pretend everything's back to normal?"

"No, of course not," he says, suddenly looking remorseful. "I was making it clear to Molly that I'm committed to you and our marriage. I don't want her thinking something is going to happen between her and me."

"I think that's the last thing on her mind. She's giving birth in a few weeks. Her focus is on that, not on trying to rekindle a romance with you."

"You don't know her like I do." His expression darkens. "In the short time I spent with her, she became very possessive of me, to the point that I became concerned."

"What do you mean by possessive?"

"Calling my phone constantly. Leaving me messages. Texting me."

"She told me you gave her a fake number. She said it didn't work."

"It didn't work because I blocked her. But before that, she wouldn't leave me alone. And I never gave her my number. She took it from my phone when I was in the bathroom. She must've seen me put in the security code to unlock it."

If that's true, I need to be more cautious around Molly. I can't let her roam freely around the apartment. I need to keep a closer eye on her.

Drew plants his hands on my shoulders. "Honey, I know you're angry with me, and you probably want nothing to do with me right now, but until Molly is gone, I think we should try our best to act like a loving couple."

"I don't think I can do that," I say, shoving his hands off of me and walking away. "I just found out you had an affair. I can barely look at you, so I don't think it's possible for me to pretend we're a loving couple."

Drew comes over to me. "Then can you at least not act like you hate me? Molly is watching us, and if she senses our marriage is faltering, she'll think there's a chance she could step in and take your place."

"You've made it very clear that's not going to happen. The moment you saw her, you told her to leave. And when she didn't, you threw her out."

"Sara, all I'm asking is for you not to shun me in front of her. If you want to spew hate at me when it's just the two of us, then fine. Go ahead. I deserve it."

I don't want to be hateful toward my husband, but I also don't want to be nice to him. I'm devastated and hurt, the pain so deep that there are moments when I feel like I can't breathe. It'd be even worse if I weren't preoccupied with Molly and all her problems. Having to deal with her has kept me from fully experiencing the feelings I'd have if I were here by myself, focusing solely on Drew and what he did, and the impact it's had on our marriage.

"If you're unable to pretend you're willing to give me another chance," Drew says, "then Molly needs to leave. Now. I'll take her to a shelter if I have to."

"The shelters are full. And I'm sure they'll remain full until the storm ends."

"Then I'll take her to the police station. They can keep her until a spot at the shelter opens up."

"The police aren't going to take her. She's not a criminal. Why don't we just get her a hotel? I know it'll be expensive, but we can afford a few nights."

"They're all booked. When I was out last night, I overheard a guy saying he couldn't get a room anywhere in town because all the flights were cancelled due to the storm. Everyone's stuck here."

"That's only temporary. Once the storm ends, the flights will start running again."

"Yes, but that may not be until tomorrow." He glances at the door, then back at me. "I want her gone today."

"I don't think that's possible."

"Then you need to try to act normal around me, or at least not act like you want to kill me."

I sigh. "I don't want to kill you. I might've imagined it, but I wouldn't actually do it."

He smiles a little, then runs his hand along the side of my face. "Do you have any idea how much I missed you last night? I was miserable. I barely slept."

I look down, not wanting to see the sad look on his face. I won't let myself feel sorry for him. He did this. It's his fault.

"You need to find out if it's yours." My eyes rise back to Drew's. "If this is really your baby, you'll be tied to this woman forever. I need to know if the baby really is yours."

He nods. "Fine. I'll take a paternity test."

"Soon. I don't want to wait until the baby arrives."

"What do I need to do? Where do I go?"

"I'm not sure. I'll figure it out and set something up."

"Even if the baby is mine, I still want Molly gone. I don't want her living here."

"Yes, I know. I don't either. I'll make some calls and see if I can find her somewhere to go."

He lowers his voice. "How certain are we that she doesn't already have a place?"

"She was living in the park. She wouldn't do that if she had a place to live."

"How do you know she was living in the park?

You're believing what she told you, which she could've made up to get your sympathy."

"Drew, the woman was filthy. It looked like she hadn't showered in days."

"Which could have been part of her plan. Make herself appear to be homeless when she's really not."

"That's ridiculous. She wouldn't choose to walk around looking like that."

"She would if it might get her what she wanted."

"Which is what?"

"You feeling sorry for her." He folds his arms. "Inviting her to live with us."

"That doesn't make any sense. If she had a place to stay, why would she be trying to live with a stranger?"

He shrugs. "Maybe you're not a stranger. Maybe she found out you're my wife and used you to get to me."

Does he really believe Molly somehow tracked him down, found out I was his wife, and then faked being homeless with the hope that I would invite her to live with us? That's an outlandish theory, especially for Drew. He's not someone who believes in conspiracies, which is what this sounds like.

"She didn't even know you lived here," I say. "You told her you lived in Baltimore. And she said you gave her a fake name."

His brows draw together. "I never told her I lived in Baltimore. She knew I lived here. She heard me complaining to the bartender about the road construction downtown and how it was taking me twice as long to get home with all the detours. That's not something I'd say if I were from out of town."

I can't tell whether he's lying or telling the truth. I'm leaning toward believing Molly's story over Drew's. Men who have affairs often make up a story to hide the truth about their actual life, not wanting the other woman to know too much about them.

"What about your name?" I ask. "What did you tell her?"

"I said my name was Andy. I didn't give her a last name."

"She never asked?"

"Sara, this wasn't a relationship. I got drunk and did something stupid. I wasn't looking to get involved with this woman." He looks at his watch. "I need to get ready for work. I have clients coming in at nine." He grips my arm and looks me in the eye. "We can get through this, Sara. I know we can." He goes to kiss me, but I back away.

"I can't," I say. "It's too soon."

He lets go of me. "What about tonight?"

"What about it?"

"Do you want me to stay here or go somewhere else?"

I pause, not sure how to answer. Part of me doesn't want him here, but we can't work on repairing our marriage if he's living somewhere else. But do I *want* that? Do I want to repair my relationship with a man who betrayed me? A man I no longer trust?

"I don't know," I tell him. "I can't give you an answer right now."

He glances at the door and lowers his voice. "I don't want you here alone with Molly. If she's staying another night, I need to be here. I'll sleep on the couch if you'd like. Please, Sara, at least consider it. For your own safety."

"Molly isn't dangerous." I roll my eyes. "You're only saying that so I'll let you stay here tonight."

He steps closer to me. "I'm saying it because I know her. There's something seriously wrong with that woman. I don't trust her, especially around you."

"What exactly do you think she's going to do?"

"I don't know, but I don't want to find out. Just be careful around her, okay?"

I nod, but still think he's crazy for worrying about this. Maybe he's saying it to convince me she shouldn't stay with us, but it's not like I want her here. I want her gone just as much as Drew does, but we can't just kick her out on the street.

As Drew goes to take a shower, I leave the bedroom, thinking of all I need to get done today. Get Molly some new clothes. Find her a place to stay. Set up a paternity test. I hope Molly agrees to the test. If she doesn't, I guess that will tell us if she's lying about the baby being Drew's.

When I walk into the living room, I see Molly standing in front of the fireplace, looking at something on the mantel.

"We have a lot to get done today," I say, going over to her. "You should go get ready."

"This is a great photo," she says, referring to the one of Drew and me last summer. We went to Martha's Vineyard for our anniversary and this nice older couple took a photo of us on the beach. "You two look really happy."

"It was our anniversary," I say, gazing at the photo. "Last June."

As I say that, I realize Drew had been with Molly just

weeks before we took that trip. I'd planned a romantic weekend for us, having no idea my husband had been with another woman. The weekend of our anniversary, Drew was so loving and attentive that I remember thinking how lucky I was to have found such a wonderful man.

How could I have been so blind not to know what was really going on? Drew wasn't being a loving husband that weekend. He was trying to assuage his guilt. He showered me with love and affection to make himself feel better.

Molly turns to me. "Do you always go somewhere for your anniversary?"

"No, but Drew thought it'd be nice to get away for a few days so I planned a weekend trip to Martha's Vineyard."

Now that I know what was going on back then, I wonder if the reason Drew insisted we go out of town was because he was worried Molly might try to find him after their affair.

"I'm going to go get dressed," Molly says.

"Oh, I washed your clothes. They're still in the dryer. I'll get them for you."

"I can do it. Just tell me where it is."

"Down here." I motion for her to follow me to the hall. I stop by what looks like a closet door and open it to show her the stackable washer and dryer. "I sprayed the stains. Hopefully, they came out." I take her clothes from the dryer and hold them up. "It looks like they did."

"Great! Thanks!" She grabs the clothing and goes down to her room.

I return to the living room, my gaze going to the photo on the mantel of Drew and me. That wasn't the first time Molly had seen it. She looked at it when I brought her here yesterday. She walked over to the fireplace and was looking at the mantel. When she saw that photo, she had to have known that Drew lived here and that I was his wife. And yet, when Drew got home, she acted shocked to see him.

Why would she do that? Why would she pretend not to know he lived here when she'd just seen his photo on the mantel? I guess it's possible she didn't think it was Drew in that photo, but how could she not? It's not like the photo was taken a long time ago and Drew's appearance has changed. That photo was taken only a few weeks after she met him.

I'm starting to wonder if Drew was right. Did Molly plan this? Did she know that Drew lived here? Did she know I was his wife?

12

"IT LOOKS like the snow has stopped," Molly says, coming into the living room. She's dressed in her now-clean clothes and her blond hair is pulled back into a loose braid. It's amazing how different she looks from yesterday. Her clean face makes her blue eyes stand out more and shows off her flawless skin. And having her hair styled like that is so much better than the messy mop that was around her face when I met her.

She's a beautiful young woman. She has the kind of natural beauty that most women can only dream of. I'm one of those women. I look terrible without makeup and it takes a lot of effort and product to make my hair look good. I see why Drew was attracted to her. But he could've been attracted to her and not acted on it. Did she really come on to him, or did he make the first move?

"Sara?" Molly says. "Did you hear me?"

"Yes, the storm has gone past us," I say, closing my laptop and setting it on the coffee table. "I just checked the forecast."

I did, but I also spent the past half hour looking for how to get a paternity test. After Molly asked about that photo on the mantel, my suspicions about her grew. I need to know if Drew really is the father of her child.

Drew left for work a few minutes ago. I didn't tell him about the photo, knowing he'd say it confirms his theory that Molly targeted us for some kind of nefarious plan. I don't want to assume that without being sure of it, and that photo isn't enough to convince me that Molly's up to no good. It's possible she didn't even notice the photo yesterday or didn't study it close enough to know the man was Drew. She stood at the fireplace for only a few seconds, which isn't long enough to say with certainty that she saw the photo and recognized the man was Drew.

"When did you want to go out?" Molly sits beside me on the couch. "I'm ready whenever you are."

I turn to her. "I need to talk to you about something." I need to talk to her about several things, but I'll start with the most important one. "Drew would like to take a paternity test. He'd like to do it soon, like this week."

"Okay. What do we need to do?"

She didn't argue about it, and she doesn't seem the least bit concerned, which tells me the father of her baby is, without a doubt, my husband. Disappointment washes over me as I realize this is actually happening. Drew's going to be a father. I was hoping it wasn't true. That Drew was right and Molly had been with other men during the time she conceived, but if that were the case, she wouldn't be so willing to take the test.

"I found a clinic in town that could do it," I say. "I was just about to call them when you walked in."

"Go ahead." She picks up my phone and hands it to me. "See if they could do it today."

She doesn't want to wait. She's eager to prove the baby is Drew's, but why? What does she think will happen once we know for sure that it's his? Does she want money? Support? Or does she want Drew?

The thought of that makes my pulse go faster. Is that why she's here? To take my husband?

"What are you waiting for?" Molly asks. "Aren't you going to call?"

"I need the number." I find the clinic's number and make the call. A woman answers and I tell her I'd like to schedule a paternity test for today, if possible. She asks me a series of questions, then schedules the test. "That should work. We'll see you then." I end the call. "Today at four."

"Won't Drew be at work?" Molly asks.

"He'll have to leave early," I say, knowing he'll drop everything to take this test. He keeps insisting he's not the father and thinks this test will prove it.

"I know you don't want to believe it," Molly says, "but the baby is Drew's. It has to be. He's the only man I was with."

"Yes, well, I'm sure you can understand that Drew and I would feel better having a test tell us that."

She looks down. "You don't trust me."

"How could I? I just met you."

"Yeah, but Drew knows me." Her eyes rise back to mine. "He knows I wouldn't lie about this."

"And yet he immediately assumed the baby wasn't his."

"He only said that because of you. He's trying to protect you from the truth."

She's probably right, but in my heart I want to believe him. I don't want this child to be his, and Molly to be in our lives forever.

"What did Drew say to you?" Molly asks. "About me?"

"What do you mean?"

"When you two went to the bedroom to talk. I know it was because of me. What did he say?"

"That he wanted a paternity test," I say, even though I was the one who insisted on it.

"What else?"

Do I tell her? Or is it best to keep quiet and believe what Drew said about us not being able to trust her? A few days ago, it wouldn't even have occurred to me that what my husband told me was a lie, but now? I feel as though I have to question everything he says.

"Sara, tell me," Molly urges. "What did he say?"

"Why does it matter?" I raise my brows. "Is there something you don't want me to know? Something you think Drew told me?"

"It's not that. It's..."

"What? Why are you asking?"

Her eyes lock on mine. "Because I think he lied."

"About what?"

"Me, and what happened last May."

"How? What do you think he said?"

She shrugs. "I don't know. He could've said anything. That's why I'm asking."

I sit up straighter. "It's really none of your business what Drew and I talked about. Even if we did discuss you, I don't need to share what was said."

"I get that, but don't you want to know if he's lying? If what he said is even true?"

"He's my husband. I'm going to believe him over a woman I've known for less than a day."

"How do you know he's telling the truth after he lied to you?" she asks, sounding genuinely curious, not like she's mocking me for believing Drew.

"I can't be certain that what he's saying is true, but the same could be said about you. How do I know your recollection of what happened isn't a lie?"

"I don't have a reason to lie. Drew does. He's trying to save his marriage."

I'm tempted to tell her what Drew said, even though the logical side of me is telling me not to do it. I should trust my husband, not this woman I just met.

"He said you lied about Baltimore," I say, deciding to call her out on her fake story and see how she reacts. "He said you knew he lived here in Boston."

She shakes her head. "I didn't. I swear. He had a hotel room. And a suitcase. Why would a guy who lives here be staying at a hotel?"

That's true. Getting a hotel room would make sense if Drew's goal was just to have sex with some random woman he met at the bar, but the suitcase seems odd. Unless Molly's right and Drew was pretending to be visiting from out of town.

"What did the suitcase look like?" I ask. "You said it was a carry-on, but what color was it? Do you remember?"

"It was blue. Navy blue with brown trim and a brown handle."

We don't own any suitcases like that, at least not that I know of. Did Drew buy a new one? If he did, where is it? It's not here in the apartment.

"What else did he tell you?" Molly asks.

I'm hesitant to keep sharing things with her, but find myself doing it, anyway. "He said he never told you his last name."

"He told me the first night we met, after he gave me that story about being in town for a conference."

She seems confident in what she's saying, which makes me think she's telling the truth. Either that, or she's an excellent liar.

"Did he ever give you his phone number?"

"Yeah, the first night we were together." She eyes me, her head cocked to the side. "Why? Did he tell you he didn't?"

"He said you took it. That you went into his phone when he was in the bathroom."

She bursts out laughing, which I find extremely irritating. What we're discussing isn't the least bit funny.

"I did not break into his phone," she says, finally settling down. "He guards that thing with his life. When he went to the bathroom, he always took his phone with him. And any time he looked at it, he'd turn the screen away so I couldn't see it."

That sounds like Drew. He's very protective of his phone, even around me. It did seem odd when he said he'd left his phone behind when he went to use the bathroom. And he wouldn't be careless enough to let Molly see his passcode.

In this instance, I believe Molly over Drew. But why would he lie about giving her his phone number?

"I don't know if it was his actual phone," Molly says. "It looked really cheap, like one of those burner phones. It'd make sense for him to use that instead of his real phone, especially if you know his passcode."

"I don't. We agreed when we got married that we

wouldn't share what's on our phones. I didn't argue about it because I trusted him. I didn't have a reason not to." I pause, my thoughts racing through my head so fast I'm having trouble focusing. "What'd the phone look like? Can you give me any details?"

What she describes is definitely not Drew's phone, or not the one he uses around me. He must have bought one specifically to hide what he was doing, although it seems a bit much to buy a phone to communicate with a woman he was only with for a few nights. Were there others? Was Molly just one of many? Or is there something else Drew's doing that he doesn't want me knowing about? Is he gambling? Buying drugs? No, he wouldn't do that. He hates gambling, and he's never touched drugs after his friend from high school nearly died while taking them.

"Now it makes sense why his number didn't work," Molly says. "He must've gotten rid of the phone after we stopped seeing each other."

"But you kept trying to reach him," I say, remembering what Drew said about her stalking him.

"No." She shakes her head. "I knew it was just a fling. When it ended, I didn't think I'd talk to him again, but then I found out I was pregnant so I called him to let him know."

"And he didn't answer," I say, confirming what she told me before.

"The number didn't work. It said it was no longer in service."

Drew must've gotten rid of the phone, assuming what Molly's saying is true and he actually had a phone I didn't know about. I don't want to believe any of this. I want to believe my husband just made a terrible mistake after drinking too much. And maybe I could believe that if it had only happened once, and if he didn't go out and buy an extra phone to use to call his mistress. That tells me he planned this. He went to that hotel looking for a woman, which makes me think Molly is telling the truth about Drew approaching her the night they met versus his version where she was the aggressor.

My phone rings and I see Drew's name on the screen. I tense up and notice my heart going faster. I shouldn't be reacting this way to a call from my husband, but I'm feeling on edge after talking with Molly. I thought I could trust Drew, but now I'm not sure that I can.

"Hey, honey," I answer in my usual cheerful tone. "I thought you were in a meeting."

"I was supposed to be, but my client cancelled. She was afraid to drive in the storm."

I glance out the window. "The storm is over. It's not even snowing."

"The roads are still bad. They were covered in ice when I drove into work. Anyway, I wanted to see if you'd made any progress in finding a place for Molly to go."

"No, not yet. Why?"

"I want her gone as soon as possible. I don't want you around her."

Why? Because she might tell me the truth and I'll find out you lied to me? That's what I'm thinking, but I don't say it.

"I'll make some calls and see what I can do." I look over at Molly. Her head is resting on the back of the couch and her eyes are closed. "I made an appointment at four today for the paternity test. Can you make that work?"

"I'll have to cancel a meeting, but yes, I'll be there. Text me where to go."

"I will. I need to get going. I have a lot to get done before the appointment."

"Sara, I'm sorry about this. I can't say that enough. I hope that someday you'll forgive me."

Forgive him for what? Cheating on me? Lying to me? Getting a woman pregnant? There are so many things I need to forgive him for, and I'm not sure I can do it.

"I love you, sweetheart," Drew says. "I'll see you at four." He ends the call.

"I need to go get ready," I tell Molly as I get up from the couch. She doesn't respond, and her eyes are still closed. I think she fell asleep.

I let her be and go down to my room. After a quick shower, I go into the walk-in closet, stopping next to Drew's section. I pull out one of his suit jackets and search through the pockets. I don't find anything, but I feel compelled to go through the rest of them, checking for any evidence that he's having an affair. I'd like to think it only happened once and that he'd never do it again, but what if I'm wrong?

I put Drew's suit jacket back, deciding not to go down this path. I'll drive myself crazy if I'm constantly looking for proof that Drew is seeing another woman. For now, I'm going to believe his brief affair with Molly was the only one, and that he'll never do it again.

13

"I'M GOING to go try everything on," Molly says when we get back to the apartment after a morning of shopping. We went to several stores and came home with more than I planned to buy, but I realized she'd need more than a few items if she'll be living in a homeless shelter. I wasn't sure how often they did laundry, or if they even had laundry service available. I don't know how any of that works. I've never been to a shelter, not even to volunteer.

"Go ahead," I tell her. "I need to make some calls."

She goes to her room while I go to mine. I get out my phone and search online for women's shelters. I find more than I thought I would, but I suppose that makes sense in a city this size. I pick the one closest to the cafe where I met Molly, assuming that's the one she went to before.

"Yes, I'm calling to ask if you have any rooms available," I say when a woman answers. "Or beds, I guess. I'm not sure how this works. I've never been to a shelter."

"Beds is correct. We put several in a shared room."

"Do you have any available? I need one tonight, if possible."

"Is this an abuse situation? Because there are shelters specifically for victims of abuse that—"

"She's not being abused. She just needs a place to stay."

"I see. So this isn't for you? You're asking for someone else?"

"Yes. I met a young woman yesterday who's been living in the park. It's far too cold for her to be outside. She needs somewhere warm to go."

"I agree, but unfortunately, I don't have any open beds right now. We filled up when the storm started and now we're having to turn people away."

"Could you recommend a place she could go? A place that might have an opening?"

"I could, but none of them will have beds until the weather warms up."

"Is it possible to add another bed? Or maybe a cot? I really need to find her a place to stay. She's nine months pregnant. She can't be staying outside."

"There are shelters specifically for pregnant women. That's where she should go. Let me give you their names." She rattles them off. "I can't promise they can get her in, but you could at least call and ask."

"Yes, I'll do that." I wonder if this woman remembers Molly. If she doesn't, it could mean Molly was lying and never went there. "By any chance, do you recall seeing her there? The woman I told you about? She's in her twenties. Blond hair. And as I said, she's nine months pregnant."

"No, I haven't seen her, but I don't work here every day."

"Is there someone else I could talk to that might've seen her?"

"I could connect you to the shelter's manager, but she's usually in the back office. I doubt she would've seen her. Why are you asking?"

"Oh, I was just curious. I'll call those other shelters you mentioned. Thank you for your help."

I call the shelters and find none of them has space for Molly, but I leave my name so they can let me know if a bed opens up. Until then, we'll have to get Molly a hotel room. The cost of that will add up quickly, but we don't have a choice. We can't have Drew's former lover living with us.

What's going to happen once she has the baby? She'll need a permanent place to live. Will Drew and I have to rent an apartment for her? How will we afford that? Rent prices in Boston are extremely high, and we're already paying a fortune for the apartment we're in now. Drew's job pays well, but not well enough to pay all of Molly's expenses along with the costs that come with having a baby. We were hoping to buy a house this year, but that's not going to happen if we have to support both Molly and her child.

I'm furious that Drew's put us in this position. Why did he have to do this? Why wasn't I enough for him? And if he was going to cheat, why didn't he take precautions to make sure something like this didn't happen?

"Sara?" Molly knocks on the bedroom door.

I walk over and open it. Molly is standing there in her new maternity jeans and the long-sleeved black T-shirt she picked out. It clings to her stomach, which is what she wanted. She said she didn't want anything baggy because it would make her look even bigger. I'm not sure why she's so worried about her appearance. It's not like she'll be dating anytime soon.

"What do you think?" She spins around.

"It looks good." I smile at her. "Did you try on anything else?"

"Yes, and everything fit." She lunges forward and wraps her arms around me. "Thank you for doing this, Sara. You have no idea how happy it makes me to have clean clothes that actually fit."

"You're welcome," I say, feeling very uncomfortable. Why is she hugging me? It's not appropriate. We're not friends. She slept with my husband. Does she think I can just forgive her and move on?

She finally lets me go. "Why don't I make us lunch?"

"You don't have to do that."

"I want to. You've done so much for me, Sara. You must be exhausted. You stay here and rest and I'll find something to make." She takes off and goes down the hall.

"Molly, I'd really prefer to make it myself," I say, following her to the kitchen. She's already opened the fridge and is moving things around. It angers me that she does things without asking. My entire kitchen, including the refrigerator, is organized just the way I like it. I have a system. And Molly is ruining it!

"How about this?" She pulls out a container of deli meat. "I could make us some sandwiches."

"You can't eat deli meat." I take the container from her. "And please stop moving things around in the fridge. I have it organized a specific way."

"I can't have a sandwich?" she asks as she watches me put things back as they were. In less than a minute, she managed to make a complete mess of my refrigerator.

"You can have a sandwich, but not with deli meat." I align the containers of yogurt, which Molly scattered all over the top shelf. "It's not allowed during pregnancy. How do you not know this?"

"No one ever told me. I've eaten it before and nothing happened. I don't think it's dangerous."

I turn to her. "It *can* be, so why risk it?"

She takes a step back, raising her hands in the air. "Whoa. Back off. I didn't know, okay? You don't have to yell at me."

Was I yelling? I didn't think I was, but I guess it's possible. She's making me very angry, and after spending all morning with her, my patience is wearing thin.

I inhale a calming breath. "I didn't mean to yell. I was just concerned about the baby. Your doctor should've told you what foods you should avoid."

"I don't have a doctor. I go to the free clinic and see whoever's working that day. Most of them aren't very good, and they have so many patients that they don't have time to talk about stuff."

"What about your mother?" I close the refrigerator door. "She didn't tell you these things?"

"She didn't know I was pregnant. I didn't want to tell her and have her worry about me. By the time I was showing, my mom was too out of it to notice. The cancer had spread and there was nothing more the doctors could do. She slept most of the day until one day she..." Molly gazes down at the floor. "She was gone."

My anger at her fades as I think of all this woman has gone through. Caring for her dying mother. Being evicted from her apartment. Ending up homeless. It's a devastating story, and I do feel bad for her, even though part of me hates her for sleeping with my husband, getting pregnant, and completely disrupting our lives.

"I'm sure that was a very difficult time," I say. "I'm sorry you had to go through that."

"I really miss her." A tear slips down Molly's cheek. "She's all I had. Now I'm all alone." She puts her hand over her stomach. "With no one to help me. How am I supposed to take care of a baby when I don't even have a place to live?"

"We'll help you," I blurt out. "Drew and I will make sure this baby has whatever he needs."

She smiles a little. "That's really nice of you, Sara. I knew you were a good person."

It's not about being a good person. If this is Drew's baby, he's obligated to provide for it, but what about his role as a father? How involved will he be in this child's life, and what will that mean for us, and the children we plan to have?

That's assuming we'll stay together. I still haven't decided if that's what I want. I'm not sure I can forgive Drew. I keep wondering if there's more he hasn't told me... and if what he's told me so far is actually true.

14

"We'll call you tomorrow with the results," the woman at the clinic says as she hands Drew the receipt for the bill.

When we arrived here, Molly and Drew were taken back to a room to do the test while I remained in the waiting area. Normally, the results take days, or even weeks, to come back, but we paid a rush fee to get them back within twenty-four hours.

"Thank you," Drew says to the woman as he stuffs the receipt in his pocket. "If I'm unable to answer the call, please leave the results on my voicemail."

She nods. "I will. Is there anything else?"

"Could you call me as well?" I say. "In case Drew doesn't answer his phone? I don't want to wait for him to check his messages."

"Honey, I don't think that's necessary," Drew says to me. "I'll tell you as soon as I find out." He looks at the woman. "Just call my cellphone."

"Yes, Mr. Tallow." She glances at me, then back at Drew, looking at us like she thinks we don't get along.

Like our marriage is in trouble. Or maybe I'm just assuming that because she knows why we're here. Couples with strong marriages aren't in need of paternity tests because of an affair. It's embarrassing and humiliating, and I find myself angry at Drew all over again for putting me through this. I keep hoping I'll wake up and find this was all a horrible nightmare.

"I'll see you at home," Drew says to me as we go out to the parking lot.

"I need to stop at the office and pick up my computer," I tell him. "I told Marie I'd try to work from home tomorrow."

I'm working from home because I'm still not comfortable leaving Molly alone in our apartment. Drew's letting her stay with us for another day. I called him earlier and told him I couldn't get her into a shelter and that he needed to find her a hotel. I could've done it myself, but then realized I was doing all the work and Drew was doing nothing. Molly is his problem, and he should be helping me deal with her.

When we arrived at the clinic, I asked him what hotel he had booked and he said he had forgotten to do it. I wanted to wring his neck. How could he forget? He keeps saying he wants her gone, and then he forgets to do the one thing that would make that happen? He took me aside and apologized, then said Molly could stay another night and we'd find her a place tomorrow. By "we" I'm sure he means me, but I'm not letting him off that easily. I'm going to make him do it, and I'm going to keep calling and reminding him until he does.

"I could go with Drew," Molly says to me, "since you need to make a stop."

"It should only take a few minutes," I tell her. "I just need to run into the building."

"I don't mind taking her," Drew says. "The car's over here." He motions for Molly to follow him.

"See you later, Sara." Molly winks at me and smiles. What's that about? Is she trying to tell me something?

She's a very odd woman. She's always doing things that have me questioning whether she's mentally sound. It could just be that she has an unusual personality, but sometimes I think it's more than that.

When I get to the office, I find a stack of folders piled up on my desk. It's research for the stories I'm working on. The office intern compiles research for all the writers. She must've seen my request in the project folder and decided to get it done today.

"Sara, I was just about to call you."

I look up and see Marie coming into my office.

"I'm just here to get my computer." I pick it up and stuff it in my laptop bag.

"Did you see my message?" she asks. "About your article?"

"No. Was it an email?"

"It was a text. I sent it around four. I thought that's why you were here."

"I didn't see it. I was at an appointment." I get my phone out and see the notification from Marie. Before I can read the text, she starts talking again.

"There was a problem with that article you did on how to get stains out of carpet. The advertiser said you didn't describe the steps in enough detail. They want you to redo it, and they're insisting we post the revised version by tomorrow. I need you to look over their notes and make the necessary edits. It shouldn't take more than an hour."

An hour? I need to get home. I don't want Drew alone at our apartment with Molly, not that anything would happen, but I'd feel more comfortable if I were there.

"I'll do it when I get home," I say to Marie.

"Could you do it now? I want to review it and have it posted before I leave for the night."

I force out a smile. "Of course." I pull out my laptop and set it on my desk. "I'll get to work."

"Great! I'll be in my office if you need me."

As I start up my computer, I call Drew.

"Hey, honey," he says. "I thought you'd be home by now."

"I'm stuck at the office. There's a problem with an article and I need to fix it."

"It's after five. Can't you do it tomorrow?"

"It's sponsored content and the advertiser wants the article revised and posted by tonight. Marie's here waiting to review it."

"How long's it going to take?"

"I don't know. I'll do it as fast as I can."

"There's no rush. Take your time. Do you care if I have dinner? I'm starving, but I'll wait if you want me to."

"No, go ahead. I'll text you when I'm on my way home."

It's almost seven by the time I revise the article and Marie okays it, a full hour later than I expected. As I leave the building, I text Drew that I'm heading home. It's only a five-minute drive, but the parking lot is always full this time of night and I spend ten minutes driving around, hoping someone will leave. I finally just park on the street.

"Drew?" I call out as I go into the apartment. "Sorry I'm late. It took longer than I thought it would."

He doesn't answer, and I notice the apartment is darker than it should be. Only the living room lamp is turned on.

"Drew?" I call out again as I turn on the lights that should've already been turned on by Drew. He knows which lights need to be turned on and at what times. I've written it down for him on a schedule since the times vary depending on the hours of daylight throughout the year. "Drew, would you come out here?"

He doesn't answer, igniting my frustration with him. I march down to the bedroom, fling the door open, and find he's not there. And the lights aren't turned on. I go over and do it myself, then go back out to the hall.

"Molly?" I knock on her door. "Do you know where Drew went?"

My question is met with silence.

"Molly, I'm coming in, okay?" I crack open the door and find her room is dark. Is she asleep? I open the door more. "Molly?" She doesn't answer. I flip on the light and see that the room is empty. Molly's not here. She's gone. And so is Drew.

My heart takes off, beating hard and fast in my chest. Where the hell is Drew? And where is Molly? Did they go somewhere? Why didn't he tell me?

An image fills my head of the two of them running off into the sunset to live happily ever after with their new baby boy. I race into the room and tear at the sheets, ripping them off the bed. I want to scream, but if

I did, one of my nosy neighbors would probably call the police.

"Sara?" I hear Drew's voice and whip around to see him standing at the door to the guest room. "What are you doing?"

I see him eyeing the balled-up sheets in my arms. "I, um, thought I'd change the sheets."

"Why?" Molly appears behind Drew. "I only slept on them for a night."

"Yes, well, they'd been on there for months and I felt they needed to be washed."

Drew comes over to me. "Honey, are you okay?"

"I'm fine." I smile and hand him the sheets. "Would you put these in the wash? I'm going to make the bed."

"Sure." He turns to leave.

"Where were you?" I ask.

He turns back. "We went to dinner. I didn't feel like making anything."

Drew took his former lover to dinner? Why would he do that? After telling me she's a liar and not to trust her? He said he didn't even want to be around her, and yet he took her out for a meal?

"It seems rather late to be getting home," I say.

"The restaurant was crowded." Molly comes into the room. "We had to wait."

"Where did you go?" I ask.

"That new Italian place that just opened up a few miles from here." Drew turns to Molly. "What was the name of it?"

"I don't remember," she says with a laugh. "But I have pregnancy brain. What's your excuse?"

"Just tired, I guess."

"Then you should get to bed," I say to Drew. "I'll meet you in the bedroom as soon as I'm done here."

"Thanks for taking me out," Molly says to Drew.

He nods, and Molly watches as he leaves the room.

She makes it sound like her dinner with Drew was a date. Is that what she thinks it was? If so, I'll be setting her straight. Drew was just being nice. I'm sure he would've preferred to go alone, but asked her to join him to be considerate.

"Can I help?" Molly asks as I take a set of sheets from the linen closet.

"I can do it." I shake out the bottom sheet and begin fitting it over the mattress. "You go ahead and get ready for bed."

"Can I wear Drew's T-shirt again? We forgot to buy pajamas, and I don't want to wear one of my new shirts to bed. They're too tight."

That's why you should've bought shirts that were looser. I kept telling her that when we were shopping, but she insisted on getting shirts that conformed to her body. She said it's the style these days, as if I were too old and out of touch to know this.

"Drew won't mind, will he?" she says. "You said he never wore that shirt, right?"

"Yes, fine, go ahead." I don't look at her as I continue to make the bed. I finish up as she comes out of the bathroom, wearing Drew's shirt and nothing else.

"What happened to the shorts I gave you?" I ask.

"The waistband was too tight. I'll just wear the shirt." She comes over to the bed. "I'm exhausted. I can't wait to get some sleep."

I step aside as she gets into bed. "So you enjoyed your time with Drew?"

"Sara, I'm really tired." She yawns. "Can we talk tomorrow?"

"Of course. Have a good night." I leave her room and shut the door, then go across the hall to my bedroom. I find Drew in the closet, getting undressed. "You took her to dinner?" I say in a harsh tone.

He turns to face me. "Is that a problem?"

"Yes, it's a problem! You're leading her on!"

He chuckles. "Honey, it was not that kind of dinner. There was no romance. It was simply two people eating a meal."

"Two people who had an affair. And are having a child together!"

Drew grips my shoulders and locks his eyes on mine. "I have zero interest in Molly. I honestly don't know why I ever found her attractive. So if you're upset because you think I still see her that way, you can relax. Nothing's going to happen. You, Sara, are the love of my life, and I will never be unfaithful to you again."

I want to believe him, but how do I know he's telling the truth? What if he and Molly reconnected over dinner and decided to rekindle their romance? He said he's not interested in her, but what if he's only telling me that so I won't suspect something's going on between them?

Is this how it's going to be now? Am I going to question everything he says? I can't live that way. I can't live in a constant state of uncertainty, wondering what's true and what's not.

Drew leans down and gives me a kiss. "I know it's still early, but I'm going to try to get some sleep. It's been a long day."

"Where are you sleeping?"

He takes a step back. "I thought I'd sleep here. In our bed."

"Do you really think I want to sleep next to you after what you did? It's been a day, Drew. One day. I'm not just going to forgive you and move on after one day."

"Sara, I told you, we need to show Molly that our marriage is strong. That's not going to happen if I'm sleeping on the couch."

"It's normal for a wife to make her husband sleep somewhere else after finding out he had an affair. It doesn't mean our marriage is doomed to fail."

"Yes, but why put ideas in Molly's head? Why even hint that there might be a problem between us? Why not just let me stay here? It's only for a night, and tomorrow, when Molly's gone, I'll go back to the couch."

I sigh. "Fine. But stay on your side of the bed."

We're both in bed by eight. Drew's snoring within minutes, which doesn't make sense to me. He has a wife who's furious with him. The woman he had an affair with is sleeping across the hall. And in a few short hours, he'll find out if he's going to be a father. How can he sleep with all that going on?

15

THE NEXT MORNING, Drew is up at six and out the door by seven. I didn't sleep well, so decide to linger in bed after he leaves. When I finally get up around eight, I put on my robe to go make coffee. I'm in the hall when I hear Molly talking in her room.

"They didn't tell me," she says. "I guess I'll just wait and see."

Who is she talking to? Herself? It doesn't sound like she's talking to the baby.

Molly laughs. "She'll find out today." Another pause. "Yeah, okay. Bye."

I lightly knock on the door. "Molly, are you up?"

"Just a minute," she calls back. Moments later, she opens the door, wearing the yellow robe she stole from me. "What do you need?"

"I was going to ask if you wanted breakfast."

"Yes, I'm starving," she says dramatically, as though she hasn't eaten in days. "I'd offer to help, but I don't want to get yelled at again."

"I didn't mean to get upset with you. It's just that I have a system, and I don't like anyone disturbing it."

"Why do you need a system? Are you like OCD or something?"

"No, I just prefer order over chaos. I find it lowers my stress level."

"What are you going to do when this little guy comes to visit?" She points to her stomach. "If he's anything like I was as a kid, he'll destroy the place." She laughs. "My mom said I used to tear the house apart."

I shudder at the thought. Drew will need to establish rules for when his child comes to visit and will need to discipline him if he misbehaves. I love children, but I don't believe they should be allowed to do whatever they please. Molly doesn't seem to agree with that, which could be a problem when this child arrives.

I'm still holding out hope Drew isn't the baby's father. I'm doing my best to be kind to Molly, but I don't think I can keep it up for the next eighteen years, or however long Molly remains in our lives.

"I'm going to take a shower," Molly says.

"Who were you talking to?"

She gives me a confused look.

"Just now," I say. "I heard you talking to someone."

"Oh!" She smiles. "My friend, Lori. I met her when I lived in New York."

"I thought you didn't have a phone."

"I do now." She pulls a phone from her pocket. "Drew got it for me. He said I might need it for emergencies."

"When did Drew get you a phone?" I say, my stomach knotting up.

"Last night. After dinner."

"Why didn't either of you mention it?"

She shrugs. "We didn't think we needed to. Are you mad he got it for me?"

"No, I just wish he'd talked to me first."

"Why? Are you one of those wives who has to approve all of their husband's purchases?"

I'm offended by her question, which implies I'm controlling of Drew.

"A cellphone involves a contract," I say. "That's a commitment. A commitment Drew shouldn't be making until he's sure he's the father of your child."

"He just added me to your plan. It's not a big deal. He could always take me off."

He added Molly to our cellphone plan? And didn't think he should talk to me first? He'd only do that if he was certain the baby was his, and that Molly would be a permanent part of our lives.

I think I'm going to be sick.

Molly's phone rings and she answers it. "Yeah, this is Molly." She listens. "Okay. Thanks for letting me know. Bye." She looks at me. "I need to tell you something."

"What? Who was on the phone?"

"It was the clinic. They got the results."

"I don't understand," I say, my mind racing as it tries to accept the news. "I thought they wouldn't know the results until later today."

"The woman on the phone said the lab they use is staffed overnight. The results were waiting for her when she came in this morning."

"And?" My heart's going so fast I feel like I might pass out. "What did they say?"

"The baby's father is Drew." Molly smiles. "Now

you don't have to wonder anymore. We know for sure that Drew's the father."

My knees are buckling and I grab hold of the doorframe for support. "Why did they call *you*? They were supposed to call Drew. The clinic doesn't even have your number."

"I texted it to them last night and asked them to call me. I'm sure Drew got a call as well."

As she says that, I hear my phone ringing from the bedroom. I race in there and grab my phone from the nightstand. "Drew?"

"Sara, are you okay? You don't sound good."

"Molly just told me the news," I say, noticing I'm out of breath. "She got the test results."

"I wanted to tell you myself. That's why I called." He sighs. "I'm sorry, Sara. I know it isn't the news you wanted."

I keep quiet, unsure what to say. Congratulations doesn't seem to fit in this scenario. Drew's going to be a father. It's something he's wanted for years, but I wasn't able to give it to him. Instead, Molly will — the woman who slept with my husband.

"Honey, say something," Drew urges. "Are you even a little happy about this? We'll finally have a baby in our lives. I know it's not the same as if it were ours, but it's still a baby. You love babies."

I do, but I didn't want this. So I can't be happy about it. Every time I see this child I'll be reminded of the affair Drew had.

"I'm going to be a father." Drew says it like he's talking to himself, not me. He laughs a little. "I'm going to be a dad in a few weeks. Can you believe it? It doesn't even seem real. I'll have a son."

I can't listen to him telling me how wonderful this is. I can't bear hearing the excitement in his voice. The joy.

"Drew, I need to go. We'll talk later." I end the call and toss my phone on the bed.

Maybe I just need to accept this and put my anger aside, not for Drew, but for the sake of this innocent child. It's not his fault he was conceived from an affair. I can't be mad at the baby, but I *can* be mad at Drew. Couldn't he at least wait a day for me to let this sink in before he expresses how happy he is about the news?

"What did Drew say?"

I turn and see Molly standing at the door. I forgot to close it. I wonder if she was listening in on my conversation.

"He said the same thing you did," I say without any emotion. I don't want her knowing how upset I am and gloating. "That the results came in and he's the father."

"How did he sound?" she asks.

"Happy, or as happy as he could be given the circumstances."

"Meaning what?"

I walk over to her. "Meaning he would rather it be us having a child and not you and him. I'm sure you can understand why he'd feel that way."

"What about you?" she says. "Are you okay? I know this isn't what you wanted."

"I'm fine." I straighten up. "I assumed the baby was his, so the news doesn't surprise me."

"What does this mean for you and Drew? Are you going to stay married?"

"Of course. It's not an ideal scenario, but we'll make it work."

I don't know if that's true. I haven't decided

whether I'm staying with Drew or leaving him. Right now, I want to divorce him, but my emotions are running high so I can't trust my judgment. I need to calm down and clear my head before I consider what to do next.

"Sara, he cheated on you," Molly says, as if I needed this pointed out. "And he lied to you. Why would you still want him after that?"

"You want me to divorce Drew?" I fold my arms across my chest. "Is that what you're telling me?"

"You can do what you want, but I don't know how you can stay with someone you can't trust. And do you really want to help raise someone else's baby?"

"It's not someone else's. It's Drew's." I glare at her. "Molly, I know what you're doing, and I find it really distasteful after all I've done to help you."

"What do you mean?" she asks, seeming genuinely confused.

"You want me to divorce Drew so you can have him for yourself."

"No." She shakes her head. "That's not what I want. I'm not even attracted to Drew. Not anymore."

"You really think I believe that?" I say sarcastically.

She grips my arm. "Sara, I'm serious. I don't want to be with Drew. I'm not even sure I want him around my kid."

"Why wouldn't you?" I ask, surprised by her comment.

She looks like she wants to say something, but doesn't, her lips pursed.

"What is it?" I ask. "Why are you looking at me like that?"

"Forget it," she says, letting go of my arm. "I

shouldn't have said anything." She turns and goes back to her room, shutting the door.

What was that about? None of what she said makes any sense. She tells me to divorce Drew, but then denies she wants him for herself? Despite what she said, it's obvious she wants to destroy my marriage so she can be with Drew. Even if that's her plan, Drew wouldn't want to be with her. She was a fling. A fantasy. She's far too young for him and acts even younger than her age. She's not college educated and lacks the social skills needed to be married to someone like Drew. He's an executive, a partner at his firm. Imagine if he took someone like Molly to a client dinner and introduced her as his wife. People would think he was having some kind of midlife crisis. He'd be laughed at. Ridiculed. His reputation would be destroyed.

I'm not concerned about Molly replacing me. I'm concerned she'll become a permanent part of our lives and expect us to support her. I don't have a problem helping her for a few months, or even a year, until she can get a job and support herself. But I'm worried she won't do it. That she'll expect Drew to support her financially and use their child to guilt him into agreeing to it.

My heart is racing and I feel pressure in my chest. I take a deep breath and tell myself to calm down. I'm getting ahead of myself, imagining the worst that could happen. I need to remain in the present. Take this a day at a time. Back when I saw a therapist, that was the advice she gave me. She said I looked too far into the future. She said that's what caused my anxiety and my need to have order in my life.

"Sara?" Molly knocks on my door. "Do you care if I get something to eat?"

I open the door. "I told you I'd make breakfast. I just need to clean up first."

"I don't mind doing it myself," she says. "I'm feeling lightheaded. I think if I ate something, I'd feel better."

"Fine," I snap. "I'll just get ready later."

Molly moves out of my way as I go past her and down the hall. I feel her behind me as I make my way to the kitchen.

"What would you like?" I ask, yanking open the refrigerator door.

"Whatever you have. I just need to eat."

I take out a container of yogurt and some fresh berries. "Will this do? I don't have the energy to make you a hot breakfast."

"I'm good with that." She watches as I rinse the berries and put them in a bowl. I add the yogurt and set the bowl in front of her.

"Could I have some sugar?" she asks, staring at the plain Greek yogurt like it's not edible. For someone who was begging for food a few days ago, she sure is picky.

"I'll give you some honey," I say, going to get it. "It's better for you than sugar." I hand her the jar. "You really should learn the basics of nutrition, for both you and your child."

"Maybe you could teach me." She drizzles the honey over her yogurt. "You seem to know a lot about it."

I'm not sure if she's making fun of me or honestly wants me to teach her. I'm having trouble figuring Molly out. One minute I think she's some naïve, clueless young woman, and the next I think she's playing me and hiding her true self, which is someone who's conniving and manipulative and would do anything to get what she wants.

"I talked to Drew," Molly says as she eats her breakfast.

I was making coffee, but stop and look over at her. "When?"

"A few minutes ago. When I was in my room."

"He called you?"

"Yeah. About the baby." She plucks a strawberry from the bowl with her fingers and puts it in her mouth.

"What did he say?"

She chews her strawberry and swallows it, then says, "He wants me to see a doctor. I missed my last two appointments because I didn't have a way to get there. Drew made an appointment for today at noon. He's picking me up."

He's taking her to the doctor? And made the appointment? Why didn't he tell me this? I spoke to him just a few minutes ago. Did he not want me to know?

"What's wrong?" Molly asks. The hurt and confusion I'm feeling must show on my face. "Are you upset that he's going with me?"

"Of course not." I force out a smile. "He's the father. It makes sense that he'd go. I assume he'll be taking you back here after your appointment?"

"I guess so. I mean, he has to go back to work, right?"

"Yes, this is a busy time for him with tax season gearing up."

"I don't understand any of that," she says, continuing to pick the berries up with her fingers. Why can't she just use a spoon? She eats like a toddler. Out of all the women Drew could've had an affair with, why would he choose her? He likes smart, sophisticated women, and Molly is neither of those things. "When Drew talks about all that tax stuff, I almost fall asleep."

That's another reason she has no future with Drew. He loves talking about his job. I admit I get tired of hearing about it, but at least I understand what he's saying and do my best to show interest in it.

What did Drew and Molly talk about when they met? She said they talked for hours before going up to the room. How could they possibly fill that much time? They have absolutely nothing in common.

I really want to know what happened that night. Was Molly the pursuer or was it Drew?

"What time is Drew picking you up?" I ask.

"Around eleven-thirty. Why?"

"I think I'll run some errands while you're out."

I won't be running errands. I'm going to that hotel and seeing if I can find out what really went on the night Drew and Molly met. There must be someone there who remembers seeing them together. Someone who can tell me the truth about that night.

16

DREW'S GOING to be here any minute to pick up Molly for her doctor's appointment. I've pretended to be working all morning, but I haven't written a single word. I haven't even looked at any emails. I don't know how I'm going to do my job when my mind can only seem to focus on Drew and what's going on with him and Molly.

"Hey, Sara," Drew says as he comes into the apartment. He texted me after I spoke with Molly this morning to tell me he was taking her to her appointment. I didn't respond. "Is Molly ready?"

"I don't know." I mindlessly type on the keyboard. "I haven't seen her since breakfast."

Drew walks over to the table where I'm pretending to work. "You're welcome to come with us to the appointment."

"I'm going to use the time to run errands." I look up at him as he stands beside me. "Do you know what time you'll be back?"

"Probably around two. I thought we'd go to lunch after the appointment."

"You're taking Molly to lunch?" I say with a strained smile. "How thoughtful."

"It's more out of convenience. I won't have time to eat when I'm back at the office so I thought I'd grab something before I went back."

"And take Molly along," I say, my gaze going back to my laptop. "How sweet."

Drew sits down across from me. "Sara, don't be like this. She's having my child. There's a lot we need to talk about."

"And by 'we' you mean you and Molly." I glare at him. "Because this has nothing to do with us. Or our marriage."

He lets out a heavy sigh. "Honey, I know we need to talk about this, but I don't think now is the time. You're too upset with me. All we'll end up doing is fighting."

That might be true, but that doesn't mean he should shut me out. A supportive husband would let me vent my feelings, even if those feelings made him uncomfortable. But that's not Drew. He hates it when I get emotional. He says if I want to talk about my feelings I should talk to my girlfriends. Except my girlfriends are all back home in Philadelphia. When I moved here for Drew's job, I lost touch with them, and I haven't made any new friends since coming to Boston.

"What are you talking to Molly about?" I ask.

"I need to find out what she plans to do after the baby arrives. I don't want her taking my son and leaving town."

"She wouldn't do that. She has nowhere to go."

"She could go wherever she gets a job. She's not tied to Boston. The only family she had was her mother, and she's gone." He leans toward me and lowers his voice.

"I've decided to hire a lawyer. I don't trust that Molly will stick around. If she ditches me and takes off with my son, I need to be prepared with legal action."

"Drew, I really don't think she'd leave. She wants you in the baby's life."

"She says that, but I don't believe her." He glances behind him to make sure Molly's not there. "Don't tell her any of this. I don't want her to know about the lawyer."

I nod. "I won't say anything."

He stands up. "I'm going to go see if she's ready. We need to leave or we're going to be late."

He goes down to her room. I hear Molly's voice, then Drew's, but I can't hear what they're saying. Moments later, they come out from the hall and head to the door.

"Bye, Sara," Molly says, giving me a wave.

"Bye," I mutter, glancing up from my laptop.

"I'll text you on our way home," Drew says to me.

They finally leave, and I shut my laptop and go to the closet to get my coat. I don't know how long this will take. I need to leave now so I'm back when Drew and Molly return.

Traffic is bad, and it takes me half an hour to get to the hotel. Since it's close to Drew's office, it's possible I could run into one of his coworkers, although I don't know why they'd be here in the middle of the day. The bar is more of an after-work spot.

As I walk into the dimly lit room and see the row of barstools, I feel sick to my stomach. Last May, Molly and Drew were sitting on those very barstools, talking and flirting with each other. Meanwhile, I was home, feeling sorry for my husband because he was working so late.

Some nights he didn't get home until midnight. I should've known he wasn't at the office.

A younger man dressed in black pants and a white button-up shirt walks up to me. "I'm sorry, but we don't open until three. If you're looking to have lunch, the restaurant's just down from the lobby."

"Actually, I was hoping to talk to someone who works at the bar."

"That would be me," he says, grinning broadly. "I'm Brandon, one of the bartenders. How can I help you?"

"I wanted to ask about one of your customers. He comes here now and then after work. His name is Drew. He's in his forties, dark hair—"

"Yeah, I know Drew," Brandon says, still giving me that broad grin. "What about him?"

"This may sound odd, but do you remember him being here with a woman? A cute little blonde in her twenties?"

"Are you talking about Molly?"

"You know Molly?" I ask, surprised he knew who I was talking about from that vague description.

"She used to work here. She was one of the housekeepers, but then she quit and I never saw her again."

"When did she quit?"

"Last summer. I think it was June."

Molly told me she interviewed here but didn't get the job. And she said she applied to work at the front desk, not clean rooms.

Brandon's smile drops and a look of concern comes over him. "What is this about? Did something happen to Molly?"

"Why do you think something happened to her?" I ask, curious as to why his mind went there.

Brandon cocks his head. "Are you a detective?"

"No, I'm..." I hesitate, not sure what to say. I decide to go with the truth. "I'm Drew's wife. My name is Sara."

Brandon's smile returns and he shakes my hand. "Nice to meet you. I've heard Drew mention you a few times."

"Oh, really? What did he say about me?"

Brandon shrugs. "I don't know. He wasn't talking to me. I just overheard him saying your name."

"Do you know who he was talking to?"

"Just people from work. Drew's here a lot with those guys, but I guess you already know that since you're his wife," Brandon says with a laugh.

Drew told me he comes here once or twice a month. I wouldn't call that a lot, which makes me think he comes here more often than he claims.

"About that woman," I say. "Molly. Did you ever see her here with Drew?"

"Yeah, but it was a while ago. Back when she was working here. Why do you ask?"

What do I tell him? Do I go with the truth or make something up? I can't tell how loyal he is to Drew. Would he cover for him and say Drew wasn't doing anything inappropriate that night? Or would he cover for Molly? If she worked here, it's possible she was friends with this man.

"Molly recently showed up in our lives," I say. "Pregnant, with no place to live."

"Molly's pregnant?" Brandon's eyes widen. "Wow. I didn't think she wanted kids."

"I don't think this was planned. Anyway, what can you tell me about Drew and Molly? When you saw them here?"

"They talked a lot, and he bought her some drinks. That's about it."

"You didn't notice their interaction was anything more than... two people talking?"

He eyes me like he's not sure what I'm asking, then a look of recognition comes over him and he says, "Shit, is Drew the kid's dad?"

"Yes," I say, clearing my throat. "And given the timing, it seems that it happened last May, here at this hotel."

Brandon blows out a breath and shakes his head. "Drew and Molly. I never would've guessed."

"So you didn't notice anything when you saw them together? Anything to make you think something was going on between them?"

"No, not at all. They were just talking. A lot of us who work here know Drew, so if he was messing around with Molly, I think he'd try to hide it. He wouldn't want us finding out and telling his wife or someone from his office."

"I suppose you're right," I say, knowing Drew and his cautious nature. He'd want to keep his dirty little secret hidden from anyone who might tell on him. I thought the alcohol would've caused him to let his guard down, but it doesn't sound like it did.

"How many times did you see them together?" I ask. "Do you remember?"

"I don't. If I had to guess, I'd say maybe four or five times."

"How well did you know Molly?" I ask.

"We talked now and then, but I didn't know her that well. She only worked here for a couple of months."

"Did you know her mother was ill?"

"No, she never mentioned her mom."

If Molly's mother was seriously ill, her coworkers would know that, wouldn't they? That doesn't seem like something she'd keep secret. She told me about her mother after I'd only known her for a few minutes.

"I need to get back to work," Brandon says. "But hey, I'm sorry all this is happening. I hope everything works out."

"You've been very helpful. Thank you. Oh, and one more thing. Could you keep this between us? I don't want Drew to know I was here."

"Yeah, okay." Brandon takes off and goes behind the bar.

As I'm walking through the lobby on my way to the door, I see Tim, a man who works with Drew, coming into the hotel with a group of men I don't recognize. I quickly turn around, hoping Tim didn't see me.

"Sara!" he calls out.

I turn back and put on a smile. "Tim. How nice to see you. It's been a while."

"Probably the Christmas party," he says, smiling back.

"Yes, that was it. Well, I was just leaving so—"

"What are you doing here? Did you meet Drew for lunch?"

"No, I was going to meet a friend, but she couldn't make it so I'm heading back to the office."

"I'm here getting these guys checked in." He motions to the three men standing next to him. "They're from the Philly office. They're here in town for some training." He looks over at the men. "This is Drew's wife, Sara. They met back when Drew was working in Philly."

We'd planned to stay there, but then Drew got promoted to partner and we had to move to Boston. I left my friends and family behind. For Drew. If I'd known he was going to cheat on me, I never would've left Philly. Or married Drew.

"Nice to meet you," I say to the men, then I say to Tim, "It was good seeing you."

"You too. Hey, you and Drew should take one of the rooms sometime." Tim winks at me. "Have a little romantic weekend."

"You mean here?"

"Yeah, the firm has rooms reserved for client visits or when we have staff here from other offices. Half the time the rooms don't get used. There's no cost. They're already paid for. You should talk to Drew about it."

"I will." I check my watch. "I really need to go. See you later, Tim."

"Yeah, have a good day!"

Drew's accounting firm has rooms reserved at this hotel? I didn't know that. Drew must've used one of those rooms when he was with Molly. It's the perfect scenario because I'd never find out. There's no credit card trail.

Now I'm wondering if Drew invited more than just Molly up to his room. All those times he said he was working late, he could've been at this hotel with any number of women, and I never would've known.

Drew never told me his firm had rooms reserved at this hotel. He didn't want me to know about them. But why? And what else doesn't he want me to know?

17

"How was the appointment?" I ask when Drew and Molly get home just after two. I'm sitting at the kitchen table with my laptop. I tried to do some work, but I couldn't. My mind was on Molly and what Brandon told me about her. Why would she lie about working at that hotel?

"The doctor said everything's good," Molly says, going to the kitchen.

"He said the baby could come any day now," Drew says, beaming like a proud father.

It makes me sick. And angry. And jealous of Molly for getting to experience all this with Drew when he should be experiencing it with me! *I'm* supposed to be the pregnant one. He's supposed to be going to *my* doctor's appointments, not hers.

"She's not due for several more weeks," I say.

"Yes, but Dr. Grant said we should be prepared for anything." Drew sits down across from me. "He said the last month doesn't always go as planned. The baby will come when he's ready, which could be on his actual due date or could be next week."

"Is it okay if I have some orange juice?" Molly asks.

"Go ahead," Drew tells her. "You don't have to ask."

Molly takes the orange juice bottle from the fridge while I grind my teeth in an attempt to remain calm. Drew knows I don't like people helping themselves to items in our kitchen. It disrupts my orderly system, which causes me to feel a great deal of anxiety. And yet he didn't even consider that when Molly asked for the orange juice.

Is this how it's going to be? Is Drew going to let Molly do whatever she wants now that he knows the baby is his?

"He seemed like an excellent doctor," Drew says. "Molly and I decided he should deliver the baby."

He and Molly decided? Like they're a couple? I want to reach over and punch Drew. He could've worded that differently. Does he not have any compassion for what I'm going through?

"This is the doctor at the free clinic?" I ask.

"No," Drew says. "I took her to see someone else. I called and got a recommendation from the fertility clinic."

"*Our* fertility clinic?" I ask, my brows rising. "The one where I had an appointment?"

"Yeah. I figured they'd be the people to ask. They recommended several obstetricians but said Dr. Grant is the best."

"They didn't find it odd that you were asking?" I say.

"I told them it was for someone at work."

I'm relieved he didn't tell them the truth. I would've

been terribly embarrassed if anyone there had found out my husband was having a baby with someone else. Then again, I don't know why I care. I'll probably never go back there. Drew won't want to continue trying to have a baby when he's having one with Molly. He'll want to wait a few years, and by then, it'll be even harder for me to conceive. It might even be too late.

Drew gets up. "I need to get back to the office."

"Could you wait?" I say. "I need to talk to you."

He sits back down. "Go ahead."

I glance at Molly standing by the counter. "Could you give us a minute?"

She holds up her glass of orange juice. "Can I take this to my room?"

"Yes," I tell her. "Just be careful not to spill."

She leaves and goes down to her room.

"Why does she keep asking for your permission?" Drew says.

"Because she's a guest in our home. She can't just do whatever she wants."

Drew sighs. "Sara, you've gotta loosen up. Molly's a grown woman. She shouldn't have to ask your permission to take a drink to her room."

I sit up straighter. "You're scolding me for setting rules in my own home?"

"It's my place too, and I'm tired of you having so many rules. I shouldn't have to stop and think before putting something away. I should be able to put it wherever I want."

"You used to like that I was organized," I say, glaring at him from across the table. "You said you couldn't live in a place that was a mess."

"There's a difference between having a clean house and having to line up the yogurt in the fridge or hang my bath towel perfectly straight."

My pulse speeds up and I feel myself getting warm. "I was trying to make a nice home for you. Most husbands would appreciate that."

"I do. But, God, Sara, enough is enough. You've taken it too far. I can't relax. I come home and have to think about every little thing."

"Is this because of Molly?" I snap. "Did she tell you to say this? Because it would make sense. The woman is a total slob. And now she's using you to convince me to let her get away with making our home a mess."

"This isn't about Molly. It's about me. I'm tired of it, Sara. I need you to loosen up on the rules and not insist that everything be so organized."

"Fine." I throw my hands up. "We'll just live in filth. Will that make you happy?"

"That's not what I meant." He stands up. "I'm going to work. We can argue about this later."

"Drew, wait." I get up and go over to him. "What are we going to do about Molly? Did you call any hotels?"

"I didn't have time."

"I can't keep missing work. We need to find her a place."

"Just go to the office tomorrow. Molly can be here by herself. She's not going to steal anything."

I stare at him, confused. "Yesterday, you told me to be careful around her, like she was some kind of criminal. And now you have no concerns about her?"

"I still have concerns, but like you said, what's she

going to do when she's nine months pregnant? She can barely get up from a chair."

"That wouldn't stop her from stealing from us. Or breaking something. Or making a mess everywhere."

"Then take tomorrow off if it makes you feel better. Sara, I can't talk about this now. I'm going to be late for a meeting."

He grabs his coat and leaves without kissing me goodbye. Without even glancing my way. Like I no longer matter to him. Like Molly is his focus now.

I hear the door to her room open and the sound of her coming down the hall. She must've heard Drew leave.

"Is everything okay?" Molly asks, going to the kitchen with her empty juice glass. "You look upset. Were you and Drew fighting?"

"It's really not appropriate for you to ask. Whatever's going on with Drew and me is private. It doesn't concern you." I type on the keyboard, hoping she'll think I'm working and go away.

Instead, she sits next to me. "Did Drew say anything about what happens after the baby gets here?"

I look up from my laptop. "What do you mean?"

"Like how involved he wants to be."

"We haven't discussed it, but I know he wants to be part of his child's life. I would think you'd want that, too."

She looks down, then back up at me. "What if I didn't? What if I didn't want him near my baby?" She protectively covers her stomach. "Would you help me?"

"Help you what? I don't know what you're asking."

She leans toward me, still clutching her stomach. "I don't want Drew around the baby. He's not a good person, Sara. I know you don't want to believe that because he's your husband, but I know a side of him that you don't. And it's not good."

Here she goes again, trying to turn me against Drew. Trying to make me leave him. I'm not falling for it. If I decide to leave Drew, it'll be because I chose to, not because Molly conned me into doing it.

"I need to get some work done," I say, looking back at my computer. "Why don't you go to your room and rest?"

"You know he lies to you. He lied to you about me, so you know he lies to you about other stuff, too."

My eyes dart back to her. "Speaking of lies, you said you never worked at that hotel. The one where you met Drew."

"Yeah?" She sits back. "What about it?"

"You worked there for several months. Cleaning rooms."

She tilts her head to the side. "According to who?"

"One of the bartenders. He was very informative."

He really wasn't, but I want Molly to think he was so she'll wonder what he told me. Maybe it'll make her fess up to whatever else she's hiding.

"Who was it?" she asks. "What was his name?"

"Why does it matter?"

She sighs. "Just tell me what this is about. What do you want?"

"The truth. I want to know why you made up that story about not getting a job there when you'd worked there for several months."

"I was embarrassed, okay? I didn't want you to know I cleaned toilets for a living."

"Why?"

"Because I'm ashamed of it. People looked down on me when I did that job. They treated me like trash. Guests would pass me in the hall and look the other way, like they were disgusted with me."

"It couldn't have been that way all the time. I've always been nice to people who work in housekeeping."

"Yeah, well, the people there were horrible to me, so I don't like telling people that's what I did. I don't ever want to feel that way again."

"Does Drew know?"

"No. I hid it from him. He never would've talked to me at the bar that night if he'd known I was the person cleaning his room."

"Why did he think you were there that night?" I ask. "What did you tell him?"

"I said I stopped in to have a drink."

"That's it? You didn't tell him what you do for a job?"

"He didn't ask, so no, we didn't talk about it."

"What about the other times you were with him? He never asked about your job?"

"No, but I told him I was taking care of my mom, so maybe he thought that's all I did."

It's strange Drew never asked. Maybe he didn't want to know too much about her. If his goal was to sleep with her and move on, he wouldn't bother trying to get to know her.

"You told me you and Drew talked for several hours before going up to the room. What did you talk about?"

She glances at the glass she left on the counter. "I need some water."

"I'll get it." I jump up and go to the kitchen to fill her glass, then bring it back to her.

"Thanks. Is it okay if I take it to my room? I want to take a nap."

"You didn't answer my question," I say, sitting back down. "What did you and Drew talk about?"

She takes a sip of water. "His job? I don't really remember."

"You do. You just don't want to tell me."

She frowns, looking at me with pity. "Because I don't want to make you feel bad. You're a really nice person, Sara, and I know he only said those things because he felt guilty for what he was doing. He was trying to make himself feel better by saying bad things about you."

"What bad things? What did he say?"

"Just the usual stuff married guys complain about."

"Like what? Can you give me an example?"

"Like saying you never want to have sex." She rolls her eyes. "It's the same excuse all guys use to cheat."

"But it's not true. We had sex all the time. We were trying to have a baby."

"He told me that, but it wasn't until later. The last night I saw him. He said sex wasn't fun anymore. That it seemed like a chore because it was all about making a baby."

I didn't know Drew felt that way. Why didn't he tell me? That's something we could've worked on.

"Other than that, did he have any other complaints?" I ask, trying to maintain my composure and not show how upset I am that my husband was confiding in her about our marriage.

"Sara, I really don't think we should be talking about this. You just got done telling me that your marriage is none of my business."

"Yes, but you're already involved in this. And I need to know what he said about me."

She chews on her lip, not saying anything.

"Molly, would you please just tell me?"

She lets out a heavy sigh. "He said he's tired of all your rules and that you get mad if he doesn't follow them. He said it makes him feel like he's a kid and you're his mom."

"You mean rules about keeping things clean?"

"That, and also the organization stuff, like how everything has to be lined up perfectly. And he doesn't like all your schedules, like for when lights need to be turned on or off."

That's another thing we could've discussed if he'd told me. Actually, he just did, before he left, but why didn't he bring it up before now?

"What else?" I ask.

Molly gives me that pity look again. "I don't want to say it."

"Why?" I ask, my pulse going faster.

She doesn't answer.

"Molly, would you just tell me?" I say, exasperated with her.

"He said he was tired of you. That he didn't want you around anymore."

"He wanted a divorce?" I nearly choke on the words.

She chews on her lip again, her eyes darting side-to-side.

"Is that what he said?" I ask when she doesn't respond. "That he wanted to divorce me?"

"No," she whispers.

"I don't understand. If he didn't want me around, what did he mean?"

She swallows, her eyes fixed on mine. "He wanted you dead."

18

"You obviously misunderstood him," I say. "Drew would never hurt me."

"How do you know?"

"Because he wouldn't. He's not a violent person. He's an accountant. Do you know what accountants are like?" I don't wait for her to answer. "They're very quiet, passive people. Maybe not all of them, but most, and especially Drew. He rarely gets angry or raises his voice. He'd never in a million years hurt anyone, and if he did, it definitely wouldn't be me."

"Did you think he'd ever cheat on you?"

"Well, no, but—"

"Then how do you know he wouldn't hurt you?" She puts her hand on my arm. "What if he's not the man you think he is? How would you know?"

"Because he's my husband! That's how." I yank away from her and stand up. "Why would you say such a horrible thing about Drew? Are you that desperate to make him yours?"

"Sara, I swear I'm not making it up. When he said

it, I thought he was joking. You know how guys will say something like, 'I want to kill my wife. She's driving me crazy.' They're just joking around. They don't actually mean it."

"Drew didn't either. If he said that, it wasn't meant as a threat. He simply said it because he was frustrated with me."

I'm certain that's all it was, but it doesn't sound like Drew. He doesn't say things like that, even as a joke.

"It's just... the way he said it." Molly glances to the side.

"What do you mean?"

She shrugs. "Forget it. I'm sure you're right. He didn't mean it." She gets up. "I'll leave you alone so you can work."

I can't work after that. I couldn't work *before* finding this out, but now? After Molly tells me Drew wanted me dead? How could I possibly focus on work?

Why did Molly tell me that? Even if Drew said it, he obviously didn't mean it. She probably made it up. She keeps saying she doesn't want Drew, but then tries to convince me to leave him. If she isn't interested in him for herself, why does she care what I do? It shouldn't matter to her.

My phone rings. I don't recognize the number but answer it anyway. "Hello?"

"Hi, this is Tammy. We spoke the other day."

"Tammy," I repeat, trying to remember this woman. "I'm sorry, but how do I know you?"

"I'm from the women's shelter. You said I should call if we had an open bed."

"Yes, now I remember. It's for the young woman

who is currently living with me. She needs a place to stay."

"Well, we have an opening if you want to bring her here. Do you know how long she'll need housing?"

"I don't. She's nine months pregnant. Is there medical care available if she needs it?"

"Not here, but the free clinic is only a few blocks away. When do you think you'll be dropping her off?"

Am I really doing this? I feel bad. I don't know what the shelter's like, but it won't be as nice as staying here. And it's quiet here. The shelter is probably noisy. What if she can't sleep?

"Are you still there?" Tammy asks.

"Could I call you back?" I say.

"You can, but the opening might be gone."

"Yes, I understand. Thank you." I end the call and phone Drew.

"Hey, Sara," he answers. "I don't have much time. What do you need?"

I feel my heart going faster just hearing his voice. It's because Molly put those thoughts in my head about Drew. It's completely absurd. Drew would never lay a hand on me, so I don't know why I'm reacting this way.

"Sara, what do you need?" Drew says, getting impatient.

"Sorry, my mind is all over the place today. I was calling to let you know there's an opening at the women's shelter."

"That's great! Are you taking her there now?"

"That's what I wanted to talk to you about." I pause. "Do you really think we should do this?"

"Do what?"

"Have her live in the shelter. I'm not sure she should go there."

"Why? You keep saying you want her to leave. And I can tell how stressed you are having her there. Just take her to the shelter."

"I don't know, Drew. It seems wrong. I mean, it's not like she's a stranger. She's having your baby."

"I barely know the woman. And what I do know, I don't like. She lies, Sara. We can't trust her."

Maybe he's right. She lied about working at the hotel. What else is she lying about?

"She can't keep staying with us," Drew says. "Take her to the shelter, or I'll do it myself."

"Okay, I'll do it."

"Good. If that was it, I need to go."

"Yes, that was it. I'll see you tonight."

I'm surprised Drew doesn't want Molly staying here. I thought he'd be more protective of her now that he knows she's carrying his baby.

He's not a good person. When Molly said that, I didn't know what she meant. I still don't, but her words have me wondering if Drew isn't the kind, compassionate man I thought he was. It makes sense that *I* wouldn't want Molly here given that she had an affair with my husband, but Drew is the father of her child. And he was so nice to her earlier—taking her to the doctor today and out to dinner last night—that I thought he'd insist she stay with us. But instead, he can't wait to get rid of her.

After I call the shelter and tell them we're coming, I go down to Molly's room and knock on her door. "Molly? Are you awake?"

"Yeah," she calls out. "Just a minute." She opens the door looking groggy, like she just woke up.

"I have some news," I tell her. "The women's shelter called and said they have an opening. They said we could go there right now."

"Oh." She sounds disappointed and a little sad, which only makes me feel worse. But Drew is right. She shouldn't be here. Drew and I need to work on our marriage, and we can't do that when his ex-lover is living with us.

"Do you need help packing? I have a duffel bag I could give you."

She nods. "Okay."

I go to the hall closet, find the duffel bag, and bring it to her. "I know this is sudden, but the shelter fills up quickly this time of year. If we wait, the spot could be gone."

She walks slowly to the drawer where she put her new clothes. She takes them out, one-by-one, and brings them to the bed.

"Let me help," I say, stacking the clothes neatly in the bag.

"I'll go get my stuff from the bathroom," she says.

While she's in there, I notice her room is a mess. The lampshade is turned on its side, the comforter is falling off the bed, and the pillows have been tossed on the floor. I go to pick them up and notice I'm holding Drew's pillow. The one from his bed. Why does Molly have Drew's pillow?

"I think I got everything," she says, walking over to the duffel bag. She adds her bathroom items to it and zips it up.

"Did Drew give you this?" I hold up the pillow.

"No, I took it. The ones in here are too soft. I needed something firm to elevate my legs."

"Why didn't you just ask me to get you a different pillow?"

"I didn't want to bother you."

I've repeatedly told her not to take things without asking, and she did it anyway. Even worse, she went into our bedroom. A private and personal space that is off limits. Did she snoop around while she was in there? Go through our nightstands? Our drawers? The things in our bathroom?

I feel uncomfortable knowing she was in our room. I've kept the door closed as a reminder that she is not to go in there, and yet she did. If she'd taken a pillow from the living room, I wouldn't like it, but I could probably be okay with it. But the bedroom? She shouldn't have done that.

This is one of the many reasons she can't stay. She doesn't respect our home. And Drew and I need our privacy. We need to be able to talk without her listening in. And I need to be able to go to work or run errands without worrying about what she's doing while I'm gone.

"I think I'm ready," Molly says, picking up the duffel bag.

"Let me carry that." I take it from her and she follows me down the hall to the living room. She's quiet as she puts on her coat, and I notice her eyes bouncing around the room, like she's taking it all in because it's the last time she'll be here.

She remains quiet on our way to the shelter. If she's trying to make me feel guilty, it's working. Maybe the shelter won't be so bad. It's better than sleeping in the park. She'll have a warm bed, bathroom facilities, and other women to talk to.

"I've heard about this place," Molly mutters as I park behind the shelter.

The concrete in the parking lot is buckled and crumbling in spots, and there's a dumpster that's overflowing with garbage. An old man with a long gray beard is slumped against the dumpster, looking like he fell asleep, his head hung to the side.

"What have you heard?" I ask.

"That it's dangerous. A lot of the women come here from prison because they have nowhere else to live."

The woman on the phone didn't mention that, but I guess that isn't something you'd want to boast about. Maybe I should've learned more about this place before bringing Molly here.

"I'll get your bag," I say as Molly gets out of the car.

We go inside and I immediately notice a stale, musty smell, like the building had experienced water damage at some point.

A young woman walks up to us. "Can I help you?"

"Yes, we're here to check in," I say, then realize I should've worded it differently. This isn't a hotel.

"You must be Sara," the woman says. "I'm Tammy." She smiles at Molly, glancing at her stomach. "And you must be Molly."

"Yeah," she mutters, her expression glum.

"Follow me," Tammy says. "We'll do some paperwork and then get you settled."

Molly turns to me. "I guess I'll see you later."

I nod, my guilt creeping back. "You have a phone now, so just call us if you need anything."

She turns back to Tammy. "Show me where to go."

I watch them walk through a door that must lead to where Molly will be staying. She'll be fine. I need to keep telling myself that. And it's only temporary. Just until Drew and I can find her more permanent housing.

On the drive home, I feel even worse about leaving Molly there. As much as I dislike having her at the apartment, it doesn't seem right to make her live in a shelter. But Drew insists that she be there. He keeps saying we can't trust her and that she lies.

I do sometimes wonder if the things she told me are true. Was she really homeless and living in the park? Drew doesn't think so, but then where was she living? If she had an apartment, she wouldn't have agreed to go to a homeless shelter... unless she wanted us to *think* she didn't have a home so that she'd be forced to live with us. She wouldn't do that, would she?

It's strange she never wanted to go back to the park to get her things. More than once I offered to take her there, but she kept saying she didn't need to. You'd think someone with very few possessions would want those things back. I could understand that she wouldn't want to go there during the storm, but we could've gone today and picked them up.

Turning the car around, I decide to go see for myself if Molly's story is true. She didn't say what park it was, but I assume it's the one near the cafe where we met. There aren't any other parks within walking distance.

The storm dropped a thick layer of snow everywhere so this won't be an easy task. I get out of my car and walk down the snowy path that leads into the park, searching for where Molly might've hidden her things. She said she'd put them behind some shrubs. To my right, I spot a row of evergreen shrubs and head over there. With my gloves on, I brush the snow away from the shrubs and search for the plastic shopping bags Molly described.

"Hey!" a deep voice calls out. "What are you doing?"

I look back and see a police officer coming up behind me. I rise to standing. "I was just looking for something."

His brows rise. "In the bushes?"

"I know it sounds strange, but I can explain," I say, brushing the snow off my gloves. "The other day, I met a homeless woman who had been living here in the park. I took her to a shelter, and now I'm here to collect her things so I can bring them to her."

"By now, whatever she had was probably stolen. When was she last here?"

"Just a few days ago. And then we had the storm, so I doubt anyone took her things. But they might now that the weather's cleared up, which is why I'm here to collect them."

"People aren't supposed to be staying here overnight. If you talk to this woman, you might want to remind her of that."

"Is there anyone here to enforce the rules? Because she never said she was told to leave."

"An officer goes through the park around ten every night to make sure no one's here. Obviously, we can't stop people from walking through it, but they're not allowed to stay overnight."

If what he's saying is correct, then Molly is either really good at hiding or she never stayed here.

"Maybe you've seen her," I say. "The woman I'm talking about. She's 26 and pregnant. Short, with blond hair and blue eyes. She said she lived here for a few weeks."

He shakes his head. "Doesn't sound like anyone I've seen. And I'd remember seeing a pregnant woman."

"Do you patrol this area regularly? Or does someone else?"

"It's usually me during the day. I'm not here all the time. I do a walk-through in the morning and another in the afternoon. We normally wouldn't, but there have been some incidents lately that caused us to step up police presence."

"What kind of incidents?"

"Men bothering women. Making them feel threatened. We think they're the same two guys, but we haven't caught them yet." His radio goes off. "I need to get going. If I were you, I'd forget about finding her stuff. Even if you locate it, it's probably damaged from the snow."

"Yes, you're probably right. I'll check a few more places and then head out."

"Suit yourself." He turns and walks off.

Molly was never here. She lied. If she'd been staying in the park for weeks, that officer, or the one that checks the park every night, would've seen her. So what's the real story? Is Drew right? Does Molly have an apartment somewhere and she made up the homeless story so we'd take her into our home?

Why is she doing this? Is it to get Drew back? Even though she insists that isn't what she wants?

19

"SARA?" Drew calls out when he gets home at six.

I go down the hall and find him by the door, taking off his coat. Seeing him, I feel a sense of unease, remembering what Molly said about Drew wanting me dead. I'm sure she made it up or Drew said it as a joke, but just having that thought in my head makes me see my husband differently.

"I was cleaning up the guest room," I say. "How was your day?"

"Good." He walks up to me and brings me into his arms. "It's even better now that things are back to normal." He kisses me. "Why don't we go out for dinner? What are you in the mood for?"

"Drew, things are not back to normal," I say, pulling away from him. "You're going to be a father soon, and we need to figure out what to do with Molly."

"Sara, she's a grown woman. Molly needs to figure out her own life. It's not up to us to do it for her."

"I understand that, but she's about to have your

child. We need to make sure she has a safe place to live and has whatever she needs for the baby."

"And we will." He pulls me close again. "But it doesn't need to be tonight." He looks into my eyes. "I've missed you, Sara. I know I screwed up, but I'll do whatever I can to make it up to you. I want things to go back to how they were." He gives me another kiss, one that lingers and implies he wants more.

How could he think I would want that after finding out he had an affair? An affair that resulted in his having a child with another woman? Does he think I can just forget about it and move on?

"No," I mutter, pushing him away. "It's too soon."

He frowns, then smiles a little. "Can I at least take you to dinner?"

"Yes, but we still need to talk about Molly. I found out some things I think you should know."

His forehead creases. "What did you find out?"

"I'll tell you at dinner. Let's go to the bistro down the street. That way we don't have to mess with getting the car."

"I don't want to wait until dinner," he says, staring at me intensely. "Tell me what Molly said."

"Let's go sit down." When we're both seated on the couch, I continue, "I went to the park today—the one where Molly claimed to have been living—and looked for her things. A police officer saw me searching the bushes and asked what I was doing. I explained about Molly and then described her to him. I asked if he'd seen her, and he said he hadn't. He's been patrolling the park after some recent criminal activity so he's been keeping a close eye on who's there, and he said he hadn't seen anyone matching Molly's description."

"I'm not surprised," Drew says. "I told you she wasn't homeless."

"But why would she make up that story? And make herself look like she was homeless?"

"To get your sympathy. So that you'd help her. Give her money."

"But she didn't even know me when I met her at the cafe."

Drew holds my hand, a slight grin on his face. "I love that you have such a good heart. It's one of the things that made me fall in love with you."

"What's my heart have to do with anything?" I ask, annoyed by his condescending tone.

"You want to see the good in people so much that you overlook what's really going on." He rubs my hand. "Molly is a scammer, Sara. I keep trying to tell you that. Maybe now that you have proof the homeless story was made up, you'll believe me."

"You're saying Molly showed up at the cafe hoping someone like me would offer to help her? Give her money?"

"I'm saying you were targeted. Because of me. She must've got my last name from the bartender at the hotel, looked me up online, saw that you were my wife, and tracked you down at that cafe."

"How would she possibly know to find me there?"

"She probably found out where we live and was keeping watch on us. You go to that cafe almost every day. Molly saw that and picked a day to meet you there."

"Drew, that's crazy. If Molly found out where you lived, she'd go to you for help, not me."

"She went to you because she knows you'd feel sorry

for a woman in her condition. I'm not like that. I'm less likely to believe her bullshit. Molly knows that, so she used you to get to me. She was hoping you'd convince me to give her whatever she wants."

"Why would she assume I'd feel sorry for her? Not every woman would."

"Because you're caring. And compassionate. And you love children. You're the perfect victim for someone like Molly. She needed someone to feel sorry for her, and unfortunately, you fell for it."

"She didn't know what I was like." I pause, eyeing Drew. "Unless you told her about me. Back when you two were together."

"Sara, anyone who searches for you online can tell what you're like. Your posts on social media show you raising money for children's charities and doing fundraisers to fight hunger."

"Those were all company-sponsored events. I did them for my job. I didn't seek them out."

"Yes, but Molly doesn't know that. And when she saw you were someone who enjoys helping others, she realized the way to get to me was to go through you. She pretended to be some poor, hungry pregnant woman, knowing you'd immediately offer to help, and sure enough, you invited her to live with us."

"No." I shake my head. "That's not what happened. It can't be. You saw how shocked she was when you came home and she saw you were my husband. And then she wanted to leave. She didn't insist on staying."

"Honey, it was all an act." Drew continues to gently rub my hand. "And it wasn't just you that got fooled. When I first saw her here, I too thought it was some strange coincidence. But after I gave it more thought, I realized she'd planned this. She's probably been planning it for months."

I'm feeling ill. Is Drew right? Was this all some elaborate scheme Molly set up to make me feel sorry for her? So I'd convince Drew to give her money? Pay her rent? Or do whatever else she wants?

"I tried to give her the benefit of the doubt," Drew says. "I told myself that maybe she really didn't know you were my wife, and maybe she really was homeless. I had to know for sure, which is why I took her to dinner last night. I wanted to find out if any of what she was saying was true."

"And what did she tell you? Did she admit it was all an act?"

"No, but she said enough that I knew she was lying."

"Like what?"

"I don't remember all the details," he says. "I just know that the more I listened to her, the more I realized her story didn't add up."

"Why didn't you tell me this last night? After you had dinner with her?"

"I didn't want you to confront her about it. I knew if you did, she'd tell you I was lying. That *I* was the one making things up. She'd try to make me the bad guy so that you'd feel sorry for her." Drew looks me in the eye. "It was working. She was turning you against me, Sara. That's why I wanted her gone."

"Did you tell her this? Did you tell her you knew what she was doing?"

"And risk her taking off with my child? No, of course not. I need to be careful in how I deal with her. And so do you. We have to be nice enough to her that she doesn't suspect we're on to her while also keeping her at a distance."

"What happens after she has the baby? What's your plan?"

"As I said before, I already have my lawyer working on making sure I get custody."

"You mean partial custody."

"No. Full custody. Molly isn't fit to be a mother."

"Drew, you can't take full custody," I say, surprised he would even consider that. "The courts wouldn't allow it, and Molly deserves to see her baby."

"Not if she's mentally unsound. Sara, she's created this made-up life for herself and gone so far as to actually agree to go live in a shelter. Do you really think a person like that should be raising my child?"

When he describes it that way, it does sound concerning. It makes me wonder if Molly has some kind of personality disorder. Maybe what she's doing isn't a scam and she really does think she's been living in the park for weeks. It would be terribly sad if that were true, but if it is, we need to get her help.

"The thing I'm uncertain about," Drew says, "is how to keep Molly around until I'm able to get custody. I don't want her skipping town with my son if I don't agree to her demands."

"What demands?" I ask. "Has she asked you for something?"

"Not yet, but she will. She'll use the baby as leverage, just like she's using you."

"Do you really think this is all an act she's putting on? Or do you think maybe she really believes she's the person she's pretending to be? Because if she's that delusional, she needs to see a psychiatrist, maybe even be admitted somewhere."

"I think she knows what she's doing, but just the fact that she's doing it shows she's not mentally sound. What kind of person would take it this far? She could've fessed up when you told her you were taking her to a shelter, but instead, she went along with it. She's that committed to her story."

"What about her mother? Do you think she really died of cancer or was that another attempt to gain my sympathy?"

"I don't know, but if her mother was really dying last year, it's odd Molly never told me. All that time I spent talking to her at the bar, she never brought it up."

"But you said she told you she was in town to see her mother."

"To *see* her, not to take care of her. She never said her mother was sick."

"Her coworker said the same thing. He told me she —" I stop, realizing I didn't want Drew knowing about my visit to the hotel. I sigh and look down. "I need to tell you something."

"I already know. Tim told me he saw you there." Drew pauses, and when I look up at him, I see him giving me that intense stare again. "What were you doing there?"

"I wanted to ask about Molly."

"If that were the case, you would've told me you were going there."

"Drew, I wasn't keeping this from you. I just didn't think to tell you."

"Or your reason for going there was less about Molly and more about me." His brows rise. "What were you hoping to discover? That I pursued her? Or that I pursued other women I met there?"

"No, of course not," I say, although that's exactly what I was hoping to find out.

"You don't trust me." Drew's jaw tightens as he says it. "I told you everything, but you didn't believe me. You had to find out for yourself."

I sit up straighter. "What if I did? I have every right to check your story. Why should I believe you after you lied to me?"

"Because I'm your husband," he snaps. "And I don't want my wife talking to strangers about our marriage. I spend a great deal of time at that hotel for business purposes, taking clients to lunch or out for drinks. Now, because of you, the staff knows all of our personal problems!" he says, his face getting red. "Do you know how humiliating that is for me? Do you understand the damage you've done?"

I move away from him on the couch, disturbed, almost frightened, by his sudden outburst. He's usually so calm, even when we're arguing. I understand that he's upset, but there's no need to shout at me.

"I went there to check Molly's story," I explain. "I wasn't even going to bring you up, but then the bartender mentioned you and—"

"He just happened to mention me?" Drew says sarcastically. "Really, Sara? You think I'm stupid enough to believe that?" Drew sneers at me. "I know you asked him about me. About that night. About my interactions with Molly."

"Drew, I didn't—"

"You did!" he shouts. "I know, because I went there. After Tim told me he saw you at the hotel, I went there and immediately noticed the staff looking at me differently. Whispering about me. Brandon stopped me and congratulated me on being a father. Do you have any idea how embarrassed I was?"

"You should be embarrassed about what you did, not what I said. You're the one who had an affair and got a woman pregnant. A woman you knew almost nothing about." I fold my arms across my chest. "Did you know that she worked there? At the hotel?"

"She didn't work there," he scoffs. "She was there to have a drink."

"She worked there. Brandon told me she was one of the housekeepers. She probably cleaned the room you were staying in. The one where you two..." I can't bring myself to finish that sentence.

He shrugs. "So why does that matter? It's irrelevant."

"Maybe, or maybe not. If she had access to your room, she could've been in there going through your personal things. Trying to figure out if you had money, or something else she wanted."

"There was nothing in that room for her to see. I didn't bring anything other than my wallet, which was in my pocket."

He's lying. Or Molly is, because she told me he had a suitcase. A navy suitcase with brown trim. It had to be Molly who was lying. We don't own a suitcase even remotely resembling what she described.

"Let's not fight about this," I say, my nerves rattled and needing a break. "Let's go out and try to have a relaxing dinner."

Drew takes a breath, his lips slowly turning up. "You're right. We shouldn't argue." He stands and offers me his hand. I get up and he pulls me into his arms. "I love you, Sara. You know that, right?"

"Yes." I want to tell him I love him back, but I'm not ready to. I'm still too angry with him for betraying me.

He leans down. I assume he's going to kiss me, but instead his lips go to my ear, and he whispers, "If you ever embarrass me like that again, you'll be sorry."

I yank back, my heart beating fast. "What did you say?"

"I said that I love you." He tucks some strands of hair behind my ear. "And that you're beautiful."

"No. You said I'd be sorry. What did you mean by that?"

"I don't know what you're talking about," he says, his brows drawing together. "I said no such thing."

"You did. Just now. You whispered it in my ear."

"You must've imagined it. It's because of all the stress you're under. It's completely understandable. Maybe you should take tomorrow off and get some rest."

I can't take another day off. I need to go back to work. And I wasn't imagining it. Drew said it. He said I'd be sorry if I ever embarrassed him again. He said it in an angry, almost threatening tone.

When Molly warned me about Drew, I thought she was making it up. The idea that my husband is dangerous was completely ridiculous. I was certain he'd never hurt me. But after what he said just now, I'm starting to question that.

20

"I WAS THINKING we should look at some houses this weekend," Drew says while we're waiting for the check.

During dinner, as I was looking across the table at Drew, I began to doubt myself about what happened before we left. Did he really threaten me or did I imagine it? He swore he didn't say it, but then why did I think he did? Is it because of Molly? Did her comments about Drew make me hear something he never actually said?

"Sara?" Drew says, getting my attention. "What do you think?"

"About houses? I thought we were going to wait and look later this spring."

"With the baby coming, I'd prefer to find something now."

"Or we could convert the guest room into a nursery. That was the plan if you and I had a baby."

Drew and I haven't discussed how his baby with Molly affects our plans to have our own. Are we done trying? Does he want to wait and try later? I haven't brought up the topic because there are too many other things going on. And I don't know if I want a baby with him, not when I'm uncertain about our marriage.

"I've given it some thought and realized we need a house," Drew says. "Just imagine how difficult it would be to go in and out of the apartment with a baby. We'd have to deal with his stroller and a diaper bag and all his other supplies. Lugging all that to the elevator, through the lobby, and out to the parking lot would be a nightmare. It'd be much easier to have a house."

"I suppose, but we'll only have the baby part of the time." I finish what's left of my wine. "I don't think we should buy a house for the few days a week that we'll see him."

"Assuming I get custody, it'll be more than that." Drew takes his napkin from his lap and sets it on the table. "We'd already planned on finding a house this year. Why wait? Why not do it now?"

How does he not know the answer to that? We can't buy a house when I haven't decided if I'm staying with him. Just a few nights ago, he was sleeping in a hotel. We haven't even discussed how to fix our marriage, and he's acting as if everything's fine and we can continue on as if nothing's happened.

"I'll take this when you're ready," the server says, setting the check on the table.

Drew pulls out some cash to cover the bill. "It's all set."

The server smiles and takes the money. "Thank you." He glances at me. "You two have a good night."

When he's gone, Drew says, "I called our realtor. She has a few houses in mind. She said she could show them to us on Sunday since I'll be working Saturday."

Drew works Saturdays during tax season, and sometimes Sundays too. That was one of the things I used to hate about his job, but now I'm looking forward to him being gone. It'll give me time to focus on myself and what I want, which may not be him and this marriage.

"I don't want to look at houses this weekend," I say, still irritated that he even suggested it.

"Why?" Drew asks, completely clueless. "Do we have plans?"

I lean toward him, lowering my voice. "We're not in a good place right now. I think we need to focus on our marriage, not finding a house."

"We can do both. They're not mutually exclusive."

"Drew, you're not getting it. I don't..." I take a breath. "I'm not sure I want a house with you. I need time to process what happened and decide what I'm going to do."

"Sara, the baby will be here any day. We don't have time to think about this. We at least need to start looking."

"I'm sorry, Drew, but I can't agree to that. Honestly, I can't believe you'd expect me to."

He shoves his chair back and stands up. "Let's go."

We leave the restaurant and head back to our apartment. The sidewalk is a slushy mess from the snow, but I didn't want to drive. Our building is only a few blocks away, and I needed the walk and the fresh air to tamp down the anger I was feeling after Drew threatened me.

"I'm still upset about what you said," I say to Drew as he walks beside me.

"About the house? Then fine, we'll wait."

"Not about the house. About how I'd be sorry if I embarrassed you. I don't know why you'd say something like that. I felt like you were threatening me."

"Sara, stop." He grasps my arm and turns to face me. "I have no idea what you're talking about. I never said that. I don't know where you even came up with it."

"Don't lie to me, Drew. I heard you say it. I didn't make it up."

"You did, because it's not what happened. I leaned down to kiss you, and you turned your head to the side. My lips touched your ear, but I didn't say anything."

I didn't turn my head. Did I? No. I'm certain I didn't. So why is he saying I did?

"I don't know why you're denying this," I tell him, "when you clearly said it. Maybe you didn't mean it, but those words definitely came out of your mouth."

"I'm sorry, honey, but it's not true." He rubs my arm. "I would never say anything like that to you. I love you. I wish you would believe that." He takes my hand. "Let's go home. It's freezing out here."

We get back to the apartment and Drew sits down to watch TV. I'm too anxious to join him, my mind trying to figure out what's going on. I know I didn't imagine what Drew said. I'm not crazy.

My phone alerts me to a text. I assume it's Marie asking if I'll be at work tomorrow, but when I look at the screen, I see the text is from Molly.

Are you okay? Let me know!

Why is she asking if I'm okay? Why wouldn't I be?

"I'll be in the bedroom," I say to Drew.

He doesn't respond, his attention on whatever sport he's watching.

I go into our room and shut the door, then text Molly. *I'm fine. Why are you asking?*

He's angry you told Brandon. He wants to punish you.

I assume she's referring to Drew, but when did he talk to her about Brandon? And why is he doing this behind my back? If he talked to Molly, he should've told me.

I text her. *When did you talk to Drew?*

My phone rings. "Hello?"

"Are you alone?" Molly asks.

"Yes. I'm in the bedroom. Drew is in the living room watching TV. When did you speak to him?"

"He called on his way home from work, whenever that was. Maybe five-thirty?"

"And what did he say?"

"That you talked to Brandon. He said you told everyone at the hotel what he'd done. How he got me pregnant."

"That is not what happened. I simply asked Brandon if he'd seen you with Drew. I mentioned you were pregnant, and Brandon asked if it was Drew's. I suppose I could've lied, but it was too late. He'd already figured it out." I sit down on the bed. "Why would Drew call you about this? Or call you at all? He says he wants nothing to do with you."

He also thinks Molly's a liar and a con artist, but I'm not going to tell her that. I haven't convinced myself she's trying to scam us. She hasn't asked us for anything, and I checked the guest room and nothing was stolen. So if she's scamming us, what's her plan? What does she want?

"He called to complain about you," Molly says. "I think he just wanted someone to talk to."

"Why would he do that? Is something still going on with you two?"

"God, no," she says like she's disgusted by the thought of that. "But he used to like talking to me back when we were together. He said I was a good listener, and that when he talked to you, you'd interrupt him or lose interest in what he was saying."

That's not true. Why would Drew tell her that? Maybe he didn't. Maybe it's another one of her lies intended to get me to leave Drew. Maybe he didn't even call her, but then how did she know about Brandon?

"What else did Drew say about me?" I ask, my pulse going faster. I'm really upset that Drew called her. It doesn't make sense. "Besides the stuff about Brandon."

"He said you haven't changed. That you're still criticizing him all the time. That nothing he does is ever good enough. It's all the same stuff he said back when we used to meet at the bar."

"But it isn't true. I mean, yes, I can be critical sometimes, but what wife isn't? And what husband isn't critical of his wife? It's human nature."

"He said you don't respect him, and that you going to the hotel today proves it. A good wife wouldn't go behind her husband's back to verify what he already told her. He said something like that, and then he said you purposely told Brandon about the affair to make him look bad."

"That is not true. I never intended for anyone there to find out."

"It doesn't matter. Drew's convinced himself that's why you did it. He was really angry. I've never heard him sound like that. I was going to blow it off and blame it on him being stressed from work and everything going on, but I couldn't let it go. I had to call and warn you."

"Warn me about what?" I ask, my stomach knotting up as my fears about Drew suddenly feel more real.

"Does Drew have a gun?" she asks.

"No," I say, noticing my hand is shaking. "I wouldn't allow it. I hate guns. Why do you ask?"

"He made this comment. He said something like, 'Sometimes I just want to shoot her'."

"That doesn't sound like Drew. Are you sure that's what he said?"

"Yeah, but I was hoping it was just a comment and didn't mean anything. This girl I worked with used to say she wanted to strangle her boyfriend for flirting with other girls, but she wasn't actually going to do it."

"Strangle and shoot are two different things. Saying you want to strangle someone is simply a phrase people use to express their anger. It's not the same as saying you want to shoot someone. If Drew said he wanted to shoot me, maybe he really does."

"That's why I told you to be careful around him. I don't think he'd do anything, but if he did, and I hadn't warned you, I wouldn't be able to live with myself. What happened when he got home? Did he get mad at you?"

"No. Not really."

"What do you mean?"

"We discussed what happened at the hotel, and although Drew was angry about it, we decided we didn't want to fight. He gave me a hug and said he loved me and then..."

"Then what?"

"Never mind," I say, deciding I've said too much. "It doesn't matter. I'm sure he didn't mean it."

"Sara, come on. Tell me."

"He, um, he whispered something in my ear." I pause. "He said if I ever embarrassed him again, I'd be sorry."

"Sara, you gotta get out of there!" Molly says in an urgent tone. "Now! You can't wait."

"I'm not leaving. Drew was fine after that. We went out for a nice dinner and now everything's back to normal, or as normal as it can be given what we're going through."

"How can you stay with him after he threatened you?"

"It wasn't really a threat," I say, although it sounded like one at the time. "I'm not even sure he said it. When I asked him about it, he acted like he didn't know what I was talking about. Like I made it up. Maybe I did. But I don't know why I'd make up something like that."

"Maybe you were thinking it in your head and thought he actually said it?"

"It's possible, but I don't remember ever having done something like that before. I'm not going to worry about it. The bigger concern is Drew calling you and complaining about me." I swallow. "Saying he wants to shoot me."

"Maybe it was just a comment, but even if it was, be careful around him. And don't believe everything he says."

The same could be said about Molly and her story about being homeless. I should confront her about that, but I don't have the energy. I'm too drained after hearing this news about Drew.

"I have to go," Molly says. "It's almost lights out.

They make us all go to bed at the same time since we're all in the same room."

"How's it going? Have you met any of the other women?"

"Well, yeah, I'm living with them. I'm kind of forced to meet them."

"Have they been friendly?"

"Some have, some haven't. This one woman got mad when I accidentally bumped into her and she tried to punch my stomach."

"That's awful," I say, shocked that someone would do that, knowing it could harm the baby.

"She's hooked on drugs," Molly explains. "A lot of women here are on drugs. They're not supposed to be, but this place doesn't seem to enforce the rules. They're flashing the lights, which means I have to get into bed. Be safe, Sara. I'll talk to you later." She ends the call.

The bedroom door opens and Drew walks in. "Were you on the phone? I thought I heard you talking to someone."

"I was." I stand up. "Molly called."

"Why?" His brows draw together. "What did she want?"

My heart races as I consider what to tell him. I can't just let this go. I have to know why he called her, and let him know he shouldn't be doing that if he's serious about saving our marriage.

"She wanted to tell me something." I pause. "Something you should've told me yourself."

21

"Why are you still talking to Molly?" Drew asks, sounding frustrated with me. "Most wives would hate the woman who had an affair with her husband, and you're acting like you want to be friends with her."

"I'm not trying to be her friend, but she's a part of our lives whether I like it or not. And I can't help but feel bad for her and the situation she's in."

"But that's what she wants. Can't you see that? She wants you to feel sorry for her so she can get you on her side."

"And whose side should I be on? Yours?"

"Of course. I'm your husband."

I walk over to him. "How can I be on your side when you don't tell me things?"

He folds his arms across his chest. "What things are we talking about?"

"You calling Molly today on your way home from work. Why didn't you tell me you called her? How can I learn to trust you again if you're keeping things from me?"

"What did Molly tell you I said?" Drew asks, his brows rising.

I'm not sure it would be wise to share everything Molly said since Drew clearly didn't want me to know. And if he finds out Molly told me, he'll be reluctant to tell her things in the future. I want to know what Drew is saying about me behind my back, and the only way I'll find that out is through Molly, assuming Drew continues to confide in her.

"She said you complained about me," I say.

"Oh, really?" He smirks. "And what were my complaints?"

"That I criticize you. That you feel like nothing you do is ever good enough."

"What else?"

"That was it," I say, deciding not to reveal any more than that. "If you have complaints about our marriage, you should be talking to me, not Molly."

"I agree."

"You do?" I say, surprised he's not trying to defend himself. "Then why did you call Molly to complain about me?"

"I didn't." He takes out his phone, swipes through it, and shows me the screen. "Look at my call list. Do you see any record of me calling her?"

I glance through the list and only see calls he made to me. "Maybe you deleted it."

"Or maybe I never called her. Maybe she made it up." He puts his phone back in his pocket. "Did you even consider that?"

"Why would she make it up?"

"To make you think I'm a horrible husband who complains about his wife. To make you think I can't be trusted. To convince you I'm still interested in her." Drew grips my shoulders and looks into my eyes. "Sara, how many times do I have to say this before you believe me? Molly is a scammer. An opportunist. She'll do whatever's necessary to get what she wants. She sees you as an easy target, so she continues to use you to her advantage. And you're allowing it."

"If you're right, then what does she want?" I ask, challenging his theory. "What is she using me for?"

"I already told you." Drew lets go of me. "She's turning you against me so you'll divorce me and she can have me for herself."

"You're assuming she wants that, but how do you know?" I ask, thinking how disgusted she sounded when I accused her of wanting Drew. "Has she done anything to indicate she wants you back?"

"Yes," he says emphatically. "She has."

"What did she do?"

"On the way to her doctor's appointment, she told me she wanted us to be a family. She and I and the baby. Not you. She told me to divorce you and then described the life she imagined us having. She talked about our wedding as if she'd already had it planned out. The colors she wanted. The flowers. What kind of cake we'd get." He shakes his head. "It was really quite sad. I honestly think she believes this fantasy of hers will actually come true."

Did that really happen or is Drew just saying it did? I don't know who to believe. I want to believe Drew, but my gut's telling me to believe Molly. What does that say about my relationship with my husband? That I would believe a woman who is basically a stranger over the man I'm married to?

"What did you say to her?" I ask. "When Molly described this future life she wanted with you?"

"I told her it was never going to happen. And I have to say, seeing how disappointed she looked, I was like you. I felt sorry for her. Despite what you may think, I'm not some cold-hearted jerk who has no feelings for this woman. But my feelings for her aren't romantic, not in the least. I feel bad for her. That's it. I feel bad that she believes this story she's created about us is actually going to come true. It's tragic and sad, but I can't indulge her. I can't let her think it's going to happen."

If Molly really believes she's going to marry Drew, then I need to stop listening to all the things she tells me about him. I assumed all along that her goal was to get rid of me so she could have Drew for herself, so why do I keep doubting it? Why do I feel like she's telling me the truth and Drew's the one making up stories?

"By believing her lies," Drew says, "you're only making it harder for her. You're giving Molly hope that she could have a future with me. She needs to know you're committed to our marriage and that nothing she says will change that."

"I haven't decided if that's what I want," I say. "It's possible I'll decide our marriage needs to end."

Drew takes my hand. "I don't want that to happen. I'll do whatever you need to make this work."

"It might be too late," I mutter, gazing down at the floor.

"If so, or if you're even considering ending our marriage, you can't tell Molly. We need to keep that between us." Drew grips my hand tighter. "Sara, I'm begging you to stop letting her get into your head. Stop listening to her lies. Stop believing what she says. Don't even answer your phone if she calls. I know you feel a need to help her, but that's not your job. It's mine, but only when it comes to the needs of the baby. I'm not obligated to help Molly, and doing so would be to my detriment. She'd see it as a sign I want to be with her on a romantic level, which is never going to be the case."

"Fine. I won't answer her calls." I say that, but I'm not sure I'll follow through. Drew doesn't get to decide who I talk to, and I don't have to tell him. I have a feeling he's not being honest with me, so I feel no obligation to be honest with him.

"Good." He smiles. "I knew you'd come around." He lets go of my hand and starts unbuttoning his shirt. "I'm exhausted. I'm going to go to bed."

"You can't stay here." I watch as he goes over to the dresser. "I made up the guest room for you."

"Why would I sleep in the guest room?" He turns back. "We're married, Sara. Married people sleep in the same room."

"Until one of them cheats," I say in a sharp tone. "I told you I need time to decide what I'm going to do. I'm not ready to go back to how things were, including having you in our room."

"Sara, I slept here last night."

"Yes, and I was very uncomfortable. I only agreed to it because Molly was here. Now she's not, and I don't want you staying here."

He turns back to the dresser, takes out his pajamas, and walks over to me. "You're letting her destroy us. And destroy our marriage. I hope you realize that. Because it's not going to end. She'll keep this up until you're out of my life. Even if she has to kill you to do it."

"She is not going to kill me," I say, thinking Drew is

more likely to kill me than Molly. I don't actually believe he would, but you know what they say. It's always the husband.

"Why won't you listen to me?" Drew demands, his eyes narrowed. "What the hell has she done to you? Why are you taking her side? Believing her lies?"

"I don't know who to believe," I say, my heart racing as I look back at Drew. I can feel his anger and it's putting me on edge. What is happening to him? Where's the calm, gentle Drew I used to know?

"If you want to keep playing her games," Drew says, "I guarantee you'll lose. I only hope you're still here when she's done with you." He storms out of the room, slamming the door behind him.

Why is Drew being like this? Why is he trying to scare me and make me think Molly is dangerous? I wonder what he'd say if he found out Molly was warning me about *him*. Saying *he's* the dangerous one, not her. I'm sure he'd deny it, then tell me it's more proof that she's trying to turn me against him.

I'm torn about what to do. I want to believe Drew, but there's a part of me that can't. I don't know if it's because I no longer trust him after finding out about the affair, or because I'm seeing a side of Drew I didn't know existed. An angry, volatile side that makes me feel unsafe and like he's capable of doing things I don't even want to imagine.

Like kill me.

22

"You're back," Marie says, smiling at me as she comes into my office. "Any chance you have the article ready for me to review?"

"No," I say with a sigh. "I'm sorry, Marie. Things have been crazy at home. I didn't have a chance to work on it. I'll do it right now and try to have it to you by noon."

She sits down across from me, leaning back and crossing her legs. "You want to tell me what's going on?"

"I just wasn't able to get to it." I look at my laptop screen and see hundreds of unread emails. "I didn't have time."

"I'm not asking about the article," Marie says. "I'm asking what's going on with Drew."

"It's... complicated," I say, not sure how else to describe it. "But I'm sure we'll figure it out."

"Talking about it might help. Sometimes you just need someone to listen."

It *would* help to talk to someone, but I don't know if that person is Marie. I feel like I shouldn't be discussing my personal life with my boss. But she already knows about Drew's affair, so I might as well tell her what else is going on. She'll eventually find out anyway when Drew's baby arrives.

"Okay, but like I told you before," I say, "I need this to stay between us. I'm not ready for everyone in the office to find out."

"You mean about Drew's affair?"

"It's more than that." I close my laptop and lean back in my chair. "Drew's going to be a father."

Marie's face lights up. "You're pregnant? Sara, that's wonderful! I'm so—"

"It's not mine," I say, interrupting her. "The baby's mother is the woman Drew had an affair with."

I tell Marie the story of how I met Molly, brought her home to live with us, and then discovered she'd slept with Drew and was having his baby.

"That's why I haven't been at work," I say. "I didn't want to come to the office and leave a woman I barely know at my apartment all day. Drew didn't want her staying with us, so I took her to a women's shelter yesterday afternoon. I don't know how long she can stay there or where she'll go when the baby arrives. It's all up in the air for now."

"Sara, I'm so sorry," Marie says, sounding both shocked and sympathetic. "How awful for you to be going through this, especially after trying so hard to have a baby of your own. And what an odd coincidence that you just happened to run into this woman who had this connection to Drew."

"He thinks it was intentional. Drew thinks Molly tracked me down and planned the whole thing. Our meeting at the cafe. Getting me to feel sorry for her so I'd ask her to live with us."

"Do you think he's right?"

"I don't know." I pause, my mind replaying my interactions with Molly. "I suppose it's possible, but if she made it all up, she's an excellent actor. She really had me convinced."

"Have you tried checking her story?"

"Yes, and unfortunately, I found out she hasn't been truthful about some things. She said she had never worked at the hotel, but she actually did, and a police officer at the park told me he'd never seen her there."

"Then that's your answer. You can't trust this woman. She's probably hoping to convince Drew to leave you and marry her instead."

I nod. "Drew claims she told him to divorce me so they can be a family."

"He claims?" Her brows rise. "Meaning you don't believe him?"

"After finding out he had an affair, I don't know if I can believe anything he says. I'm sure you can understand what that's like. Not being able to trust someone after you've been betrayed."

"Of course. I've been there myself with my ex. But we're talking about Drew's word over some woman you barely know who you just admitted lied to you."

"Yes, but how do I know Drew isn't lying? Am I just supposed to trust he's telling me the truth about Molly?"

"What reason would he have to not be truthful about her?"

"To make her look bad. To make me not believe the things she says about him."

"What does she say about him?" Marie asks.

"I shouldn't talk about it." I pick up a pen and nervously tap it on the table, watching it move up and down. "It's ridiculous. I don't know why I even let my mind entertain the idea."

"What idea? What did she say about Drew?"

"Forget it. I'm sure it's nothing."

"If it were nothing, you wouldn't be drilling that pen into the table." Marie grabs my hand, stopping the tapping motion. She waits until my eyes rise to hers. "Tell me what she said."

I swallow. "She said I should be careful around him. That he might... harm me."

Marie rears back. "Drew? He's the mellowest person I know. I can't imagine him hurting an insect, so I certainly can't imagine him hurting his wife. He loves you, Sara. You know he wouldn't hurt you."

"I thought that too, but now?" I pause, not sure if I should tell her.

"Now *what*?" she cautiously asks. "Did something happen? Did Drew get violent with you?"

"No. But he did say something that frightened me."

I tell her what Drew said about how I'd be sorry if I ever embarrassed him. Then I tell her about Molly's text and what we spoke about on the phone.

"If I were you," Marie says, "I'd ask Drew to move out. If you don't feel safe with him there, he needs to leave."

"The thing is, I don't know if he actually threatened me or if I imagined it. He told me he didn't say anything, but I swore he did."

"You wouldn't imagine something like that."

"I didn't think I would, but what if I did? What if Molly's warnings about Drew have me so on edge that

I imagined him saying something he didn't actually say?"

"Stress doesn't make people hear things that aren't real. You're not delusional, Sara. You're very levelheaded. So unless you'd taken some kind of hallucinogenic drug, I'd be pretty certain Drew said it."

"Then why would he say he didn't?"

"Exactly." She eyes me. "That's what you need to be concerned about. I don't know what he's up to, but I think you need to watch what you say around him. And if you can, get him to move out. Tell him it's because you're upset about the affair and having him there is making it harder on you."

"I don't think he'll agree to that."

"He will if he knows it might save his marriage. He should be groveling and begging for your forgiveness, and if you tell him to move out, he should do it without arguing."

"That's not Drew. He always insists he knows what's best for us, and in this case, he thinks living together is the only way to save our marriage."

She shrugs. "You can do what you want. I'm just saying what I would do. He's shown you he can't be trusted by being with this other woman. And now he's making threats. You really want a man like that staying with you? Sleeping next to you in bed?"

"He's staying in the guest room. He's not happy about it, but I insisted." I pause. "He's changed. This past week, Drew's really changed. I don't know if it's the stress of my finding out about his affair, or if it's because Molly showed up and told him he's going to be a father. Whatever it is, he's not the same as he was before."

"Do you think there's more he's hiding?"

"Yes," I say without hesitation. "I just don't know what."

"Then you need to find out." Marie plants her hands on the desk, her eyes on mine. "You need to hire a private investigator. I did it with my ex, and you wouldn't believe all the stuff he was hiding from me."

"I don't think it's necessary to hire an investigator. And I'd worry that Drew would find out."

"Then investigate him yourself. Go to his office and look around. See if he's hiding anything there. Search his car. Go through the pockets of his suits."

"For what? What do you think I'm going to find?"

"Hopefully, nothing. Or maybe you'll find out Molly wasn't the only one. Maybe there were others. Maybe there still are."

"I hope not," I mutter, my shoulders slumping.

"Sara, I'm sorry. I shouldn't have said that. I just know a lot of women who have been through this and forgiven their husbands for an affair, only to find out he'd been cheating on her for years, or that he was hiding money from her, or had a huge gambling debt. I'm not saying Drew is doing those things, but wouldn't you feel better if you did some investigating so you can stop wondering if there's more he hasn't told you?"

"Yes, and I've thought about doing it. I'm just afraid of what I might find. I think that's what's holding me back."

"That's understandable," she says. "But the sooner you do it, the sooner you can make a decision about how to move forward."

"I've already searched the closets and drawers, and I went through all of his suits."

"You didn't find anything?"

"No, but I didn't think I would. Drew isn't careless like that. He wouldn't leave evidence of an affair, or whatever else he might be doing, around the apartment." I sigh. "I can't believe I have to do this. I shouldn't have to spy on my husband or snoop through his things to find out if something's going on with him. If Drew found out I'm doing this, he'd be furious."

"Tell him he lost the privilege of privacy when he lied to you and cheated on you. He'll get his privacy back when he earns back your trust."

"Telling him that would just anger him even more."

"What happens if you divorce him? Is there a prenup?"

"No, but Drew wanted one. We argued about it, and he eventually gave up on the idea."

"Since you've been married, he's become partner at his firm. I'd have to check the laws, but I'm almost certain you'd get part of the firm in a divorce."

"Even if that's true, Drew would never let it happen. He'd fight me in court. He worked his whole career to make partner. He'd rather see me dead than have to give me—" I stop, wondering if there's any truth to what I just said.

"I doubt he'd win," Marie says, not getting the significance of what I said. But she doesn't know what Molly told me about Drew wanting me dead. I left that part out. I'm sure Drew didn't mean it. He would never kill me. He has a wonderful career and a baby on the way. He wouldn't do something that would result in him spending his life in prison.

"I need to go," Marie says, checking her phone as she stands up. "I have a meeting starting in a few minutes."

"Go ahead." I give her a smile. "And thanks for the talk. You were right. It felt good to be able to say all that. I think I'll be able to focus on work now."

She frowns. "You won't. This is going to consume you for weeks, and probably months. But do the best you can. If you need to take a leave of absence, we can discuss that later. For now, see if you can get that article to me, and then maybe take the rest of the day off. You know what Fridays are like around here. Half the office leaves early. No one will notice you're gone."

"Thanks, Marie. I might just do that."

She leaves and I wake up my laptop. I find the article I'd started on Monday and open the file. Monday seems like a lifetime ago. In a way, it was. I didn't know about Drew's affair. Didn't know about Molly. Didn't know about the baby.

My life was so much simpler back then. I was certain about my future with Drew, dreaming of the baby we'd have someday. The house we would buy.

And now, just a few days later, my life has completely changed. I no longer trust Drew. I'm questioning our marriage. Questioning our future together.

How could everything fall apart so fast?

23

"SURPRISE!" I say, standing at the door to Drew's office holding a sack from the deli down the street.

"Sara, what are you doing here?" Drew scrambles up from behind his desk and comes over to me.

"I brought you a sandwich." I hold up the sack. "Turkey on rye. Your favorite."

"Why aren't you at work?"

"Marie said I could leave early. I was driving home and decided to stop here and surprise you with lunch. Remember how I used to do that when we were first married?"

"That's very sweet of you, but I don't have time for lunch. I was just heading to a meeting."

"Go ahead." I go past him and sit down on one of the chairs in front of his desk. "I can wait."

"It's not a quick meeting." He walks over to me. "It could take hours. Just leave the sandwich. I'll eat it later."

"Okay, but mine's getting cold. I got the turkey melt. I'll just eat it here and then head out."

Drew purses his lips and his jaw tightens. "Sara, I'd really prefer if you ate somewhere else. Why don't you go down to the first floor? They have tables set up. We've eaten there before. You know where it is."

I shake my head. "I don't like it down there. It's too loud." I smile at him. "I'll just stay here and enjoy the view."

Drew's office looks out at a wooded area that's currently blanketed with snow. The sun's glistening off it, making it look almost magical. It's a beautiful view, and the reason Drew picked this office when he was made partner at the firm.

"The clients are in the conference room," a woman says. I look back and see Jan, Drew's assistant, at the door. She smiles when she sees me. "Sara, what a surprise! Drew didn't mention you were coming to the office today."

"I didn't tell him." I hold up my sandwich. "I brought him lunch."

"Which I don't have time for," Drew says, seeming flustered as his eyes bounce between Jan and me.

"Go to your meeting," I tell Drew. "I'll close the door on my way out."

He sighs. "Fine. I'll see you at home." He grabs a stack of files from his desk and races out of the office.

"So how have you been?" Jan asks, walking over to me.

"Good," I say with a smile. "Of course, this time of year is always hard on me with Drew working so much. I always dread tax season."

I used to, but now I don't. I'm actually happy Drew has to stay late at the office.

"It's better than it was before," Jan says.

"What do you mean?"

"Just that Drew is home more now that he isn't coming into the office every weekend. I think he's only worked one Saturday this tax season. That's a big change from years past."

Drew hasn't been coming to the office on weekends? If he's not here, where has he been going? And why didn't he tell me?

Jan leans down to me and says in an excited tone, "Do you have any baby news? Drew never gives me any updates, but I know he can't wait to be a father."

He won't have to wait much longer. His baby could arrive any day now. How will he explain that to his staff? He portrays himself as the perfect husband. What will they think of him when they find out he got a woman pregnant? A woman who is not his wife? Will he even tell them, or will he try to hide it? Part of me wants to tell Jan right now and expose Drew for the man he really is, but that would be petty and immature. I'm better than that.

"I'm afraid I don't have any news to share," I say. "I guess the timing isn't right."

She pats my shoulder. "It'll happen. Don't lose hope. My daughter tried for years before she had her son."

"Yes, I just need to be patient."

She straightens up. "Well, I'll let you eat your lunch. I should get back to work."

"Bye, Jan."

When she's gone, I get up and shut the door. There's a narrow pane of glass next to it that could be a problem if one of Drew's coworkers walked by. If they saw me going through his things, they might tell on me. I'll have to keep an eye out for anyone.

I hurry over to Drew's desk and begin searching through the drawers. All I see are pens, pencils, notepads, and other office supplies. I don't find anything suspicious or out of the ordinary.

Moving to the top of his desk, I quickly flip through the paperwork and files stacked up next to his computer. It's a mix of client records, spreadsheets, financial forecasts, and invoices. All legit business paperwork.

My gaze moves around the room as I try to decide where to search next. Drew's coat is hung on a rack by the door. I go over to it and search all the pockets. I find nothing. Not even a tissue or gum wrapper. That's because of me. I've trained Drew to clean out his pockets after he left a piece of red candy in his dress shirt and it bled all over our laundry, ruining my favorite blouse.

Looking to the right of Drew's desk, I notice a pair of closed doors that I believe hide a storage closet. I go over there, open the doors, and see metal shelves holding boxes of files. The shelves end a few feet from the floor, leaving room for more storage. I kneel down and see more file boxes lined up. Looking past them to the corner of the closet, I notice something pushed way back against the wall. I get out my phone and turn on the flashlight, aiming it at the corner. I gasp when I see what's back there.

It's a suitcase. A navy suitcase with brown trim, exactly like the one Molly described seeing in Drew's hotel room. She wasn't lying. Drew brought a suitcase to the hotel. He was pretending to stay there, like he was visiting from out of town.

Molly was right. Drew made up a story about who he was and where he lived. He did it so she wouldn't try to find him, or try to find me. But somehow she did, despite the fake name he gave her. How did she do it? How did she find him?

Maybe she didn't. Maybe meeting her in the cafe really was a coincidence. But I swear she saw that photo of Drew and me on the mantel. If she really believed he didn't live in town, she would've reacted with shock when she saw it. She would've asked me about it. She would've wanted to know why I have a photo of a man who supposedly lived in a different state.

I pull out the suitcase, which is surprisingly heavy. I thought it would be empty. What is Drew keeping in here?

I glance at the pane of glass to make sure nobody's watching me, then unzip the suitcase. Inside is a small black case with a handle. I undo the latches and open the case. My heart nearly stops when I see what's inside.

Why does Drew have a gun? He swore to me he'd never get one. He knew how much they frightened me, and he agreed we'd never have one.

He lied. Again. How long has he had a gun? And what does he plan to do with it? Was he serious when he told Molly he wanted to shoot me? But why would he do that? If he wasn't happy, he could just divorce me.

My mind flashes back to the conversation I had earlier with Marie about Drew having to give me part of the accounting firm if we divorced. Would he use that as a reason to kill me?

No, he would never do that. I'm letting my mind take me places it shouldn't go. Drew is not a murderer. I refuse to believe he's capable of harming someone, especially me. But I also didn't think he was capable of having an affair, and then found out he did.

It's not the same. An affair and murder are two separate things. Drew cheated on me, but that doesn't mean he'd kill me. Men cheat all the time, but they don't follow it up with murder. Well, some do, but most don't.

I hear someone in the hallway and quickly close the gun case. With trembling hands, I zip the suitcase shut and put it back where I found it. I stand up and shut the closet doors.

A knock on the door startles me. I look over and see Jan walking in.

"I just need to drop off some files," she says, heading straight to Drew's desk. She sets the files down as I hurry to get my purse from the chair.

"Sara, are you okay?" Jan asks, gripping my arm.

I look at her and smile. "I'm fine. I just realized I need to get going. I'm meeting a friend, and if I don't leave now, I'll be late."

"Are you sure you should drive?" Jan asks, still holding onto my arm. "You're very pale. You look like you might pass out."

"I feel great," I say with a laugh. "I just need to get some sun. I always look pale in the winter."

"You're shaking," she says, glancing down at my arm. "I really think you need to sit down and rest."

"Jan, I'm fine. Really." I pull my arm from her grasp. "I need to go, but it was nice seeing you. Have a good day!"

I race out of there and hurry down the hall to the elevator. I take it to the first floor and go out to my car. I'm feeling shaky and lightheaded. Maybe Jan is right and I shouldn't drive.

I get the car going and turn on the heat. I take some deep breaths and close my eyes, trying to imagine myself somewhere peaceful, like a tranquil beach. But all I can see is an image of Drew holding that gun, pointing it at me.

My eyes pop open and I put my hand to my chest, focusing on my breath. Everything's fine. Drew is not a killer. He's my husband, and he loves me. He would never hurt me.

I have to believe that's true. Because if it's not, I'm in serious danger.

24

"HEY, honey, I'm just checking in," Drew says when I answer his call.

It's almost five. I've spent all afternoon trying to decide what to say to Drew. I almost didn't answer his call, but I need to know when he'll be home.

"Are you leaving soon?" I ask, my heart pounding at the thought of him being here.

"I need to finish a few things and then I'll head out. I'll probably be home around six."

"Okay, I'll see you then."

"Sara, wait," Drew says. "What happened today?"

"What do you mean?"

"Jan said you didn't look well. Are you sick?"

"No." I nervously laugh. "I don't know why she told you that. I feel fine."

"She said you were pale and shaking. That doesn't sound fine to me."

"She's exaggerating. I wasn't shaking, and I'm pale because it's winter and my skin's in desperate need of some sun. She just hasn't seen me for a while."

"Are you sure that's all it is?" He pauses. "You wouldn't lie to me, would you?"

"Of course not. You're worrying about nothing. Don't listen to Jan. You know she tends to overanalyze everything and create drama."

"Yes, I suppose you're right. I just wanted to make sure you're okay."

"I am. I'll see you tonight." I end the call before Drew could pick up on how nervous I am just speaking with him. What am I going to do when he gets home? I'm afraid to be around him. Maybe I need to leave. Go stay somewhere else.

My phone rings. I answer it without checking who's calling. "Hello?"

"Hi, is this Sara?"

"It is. Who's this?"

"Tammy. I work at the shelter. We met yesterday when you dropped off Molly."

"Yes, I remember," I say, wondering if she's calling to tell me Molly went into labor. Maybe she's already at the hospital. "Is everything okay?"

"I'm afraid not. There was an incident this morning between Molly and one of the other women. It seems they got into an argument and Molly was injured."

"Injured how?" I ask, thinking back to what Molly said about some woman trying to punch her in the stomach.

"I don't know for sure what happened. I wasn't there, but Molly said the woman involved took out a pocketknife and slashed her arm."

"That's awful! Is she okay?"

"She's fine. It wasn't a deep cut. We patched her up, but she doesn't want to stay here after what happened."

"What about the woman with the knife? Was she arrested?"

"No, Molly decided not to press charges. We searched all over for the knife and couldn't find it. The woman involved swears the knife wasn't hers and claims she never attacked Molly. We don't have any witnesses, so it's hard to say what really happened."

"When I spoke to Molly last night, she said a woman tried to punch her in the stomach. Do you think it's the same person?"

"It's possible, although Molly didn't mention that when I talked to her. I told her we could switch her to a different room, but she said she'd rather leave. She doesn't feel safe here, and she's worried the stress is hurting the baby. I think it's a valid concern. Is there any way you'd consider letting her stay with you again? Molly didn't think you'd agree to it, but I wanted to at least ask before I called around to other shelters. I worry she'll be just as stressed somewhere else, thinking something like this might happen again."

Drew won't like that I'm agreeing to this, but I'm not concerned about him. I'm concerned about the baby and how all this stress is affecting his health.

"I'll come get her," I say. "I'll leave right now."

"Wonderful!" Tammy says, sounding surprised. "I'll tell Molly. See you soon!"

When I arrive at the shelter, Molly is waiting just inside the door. She sees my car pull up and races outside with her duffel bag. I jump out of the car to help her.

"Let me take that," I say, grabbing her bag.

"Thank you for doing this," she says, sounding

relieved. "I couldn't keep staying there, knowing that woman might try to hurt the baby."

"Yes, it's best that you leave." I put her bag in the trunk. "Go get in the car. It's freezing out here."

"I'm really sorry about this," Molly says as we drive away from the shelter. "I know it's not what you wanted. You finally got rid of me, and now this happens."

"It's not your fault. Clearly, that place needs to do a better job of screening people. They shouldn't allow drug addicts to live there. That woman needs to be in a treatment center. Was she the same woman who threatened you last night?"

"Yes." Molly shudders. "I was so afraid she'd do something to me that I didn't even sleep last night."

"You can take a nap when we get home. I haven't figured out dinner yet. I'll probably just order something in."

Dinner's the last thing on my mind. I'm not even hungry. I lost my appetite when I discovered that gun in Drew's office. I can't just pretend I didn't see it. I have to talk to Drew about it. I don't have a choice.

"What did Drew say?" Molly asks. "About me moving back in?"

"I haven't told him." I stop at an intersection. "I didn't have a chance. I left as soon as Tammy called."

"He's going to be mad." Molly looks down. "He'll make me go to another shelter."

"The apartment belongs to both of us," I say, continuing through the intersection. "If I want you to stay, Drew will have to accept that."

"But why would you want that?" Molly looks at me. "I thought you hated me."

"I don't hate you. I hate what you did." I hit the button to turn up the heat.

"But you don't like me," she says as though it's a fact.

"I don't really know you." I glance at her. "So I can't say whether I like you or not."

"I don't really know you either, but I like you. You're a great person, Sara. Way better than Drew."

I'm tempted to ask what she means by that, but decide not to. I don't want to talk about Drew.

Back at the apartment, I bring Molly's bag to the guest room.

"Has Drew been staying in here?" Molly asks, seeing Drew's suits in the closet.

"He has, but obviously he won't be any longer."

Molly sits on the bed. "How are things going with you two?"

"I'd rather not talk about it." I go into the bathroom to collect Drew's things.

Molly appears at the door. "Do you have any bandages? I should probably change this." She lifts up her sleeve and peels back the bandage on her forearm, exposing a three-inch-long cut.

"Oh, Molly, I'm so sorry that happened to you," I say, gently taking hold of her arm. "This is a serious cut. Maybe you should see a doctor."

"I don't need to. It'll heal. I just need to keep it clean so it doesn't get infected."

"I'll go get the bandages. I'll be right back." I take Drew's toiletries back to our room, then go to the hall closet and get the first aid kit.

When I return to the guest bathroom, Molly is

leaning against the counter, her eyes squeezed shut, her hand on her belly.

"Is something wrong?" I ask.

Her eyes open. "I keep getting these pains, but I think it's because I'm stressed."

"The pain could be something serious. I'm taking you to see a doctor tomorrow."

"Sara, I'm fine. Really. I just need to get some rest."

"Let me take care of this," I say, taking the bloody bandage off her arm. "Then I'll get the sheets changed so you can lie down."

"You don't need to change the sheets. I don't care that Drew slept on them."

"I'd prefer that they were clean. It won't take me long to change them." I spray a disinfectant solution on her arm, then cover it with a new bandage. "Okay, you're all set."

She smiles at me. "You'll make a great mom someday. Better than I'll be."

"Molly, don't say that," I say, putting everything back in the first aid kit. "I'm sure you'll be a wonderful mother."

I'm being nice. I don't think she'll be a good mother, but hopefully she'll do her best.

"It's too bad my mom's not around to help me," Molly says. "I always imagined her showing me what to do if I ever had kids."

"I'm sure it's hard for you not having her here." I close the first aid kit and set it on the counter. "When did you say she died?"

"In December, a week before Christmas."

"That's awful," I say, my heart going out to her. "It's

sad to lose someone at any time of the year, but Christmas is especially hard."

Molly shrugs. "I didn't see it that way. I've never liked Christmas. My dad left us during the holidays so it's always been a bad time of year for me. I was almost relieved it happened then. It's just another bad memory of the holidays. I'd rather have them all at once than throughout the year."

"When did your father leave? How old were you?"

"Six. He left on Christmas Eve. He told my mom he was going to go pick up her present and never came back."

"And you're sure nothing happened to him? He wasn't in some kind of accident?"

"He was fine." She lets out a harsh laugh. "My mom's friend saw him at a bar, getting drunk and making out with some woman. Her friend thinks it was a hooker, but who knows? We never had money so I don't know how he paid her."

What kind of man would leave his family on such a significant night in a child's life? And then he spends it at a bar with a prostitute? Poor Molly. She's gone through so much, assuming she's telling the truth.

"We never saw him again after that," Molly says. "A few years ago, I looked him up online and found his obituary. It didn't mention him having any kids, so I guess he forgot about me."

"I'm sure he didn't," I tell her in a comforting tone. "He just didn't know how to be a father. Not everyone is meant to be a parent."

She pushes away from the counter. "I think I'll lie down. I'm having trouble staying awake."

"Let me just change the sheets." I take a new set from the linen closet and go back to the bedroom.

"I really like it here," Molly says, watching me make the bed. "This is a great apartment, although anything seems great after sleeping outside."

I was about to put the sheet on, but stop and turn to Molly. "About that. I need to tell you something."

"What is it?"

"I went to the park to get your things, but they weren't there."

"Someone probably stole them."

"Maybe, but then I spoke with the police officer who patrols the park and he said he'd never seen you."

"Because I'd hide whenever he was there. I knew he'd kick me out if he saw me."

"You hid all day? That doesn't seem possible."

"It wasn't all day, and sometimes I'd leave the park before he got there."

"You're talking about the park by the cafe, right?"

"No, there's another one a few miles away. It's small, so you may not even know it's there. It's just a neighborhood park."

"Are you saying you walked several miles the day we met?"

She shrugs. "What else was I going to do? I was bored. I used to walk all the time, but I'd take a lot of breaks. I'd get out of breath or my feet would hurt."

So she wasn't lying about being homeless, or she was, but she changed her story after I told her the officer had never seen her before. I need to go find that other park to see if her things are there, although by now they're probably gone.

I finish making the bed and hear Drew calling out from the other room. "Sara, I'm home."

"Wait here," I say to Molly. "I don't want him seeing you until I've told him why you're back."

I race out of the room and shut the door just as Drew appears in the hall.

"What are you doing?" he asks, glancing at the guest room.

"I need to talk to you." I walk up to him. "Let's go to our room."

"*Our* room?" His brows rise. "Are you saying I'm allowed back in our bedroom?"

"I'm saying I need to talk to you." I pull on his arm. "Come on. This can't wait."

Surprisingly, I'm not as fearful of Drew as I thought I'd be. I think it's because of Molly and what happened to her at the shelter. It distracted me from the gun incident that had been taking up my thoughts.

My mind is overwhelmed by everything that keeps happening. I feel like I'm experiencing one stressful event after another. I can't keep track of them all. It's hard to believe Molly showed up in our lives just a few days ago. It feels like weeks. So much has happened since she arrived.

"What is this about?" Drew asks, undoing his tie.

I shut the door and go over to him. "Molly. She's back."

"Back where?" He stops messing with his tie. "Here?"

"Yes, and before you get upset, she was injured. A woman at the shelter attacked her with a knife, leaving a large cut on Molly's arm. She didn't want to stay there after that, and I don't blame her. It's not safe."

"So we'll take her somewhere else. We'll find a different shelter."

"Drew, no. The stress she'll experience there isn't good for the baby."

"Then we'll get her a hotel, or find her an apartment."

"Let's just keep her here until the baby comes. She shouldn't be alone right now. What if she needs medical help?"

"Then she can call for an ambulance." He rips his tie off and tosses it on the floor. "I got her a damn phone. She just needs to use it." He takes his suit jacket off. "It's better we find her a place now than later. She needs a place to go after the baby's born."

I keep quiet, knowing he'll be upset if I even suggest it.

Drew sighs. "Sara, she is not staying here with the baby. You better not have told her she could."

"I didn't, but why wouldn't you want her to stay? You'd get to be close to your baby. You'd see him every day."

"We'd also see Molly, which is not going to help our marriage. It would only make things worse." He heads to the walk-in closet.

I follow him in there. "She'd only stay for a few weeks. Drew, she has no idea how to care for an infant. Do you really trust her to care for him on her own?"

"I'm sure she'll figure it out," he says, hanging up his suit jacket. "Women have been doing it for centuries."

"Yes, but it would be better for the baby if she had someone to help her. Those first few weeks are exhausting for a new mother. She can't do it alone."

Drew turns to me. "This is about you, isn't it?"

"I don't know what you mean."

"You want to care for the baby. It isn't about helping Molly. It's about you wanting a baby."

I don't answer him, knowing there's some truth to what he said.

He steps closer to me. "Honey, I know how much you want this baby to be ours, but it's not. Molly is his mother. You can't change that."

"I'm not trying to. But you know I would be a better mother than her. She's going to ruin that child's life."

"You seem to be forgetting I'm his father. Do you think I'll have no influence on him and how he turns out?"

"No, but we both know you're never around. He'll spend most of his time with Molly."

Drew lowers his voice. "I told you I'm working on getting full custody. If I do, Molly will only see him when I allow her to."

"A judge is not going to take a child from its mother."

"He would if I could prove she was dangerous."

"She's not dangerous," I scoff. "She would never hurt her child."

"Sara, you just met her. You know nothing about her." He unbuttons his shirt. "I honestly don't understand why you keep defending her and acting like you two are friends. Even if you don't believe me when I tell you she's deceiving you, she was a willing participant in our affair. She knew I was married, and it didn't seem to bother her. She didn't feel an ounce of guilt."

"Neither did you," I point out.

"Of course I did. I still do. I deeply regret the pain I've caused you."

He says it so sincerely, and is looking at me in such a loving way, that I feel like he actually means it. Or maybe I'm just seeing what I want to see.

"I'm sorry, Sara, but Molly needs to go," Drew says. "We can do a search online this weekend and see what apartments are available."

"Maybe I'll go live there with her," I mutter.

"Is that some kind of joke?" Drew says in a harsh tone. "Because it's not funny. I don't trust her around you. I'm worried about what she might do, which is why I want her out of here as soon as possible."

"Molly wouldn't hurt me." My eyes go to Drew's, my heart pounding in my chest. "But you might."

"What are you talking about? Why would you even say that?"

"I saw it, Drew." I swallow. "I saw the gun."

25

"THAT'S why you were at my office?" Drew says. "To spy on me? Go through my things?"

That is not the reaction I was expecting. I thought Drew would be panicking, racing to explain why he has a gun. But he's strangely calm, not seeming at all concerned that I found a firearm in his office closet.

"Don't make this about me," I snap. "Tell me why you have a gun!"

"Tell me why you were looking for it."

"I wasn't. I opened your suitcase and there it was." I put my hands on my hips. "Why do you have a gun? And why are you hiding it from me?"

"Because I know you don't like guns." He takes off his shirt and tosses it in the hamper. "I kept it at my office because I knew you wouldn't want me keeping it here. And I didn't tell you about it because you'd tell me to get rid of it."

"You're right. I want you to get rid of it."

He shakes his head. "I'm sorry, Sara, but I'm keeping it."

He takes a shirt from a hanger and puts it on, going about his routine as if this is just some normal conversation. Does he not get how serious this is? Or how concerned I am that he has a gun?

"Why do you need a gun?" I ask, my heart beating fast. "Are you planning to use it to... to kill me?"

Drew's eyes widen. "Kill you? Sara, you can't be serious."

"You know what they say when a wife turns up dead. It's always the husband. What did you expect me to think after finding a gun at your office?"

"I expect you to let me explain why I have it, not accuse me of trying to kill you." He looks down, shaking his head. "What the hell, Sara? Do you really think I would do that? That I would kill you?" He looks back at me. "Because if you really believe that, then maybe we shouldn't be married. Maybe we should consider getting a divorce."

His words feel like a dagger slicing through my heart. It's not like I haven't thought about divorcing him since learning about his affair, but I wasn't ready to go there yet. I didn't think he was either. He said he loves me and would do anything to save our marriage. And now he's bringing up divorce?

"That's not what I want," I say. "I'm not giving up on our marriage."

"You act like you already have." Drew folds his arms over his chest. "You can barely look at me since you found out about the affair. You don't want me to touch you. You don't want me in our room. Our bed. Hell, you don't even want me in our apartment."

Why is he turning this around and making *me* the bad guy? He cheated. Of course I'm going to be cold to him and not want him touching me or sleeping next to me in bed. I'm still extremely hurt and angry that he had an affair and got some other woman pregnant.

"A lot has happened this week," I say. "Things I never expected. I would think you'd understand why I don't want to be around you right now."

"I get that, but what you said about me hurting you? Or..." He cringes. "Killing you? I don't know how to get past something like that." His eyes lock on mine. "My job as your husband is to protect you. To take care of you. So for you to think I would harm you in any way is just..." He shakes his head. "I don't know why we'd keep doing this."

My throat burns as I fight back tears. Is Drew saying he wants a divorce? I'm not ready for that. Despite everything he's done, I still love him. I'm not ready to give up on us, not yet.

"Let's not talk about this now," I say. "We're both stressed and not thinking straight." I pause. "I do still love you, Drew. That hasn't changed."

But part of me wishes it would. If I no longer loved him, it would make things a lot easier. I could divorce him and move on with my life, and try to forget this whole nightmare with Molly ever happened.

"The reason I have the gun," Drew says, "is because..." He takes a breath.

"Because what?"

"Because I was almost killed one night after work."

I look at him in disbelief. "When did this happen? And why didn't you tell me?"

"I didn't want you to worry." He looks down, then back up at me. "It was about a year ago. I went out to my car after work and this guy came up behind me and demanded I give him money. I turned around and saw he had a gun pointed at me. I told him I didn't have any cash and he got angry. He was about to shoot me when a police car drove by. The sirens went off, and the guy must've thought he'd been caught because he ran away and I never saw him again."

"Oh my God." I grip Drew's hand. "I wish you'd told me. I'm your wife. I should've been there for you when you were dealing with this. You must've been reliving it for months."

"I was, but talking about it wouldn't have helped. The only thing that did was buying the gun. It made me feel safe, like I had some control if something like that ever happened again. I'd bring it with me when I went out to my car at night, and then when I got home, I'd put it in the trunk."

"Are you still doing this? Taking the gun with you?"

"I do, but not every night. I probably should, though. I want to believe it won't happen again, but I know there's a chance it could. If it happened once, it could happen again."

"Did you tell the people at your office?"

"No, I didn't want to alarm anyone."

"Drew, they need to know so they can be careful when they're walking to their car."

"Everyone parks in the lot behind the building, which has security. I usually park on the street because by the time I get to work, the lot is full."

"Then you need to go to the office earlier."

"I'd rather spend a few extra minutes with my wife in the morning." He smiles a little. "I like our routine."

When our schedules allow it, Drew and I have breakfast together before going to work. We talk about our day and what we have planned. It's a way to connect with each other before going our separate ways.

"Your safety is more important than our routine," I say, angry that our silly morning ritual almost got him killed.

"Sara, I'm fine. Nothing has happened since then." He takes off his suit pants and hangs them up.

"Except that now you're carrying a gun."

"Yes, but it will never come into our home."

"I still don't like that you have it," I say as he takes a pair of jeans from the shelf.

"Am I going somewhere tonight?" he asks, putting on his jeans. "I need to know if I should pack a bag."

I was going to tell him to get a hotel, but that was when I thought he had bought the gun to kill me. I feel bad for assuming that, but then forgive myself, realizing I'm not thinking clearly this week. I'm exhausted and overwhelmed and completely stressed. I'm not surprised my mind jumped to the worst possible scenario.

"You can stay," I tell him.

After finding out I almost lost him, I want Drew here with me. If he'd been killed that night, I'd be a widow. Molly wouldn't be here. There wouldn't be a baby. Our lives would've been changed forever.

"Are you sure?" he asks.

I nod. "But I'd like you to stay on the couch." I glance at the bed. "I'm not ready for more than that."

"Sara, our relationship isn't going to get better if we're apart. And with Molly here, we need to make it appear that we're getting along."

"Molly knows we're having issues. We don't need to try to hide it from her."

Drew's brows rise. "You've been talking to Molly about us?"

"No, but it only makes sense we'd have issues after I found out you had an affair."

Thinking about the affair reminds me of the suitcase. The one I found in Drew's office. The one that had the gun in it.

"Why do you have that suitcase?" I ask, my pulse racing because I'm not sure I want the answer. I keep thinking there's more Drew's hiding from me. More women. More lies.

"What suitcase?" he asks.

"The one in your office. The one hidden in the closet."

"You already know why I have it. You saw what was inside."

"That's it? You're using it to hide the gun?"

"For now, yes."

"Why are you lying?" I say. "Why can't you just tell me the truth?"

"I am. I don't know what you're referring to."

I'm so exhausted by his lies. Why can't he be honest with me? How am I supposed to trust him when he keeps denying what I already know is true?

"Molly told me about the suitcase," I say. "About how you had it in the hotel room so she'd believe your story about being from out of town. She described the suitcase to me. It wasn't like any of the ones we have, so I assumed she was lying. But then today, I found it in your office, hidden where you thought I'd never see it."

Drew steps up to me, a concerned look on his face. "Honey, are you feeling okay?"

"Yes. Why are you asking?"

"You've seen that suitcase before. You're the one who picked it out. You bought it a few years ago for our trip to New York, but then I had to work and we never went on the trip. I kept the suitcase at the office because we didn't have room for it here."

I didn't buy that suitcase. I've never even seen it before. Or have I? Did I forget that I bought it? I remember the trip to New York. We planned it but never went, just as Drew said. I guess it's possible I bought a suitcase back then, but why don't I remember it?

"Are you sure you didn't buy it?" I ask.

"Sara, when have I ever bought us luggage? Even if I wanted to, you wouldn't let me. You're very particular about the types of bags we buy."

It's true. I like to have a certain number of compartments in varying sizes and zipped storage pockets on the outside. I also have preferences for color and material.

"I would never buy a suitcase like that," I say. "You had to have bought it."

He puts his hand on my shoulder. "Honey, you're worrying me. This wasn't that long ago. You should be able to remember buying that suitcase."

"Well, I don't. Maybe all this stress is affecting my memory."

It has to be, because Drew seems certain I bought the suitcase for that trip. I hope it's stress and not something more serious, like some kind of problem with my brain.

"I'm starving," Drew says, walking to the bathroom. "Do you have any ideas for dinner?"

"No, I haven't thought about it." I stand outside the

bathroom as he washes his hands. "Were you using that suitcase to trick Molly into thinking you were from out of town?"

Drew sighs, grabbing the hand towel and turning toward me. "Sara, can you please stop questioning me like this? I feel like I'm constantly under attack."

"Just answer the question."

"No, I did not bring a suitcase to the hotel," Drew says, drying his hands on the towel. "Why do you keep believing her? She tells you some made-up story and you automatically assume she's telling the truth and I'm not." He tosses the towel on the counter. "You can't keep doing this. If you trust some stranger more than me, then it's like I said before, maybe this isn't going to work."

"Why do you keep bringing up divorce?" I pause. "Is that... is that what you want?"

"Of course not," he says, coming over to me. "But I don't know how we can have a marriage when you're constantly questioning everything I do, and believing some woman who you know for a fact lies. Sara, she lied to you about being homeless. That alone should tell you she's crazy. Who the hell does that?"

"I'm not certain she lied about that. I asked her about it, and she said the park she was living in wasn't the one I went to. It was a different one. I'm going to go there this weekend and see if her things are there."

"Why bother?" he scoffs. "You know it's just another lie."

"If it's a lie, then where does she live? Where's her apartment? She doesn't have a job, so how is she paying rent? And why would she keep paying rent if she's not living there?"

"Who the hell knows? Maybe she was staying with a friend. Crashing on their couch. Sara, you have got to stop believing the things she tells you. And do not talk to her about us, even if she asks." He glances at the bedroom door. "I'm going to go speak with her."

"About what?"

"About what she's doing. I'm not going to let her continue to fill your mind with lies about me. It needs to stop." He heads to the door.

"Drew, wait. I'll go with you."

"No, I need to talk to her alone. Just wait here."

He leaves, while I remain in the bedroom. I want to hear what he says to her, but it's probably best if I stay out of it. Knowing Molly, she'll tell me what he said. She's been very open with me, unlike Drew, who keeps deflecting my questions or getting annoyed with me when I ask them. I think that's why I keep taking Molly's side over Drew's. I feel like she's telling the truth, like with that suitcase. If Drew didn't have it at the hotel, then how did she know what it looked like? When else would she have seen it? Did she go to his office? Look in the closet? I doubt it, which makes me think Drew was the one lying.

I want to believe my husband. I really do. So why is he making it so difficult?

26

"THANKS FOR DINNER," Molly says, getting up from the table.

After Drew talked to Molly, I joined them in the kitchen and we ordered takeout. Molly didn't say much during dinner, and she never once looked at Drew. It was almost as if she were afraid of him. It makes me wonder what he said to her.

"You're welcome," I say. "Are you going to bed?"

"Yeah, I'm not feeling well."

"What's wrong?" I ask with concern.

"She's fine," Drew says, glaring at Molly. "She's just tired. Right, Molly?"

She nods, then cringes as she rubs her stomach.

"Molly, what is it?" I get up and go over to her. "Are you in pain?"

"It's nothing," she says with a weak smile. "I'm sure it'll go away."

"Drew, we should take her to a doctor."

"She just told you it's nothing," Drew says to me. "Molly, go to your room. You'll feel better if you sleep."

She walks off, her shoulders slumped like a child who's just been scolded.

"What is wrong with you?" I say to Drew. "She's obviously in pain and you just dismissed it, like it was nothing."

"Sara, she's faking it. She's pretending to be in pain so we'll let her stay."

"And what if she's not pretending? What if there's something wrong with the baby? Are you willing to risk your baby's health because you're too stubborn to admit she might be telling the truth?"

He lets out a frustrated sigh. "Honey, it's all an act. I told her I'm taking her to look for apartments tomorrow so now she's doing whatever she can to convince you to let her stay."

"You're taking her to look for apartments? What about work?"

"I'm not going into the office tomorrow. This is more important. We have to get her out of here."

"I'm going with you, right? To look at apartments?"

"No." He gets up and gathers our plates from the table. "If you go, you'll find fault with every place we look at and convince Molly she can't live there."

"Drew, that's not fair. I'm not that picky."

His eyes widen. "Are you kidding? It took us forever to find this place. We looked at apartments every weekend for a year."

It wasn't that long, but it was close to a year. When we moved here from Philadelphia, Drew's firm paid for our housing until we could find a place to live. After three months, the firm said we were taking too long and would no longer cover our rent. Drew was annoyed with me at the time, but it's not easy to find an apartment in

Boston that would fit all our needs. We needed to wait for the right one to become available.

"I knew we'd be here for a while," I say. "I didn't want to pick the wrong place and have us regret it."

"And you'll do the same thing with Molly's place. You'll say it's not good enough for the baby. Or not safe enough." He takes the plates to the sink. "I'm sorry, Sara, but I'm doing this without you. I'm not arguing about it."

I don't like the idea of him going without me. I'm much better at things like this. Why does he have to be so stubborn? It infuriates me when he won't even consider my advice.

Drew loads the dishwasher, doing it just the way I told him. At least he listened to me about that. It's not the same as listening to me about an apartment, but at least it's something.

"I'm going to watch some TV," he says, drying his hands on the towel.

I walk over to him. "What did you say to Molly? She was really quiet during dinner."

"Because she knows I'm on to her. I don't know what she wants from us, but I told her I'm done playing games. And so are you. You need to stop giving her your attention and sympathy. You did it just now, when she was pretending to be in pain."

"Maybe she was. How do you know she was pretending?"

"If she were really suffering, she'd insist we take her to see a doctor. She didn't, because she knows the doctor wouldn't find anything wrong with her, which would prove she made the whole thing up."

It's a good point. Maybe Drew's right and she was

faking her pain, but why? Drew's made it clear he has no interest in continuing their relationship. That's the only reason I can come up with for why she'd want to stay here. To be close to Drew, so she could convince him to leave me and marry her. But if he's told her that's not happening, then what's her reason for wanting to stay with us?

"Are we done now?" Drew asks. "Because I want to watch the game. It started ten minutes ago."

"Just one more thing."

"What?" he says with a sigh.

"Jan said you haven't been going to the office on weekends." I study him to see if his body language changes, indicating he's been caught doing something he shouldn't. But his expression hasn't changed, his hands remain at his sides, and he's not looking away.

"I'm still going to the office, just not as much," he says.

"Then where have you been going on Saturdays?"

"I've been taking my laptop to a coffee shop and working there. Jan doesn't know because I didn't tell her. I don't know why she cares whether I'm at the office or not. She's not even there on weekends. I'll have to have a talk with her."

"No, don't. I don't want her getting in trouble for this. She only mentioned it because I said something about you never being around this time of year."

"She still shouldn't be talking about me. Look at the damage it caused. You've been worrying about this since she told you." His brows rise. "Did you assume I was with a woman?"

"Maybe," I mutter.

"Then I'm definitely having a talk with her. Jan's a

nice woman, but she doesn't know how to mind her own business. She's always gossiping about people in the office and it needs to stop."

"She wasn't gossiping. She simply made a comment about you not being there on Saturdays. It was completely innocent."

"And yet it had you thinking I was having an affair. Worrying about it. Being stressed. And now we're arguing."

"We're not arguing." I take a calming breath. "Go watch your game. I think I'll go into the bedroom and read."

Two hours later, I find myself dozing off and decide to go to sleep. When I wake up, it's after midnight and I find I'm alone in bed. Drew must've decided to sleep on the couch. I was hoping he would. I don't feel comfortable having him next to me. It could take weeks, or even months, before I want Drew back in our bed. What will that mean for our marriage? Will Drew decide he wants a divorce? He's already talking about it, and it hasn't even been a week since the news of his affair damaged what was once a strong marriage. I guess it wasn't that strong if he cheated.

I turn on my side and try to shut off my thoughts, knowing if I don't, I'll never go back to sleep. The minutes tick by, then an hour passes. No matter how hard I try, I can't quiet my mind, so I get up and go to the bathroom to take a sleeping pill. I'm walking back to bed when I hear something in the hall. It sounds like a door opening. It must be coming from Molly's room. What is she doing up at this hour?

I make my way to the door and quietly open it. I go out to the hall to see where she went, but then hear her talking in her room. That's odd. I swear I heard her door open.

"Stop telling me what to do," she says.

I assume she's talking to herself until I hear Drew's voice.

"Quiet down!" he scolds in a much softer voice than Molly's. "You're going to wake up Sara."

"Good. Let's ask her to join us. It'd make things more interesting. Don't you think?"

"Stop this right now!" Drew says in a harsh tone. "You've done enough damage. Leave Sara alone. If you need something, you come to me, not her. Do you understand?"

"Fine, but I don't know why I have to move out. Why can't I stay here?"

"Because I can't trust you not to cause problems."

"Like what?"

"Like making Sara think you're some sweet, innocent girl who needs saving. Trying to get her on your side. You realize that doing this isn't going to get you what you want."

"Maybe it has nothing to do with that."

"Then why do it? Just leave Sara alone. You hear me? I'm not discussing this again."

"You know, you should be nicer to me since I'm the one who–"

"We're done here." Drew's footsteps sound on the wood floor as he walks to the door.

I sneak back to my room as Drew leaves the guest room. Should I talk to him now or wait until tomorrow? It has to be now. I won't sleep with this on my mind.

Leaving the bedroom again, I go down to the living room. Drew is on the couch, a blanket draped over him.

"Drew?" I whisper.

He startles and sits up. "Sara. What are you doing up?"

"I couldn't sleep." I motion for him to move over on the couch, then sit beside him. "I got up to take a pill and heard you and Molly talking in her room."

He leans forward and rubs his head. "I'm sorry about that. I told her to be quiet."

"Why were you in her room at this hour?"

"She texted me and said she needed help. Like an idiot, I fell for it and went to her room. I should've known she was faking it to get me to go to her."

"What did she want?"

"To demand I let her stay with us until after the baby's born. But it's not happening, Sara. I want her gone. I don't want to wait."

"She obviously has a reason for wanting to stay. Maybe she's worried about being alone so close to her delivery date."

"God, Sara, would you stop making excuses for her?" He turns to me. "She's destroying our marriage. She hasn't even been here a week and we're talking about divorce."

"That isn't because of Molly."

"You don't think the things she tells you about me affects how you see me?"

"What things? You don't know what she says."

"It doesn't matter. It's all lies to turn you against me so you'll divorce me and she'll have me all to herself. The woman is crazy. I keep telling you that and you still don't believe me."

"She's not crazy, and you really shouldn't use that word to describe people with mental health issues."

"Fine, she's delusional," he says, tossing his hands up. "Is that better?"

"What is it she wants?"

"What do you mean?"

"I heard you say she wanted something, or I think that's what I heard."

"She wants me to pay for a year of her rent. I said I'd do it if she left us alone, meaning no unexpected visits, no calling us at all hours of the day and night, no demanding we buy her things. I'm putting all this in writing, and if she doesn't abide by the rules, the deal is off."

"You really think that's necessary? I think just telling her that should be enough."

"You're not getting it, Sara. Molly does whatever she wants. She doesn't listen. She agrees to something, then doesn't follow through." Drew leans back on the couch and rubs his eyes. "I need to get some sleep. I'm exhausted."

"We can talk about this tomorrow," I say, getting up.

"I can't. I need a break from talking about Molly. It's all we do."

Because we need to. This affects both of us. I don't want Drew to leave me out of decisions or not tell me what's going on. If I hadn't overheard that conversation in Molly's room, I'm sure Drew wouldn't have even told me about it.

That bothers me. And it makes me wonder what else he's neglected to tell me.

27

"How's the apartment hunt going?" I ask when Drew answers my call. It's noon, and he's been out with Molly for several hours.

"Slow," he says. "We've only seen three places so far, and none of them were like the description online."

"That's not surprising. It was the same when we were looking. I wouldn't get your hopes up about finding a place today. It could take a few weeks."

"We don't have a few weeks. I'm just going to pick one and she'll have to be okay with it. She's not paying for it, so she really can't complain."

"You can't just pick one. It needs to be something that's been updated and is clean. And it should be in a safe neighborhood."

"Sara, I told you to stay out of this. I will find her a decent place to live. It may not be up to your standards, but your standards are extremely high. Just look at who you married."

I smile at his joke. "Well, good luck. I'll check in with you later." I end the call and go to the kitchen.

I'm not hungry, but I should probably eat since I didn't have breakfast. I open the refrigerator and feel a surge of anger when I see that everything's been moved around. The yogurts aren't aligned, and some of them are on different shelves! The milk container is on its side instead of being upright in the door. The condiments, which are supposed to be in alphabetical order, are all mixed up, and the produce is no longer in the produce bin.

"Who did this?" I say aloud to myself as I hurry to rearrange everything. Drew wouldn't have done it. He knows better. It had to have been Molly, but why would she do something she knows would upset me? I've gone out of my way to be kind to her, and then she does *this*? Does she think it's some kind of joke? If so, it isn't funny. My pulse is racing and my chest is experiencing a sharp pain. I almost feel like I'm having a heart attack. That may sound overly dramatic, but chaos and disorganization cause me a great deal of distress.

I'm glad Molly is gone. I can put my house back the way I want it. I haven't been in her bedroom yet. I'm sure it's a mess, but I didn't want to clean it in case she ends up staying here tonight. I really don't think Drew will find a place today, and if he does, he'll have to wait for the paperwork to be done before Molly can move in. That could take several days.

When my refrigerator is back as it was, I take out the deli ham to make myself a sandwich. I open the cupboard to get a plate and see that the plates have been replaced with coffee mugs. Did I open the wrong cupboard? I take a step back to check. No, this is definitely the cupboard that holds the plates, or it used to be.

I open all the cupboards, gasping when I see they've all been rearranged. I yank open the drawers and see that they, too, have been rearranged.

"I'm going to kill her," I mutter as I assess the damage she's done. I'll have to take everything out and put it all back. That could take hours!

When did she do this? And why? Does she secretly hate me? Maybe Drew was right and Molly has been putting on an act this whole time, pretending to like me when she really can't stand me. I don't know how else to explain why she'd do this.

My phone rings, waking me from my state of shock. I grab it from the counter, still eyeing the disaster that is now my kitchen. "Hello?"

"Sara, it's Marie. I realize it's the weekend and you're probably out and about, but I just wanted to check in and see how things are going."

"Not well, unfortunately. I just discovered that Molly moved everything around in my kitchen. It's a complete disaster. I don't know what she was thinking. It's either some kind of immature prank or she's extremely inconsiderate and wanting to hurt me."

"Hurt you?" Marie says, sounding confused. "By moving things around?"

"You don't know this about me, but I have a very precise system for organizing my kitchen. Well, it's all rooms, actually. I can't stand when things aren't where they should be. Drew knows this and would never dare mess with my system, so it had to be Molly, although I clearly told her that she is not to move things out of their given place. And she still did it!"

"Sara, I think you might need a break," Marie says,

sounding concerned. "Forget the kitchen and go take a bath. Or maybe get a massage."

"No, I need to fix this. It's the only thing that'll make me feel better."

"Maybe Drew could help."

"He's out looking for apartments with Molly. He's hoping to find one today, but I can't imagine he will. It's nearly impossible to find a place on short notice. Even if he manages to, she won't be able to move there today."

"Is he looking for a furnished place? Because that can be even harder to find."

"I hadn't thought about that. I assume Drew's looking for unfurnished, which means we'll have to buy her everything she needs."

"That'll add up fast," Marie says.

"Yes, it will. And Drew has offered to pay her rent for a year. There goes the savings for our house."

"I'm sorry. I know how much you were hoping to buy one this year."

"Yes, well, it's not going to happen." I pace the floor, feeling more and more anxious as I think of how much Molly's going to cost us. Add to that the mess she made of my kitchen and I feel like I'm about to have a stroke.

"How are you and Drew getting along?"

"We're not really arguing, so I guess that's good."

"Have you been talking much?"

"Not a lot. I keep asking him things, and he answers, but I'm not sure if he's telling the truth."

"It's normal to feel that way. He lied to you, so now everything he says is going to seem like a lie. He needs to rebuild your trust."

"He does, but until that happens, I don't know what

to believe. He'll tell me something, and then Molly will tell me the opposite."

"You can't believe Molly. She sees you as the enemy. She's not going to tell you the truth."

"I'm not the enemy. I've been nothing but nice to her."

"Yes, but you have what she wants. You have Drew."

"She doesn't want Drew, and if she did, he's repeatedly told her he has no interest in her."

"That doesn't mean she won't still try." Marie lets out a sigh. "I shouldn't be saying all this. I'm basing it on my own experience, not yours. You know this woman better than I do. If your gut's telling you she's not after Drew, then I'm sure you're right."

I stop pacing and look at the open cabinets, anger filling my veins. "Marie, I'm sorry to cut this short, but I need to clean up this mess Molly made. I can't take seeing my kitchen this way."

"Okay, but don't work too hard. Take some time to rest. I'll see you on Monday." She ends the call.

Take time to rest? If she saw my kitchen, she'd see it isn't possible to rest until everything is put back in its proper place.

Where do I even start? There's so much to do! I decide to fix the cupboards first, then the drawers, and I'll end with the refrigerator. My stomach growls, reminding me I never made myself that sandwich, but I don't have time now. This mess must be dealt with before I lose my mind.

I cannot let that woman back in my home. If Drew can't find Molly an apartment, she'll have to go to a hotel. She can't return here, not after what she did. She clearly hates me, and because of that, I no longer feel safe around her. Drew told me she was crazy, and although I didn't want to believe him, what she's done to my kitchen is proof that the woman needs help. What sane person would do something like this?

I've only emptied one cupboard when I decide I need to rid the guest room of Molly's things for my own sanity. So that I feel like she's gone.

Hurrying down the hall, I fling open the door to her room and see it's an even bigger mess than before. Her clothes are scattered everywhere, the bed is unmade, and she has bottles of lotion on the nightstand and dresser. As I'm gathering up the lotions, I notice they aren't the ones I had in the guest room. They're mine. The ones I had in my room, in the bathroom, in a container under the sink.

When was Molly in my room? Snooping through my things? After she took my robe, I told her she is never again to go in my room. But she did it anyway! What is wrong with her? Why is she doing everything possible to turn me against her? I was on her side. I stood up for her when Drew said we couldn't trust her. I encouraged him to let her stay here.

What a fool I've been. She's been playing me this whole time. Using my kindness to her advantage. Well, no more. I am done being nice.

I gather up all the bedding and bring it down to the washer. I return to the guest room, take out Molly's clothes, and pack them in her duffel bag. Then I snatch up the bottles of lotion and take them back to my room. I put them in their designated spots under the sink, letting out a sigh of relief when I see that nothing's been rearranged. I was worried Molly might've destroyed my bathroom the way she destroyed my kitchen, but thankfully, that didn't happen.

Going back to the guest room, I'm about to start cleaning it but change my mind and decide to do it later. The kitchen is my priority. I can't bear to see it in such disarray.

I grab Molly's duffel bag and bring it to the door so it's ready to go when Drew gets home. I need to call him and tell him to take Molly directly to a hotel if he's unable to find her an apartment today. I don't want her coming back here. I can't be around her right now. I'm too angry.

My eyes dart to the kitchen and I race over there, focused on the job I need to do. I empty each cabinet, lining everything up on the counters. Two hours later, I've got all the cabinets back as they were. I'm working on the drawers when Drew calls.

"Did you find an apartment?" I ask, desperately hoping he did.

"No," he says with a sigh. "I'm at the hospital."

28

"Why are you at the hospital?" I ask. "Is Molly having the baby?"

"No, but she started having pain and thought it might be labor pains so I took her to the hospital. They said she's not in labor, but they're recommending she be on bedrest for a week."

"Why? What's wrong with her?"

"They don't know, but just to be safe, the doctor doesn't want her moving around. She's filling out some paperwork, and then I'll take her home."

"You mean here?" I say with dread.

"Well, yeah. I don't have anywhere else to take her. And she can't be alone. The doctor said we need to keep an eye on her."

My shoulders slump in disappointment as I realize what this means. Molly's coming back to live with us, probably until she has the baby.

"Sara?" Drew says. "You still there?"

"Yes, I'll have to get her room ready. I'd already taken all the bedding off, assuming she wouldn't be here tonight."

"I'm sorry, honey. I know this wasn't the plan, but there's really nothing I can do about it. I was given strict orders to keep watch on her until the baby arrives."

"I thought you said the bedrest was only for a week. The baby isn't arriving that soon."

"He might. And if he doesn't, are you suggesting we kick her out right before her due date?"

Part of me would like to, but that wouldn't be right. I need to set aside my anger at Molly and think about her health and the health of the baby.

"No, of course not," I say. "She'll need to stay here. I'll go make up the bed."

"Sara, are you okay? You sound upset."

"We can discuss it when you get home," I say, heading down the hall.

"Just tell me now. What did I do?"

"This isn't about you." I go into the guest room and straight to the linen closet where I take out a set of sheets. "It's Molly. She did something that upset me."

"What did she do?"

"She rearranged the entire kitchen, including the refrigerator." I bring the sheets to the bed and put the phone on speaker, setting it on the nightstand. "It was a complete disaster." I shake the fitted sheet out and pull it over one corner of the bed. "I've spent the past two hours getting the cabinets back as they were, and was just starting on the drawers when you called."

"Molly wouldn't do that. She couldn't have. She's been out all day."

"She did it last night." I yank the sheet over the opposite corner of the bed, nearly ripping it as my rage reignites over what Molly did. "She obviously hates me.

Being nice to me was all an act. What for, I don't know. Maybe so I'd convince you to let her stay with us? But if that's the case, why would she destroy my kitchen? She had to have known how much that would anger me." I finish with the bottom sheet and grab the top, shaking it out until it lies evenly over the bed.

"Are you sure you didn't—" Drew stops abruptly.

"Didn't what?" I pause, letting go of the sheet.

"Nothing. Forget it."

"No, what were you going to say?"

He clears his throat. "I heard you in the kitchen last night. Around midnight. When I was on the couch."

"I wasn't in the kitchen," I scoff. "I was asleep. In bed."

"Sara, I talked to you. I asked what you were doing. Don't you remember?"

"No, because it didn't happen," I say, thinking he must've dreamed it.

"I asked what you were doing and you told me not to worry about it. To leave you alone."

"I don't know what you're talking about. That never happened. You must've been having a dream."

"I wasn't dreaming. I was wide awake, listening to you make noise in the kitchen for two hours. I eventually put in earbuds and played some music to drown out the sound."

"Drew, I was not in the kitchen last night," I insist, going back to making the bed. "You were obviously dreaming. Why are you telling me this? We need to talk about Molly and what she did."

"Except... I don't think she did it. I think maybe you did."

"Me?" I drop the sheet I was tucking in and rise to standing. "You can't be serious."

"Why else were you in the kitchen? You were doing something in there."

"I was not in the kitchen. It had to have been Molly. That must've been when she rearranged everything. She did it in the middle of the night so I'd wake up to a mess. But then I didn't have breakfast and didn't find out until later what she'd done." I huff. "She's even crazier than I thought. Who does something like that?"

"Sara, it was you," Drew says in a soft, gentle tone. "I know it was you. I saw you."

"I don't know why you keep saying that when you know it's not true." I lean down and tuck the sheet in. "Molly destroyed my kitchen, and I am furious about it!" I take a breath. "But I will do my best to be civil to her."

"Speaking of Molly, they just let her go. I'm going to help her out to the car. We should be home in half an hour or so."

"Yes, fine." I end the call, enraged that Drew would even think of accusing me of messing up my own kitchen. Is he out of his mind? Why in the world would I do that? He knows I wouldn't, which means he's either confused or he's trying to protect Molly.

If he did it to protect Molly, I find that very concerning. It means he's taking her side over mine. Blaming me for something she clearly did.

Why would he do that? Is he having feelings for Molly? Is seeing her carrying his baby making him change how he feels about her? I hope not, but I'm worried that might be what's happening. Why else would he make up that ridiculous story in an attempt to cover up what she did?

After I finish making the bed, I get the duffel bag I'd set by the door and bring it back to the guest room. I put Molly's clothes away in the dresser, then leave the room, shutting the door behind me. I return to the kitchen and quickly configure the drawers the way they should be, finishing up just as Drew and Molly get home.

"I'll be in my room," Molly says to Drew, hunched over and clutching her stomach.

"Yes, go ahead," he tells her. "I'll check on you in a few minutes."

Molly doesn't even glance at me as she heads to the hall. I'll admit, she doesn't look well. I thought she might be faking her condition, but she saw a doctor who was concerned enough to order her to stay off her feet, so perhaps I shouldn't be so judgmental. I'm usually not, but Molly's bringing out the worst in me.

"Does she need anything?" I ask as Drew joins me in the kitchen.

"She says she doesn't, but I'm going to bring her some water. The doctor said she was slightly dehydrated."

"Has she eaten anything?" I ask.

"Yes, I took her to lunch around eleven. She was feeling lightheaded. I thought it was because she needed to eat." He takes a glass from the cupboard, the one I just put back in place with all the glasses perfectly lined up. "I hope it wasn't something more serious." He glances at me. "The lightheadedness."

"I'm sure it wasn't. If it was, the doctor would've told you."

Drew fills the glass with water, then turns to me. "I was really worried, Sara."

"About Molly?"

"And the baby." He sets the glass down. "I haven't been that panicked in a long time. I had all these thoughts going through my head about what might be wrong. At one point, I worried the baby might not make it." He chokes on the words.

"Drew, relax," I say, rubbing his arm. "Everything's fine. Molly's just having some pain. I'm sure it'll go away and you can stop worrying."

He nods. "I wasn't prepared for this. She was fine this morning, when we were looking at apartments, and then the next thing I know, she's in the hospital."

The timing seems rather suspicious. The day Drew goes to find Molly an apartment just happens to be the day she has mysterious pains and ends up at the hospital? And the doctor isn't sure what's wrong?

I shouldn't think that way. I'm sure Molly really was in pain, and seeing her just now, it looks like she's still in pain. I guess the timing was just a coincidence.

Drew picks up the glass. "I'm going to go bring her this and see how she's doing." He takes off and I hear him going into her room. Several minutes pass before he returns. "She's going to rest."

"That's good," I say, wiping up the counters. "I'm sure she needs it."

"Hey." Drew comes over to me. "Can we talk?"

"About what?" I ask, wondering why he has such a serious look on his face.

"Several things." He glances at the dishcloth I'm using. "Stop cleaning and come sit down."

I reluctantly follow him to the couch. As I sit down beside him, he checks his phone.

"I got a text from one of the apartments Molly and I looked at," Drew says. "It's been leased to someone else."

"Well, you don't need it now so it doesn't matter."

Drew sets down his phone and turns to me. "I'm sorry you're having to go through all this."

I shrug. "There's nothing you can do about it. We just have to get through it."

"We? Meaning you're not planning to leave me?"

"I haven't decided what I'm going to do." I straighten my shoulders and look away. "This all happened so fast. I still can't believe it's true. I keep thinking I'll wake up and realize none of it was real."

"But it is." Drew takes my hand. "Molly is going to have the baby soon, and when he arrives, all of our lives will change."

Why is Drew telling me this? I know everything's going to change. I don't need to be reminded of it. His words are causing me to feel *more* stressed, not less. He knows I don't like uncertainty, and everything with Molly and the baby is uncertain. We don't know where the two of them will live, what the custody arrangement will be, or how much money we'll need to spend to support them. It's all up in the air, which keeps me in a constant state of anxiety.

"I know things will change," I say, looking back at Drew, "but how? Do you have a plan for what happens after the baby arrives?"

"Molly and I talked about that today, but we didn't get anywhere."

"You talked about it with her but not me?" I say, hurt that he didn't even consider including me.

"We talked specifically about our son," Drew says. Hearing him say "our" in reference to him and Molly causes an ache in my chest. It's incredibly painful to know his firstborn child will be with her, the other woman. I wish he'd stopped saying "our son" or "our baby".

"What about him?" I ask.

"We talked about how we'll handle his care once he's here. I told Molly I'd like to share in the responsibilities. But that'll be difficult to do if she lives across town."

"Share in what responsibilities? What do you mean?"

"Feeding him, changing his diapers, rocking him to sleep," Drew says in a wistful tone. "I want to be part of all of it." He smiles a little. "I don't want to miss a thing. This is what I've been waiting for. To be a father. I want to be there for all the moments, big and small. If that means Molly has to live closer to us, then I guess I'll just have to be okay with it."

"What about me?" I ask in a sharp tone. "Shouldn't you be asking if *I'd* be okay with it?"

"Of course, but I assumed you'd be fine with it. You get along with Molly. You even seem to like her, which I must say is very mature of you. Most wives in your situation would hate Molly, but you've accepted her and gone out of your way to help her."

"Yes, but now I'm not sure about her. I think you were right in saying we should be cautious around her. What she did to our kitchen is bizarre and disturbing. It makes me think she might have some mental health issues, like you said."

"Honey, I know you don't remember it," Drew says, taking my hand gently in his, "but it was you in the kitchen last night. It wasn't Molly. I thought maybe you couldn't sleep so you decided to go on one of your organizing binges. Remember when you used to do that?"

He's referring to the time when we moved here. Having to leave my old life behind and start somewhere new was overwhelming and stressful. I needed to feel grounded and like I had a sense of control, so I became obsessed with organizing things. As Drew described, I went on organizing binges that sometimes went on for hours. But that is not what happened last night. I would've remembered it.

"I was not in the kitchen," I say emphatically. "And I don't like that you keep insisting you're right about this when you're not."

"Let's just agree to disagree," he says, which only annoys me more. Why doesn't he believe me?

"Drew, I promise you, I did not—"

"Forget it," he says. "I don't want to fight about it. That's not what I wanted to talk about. Can I continue?"

"Go ahead," I tell him, but I'm irritated he's moving on when I'm still upset he accused me of something I didn't do.

Why would I rearrange my kitchen in the middle of the night? There's no logical answer, because I'd never do it. But Molly would, and I'm certain she did.

So why is Drew insisting it was me? Why is he covering for her?

29

"What do you want to talk about?" I ask.

"The thing we've been avoiding. The thing I know is bothering you, and yet you haven't said anything, which concerns me."

"What are you referring to?" I ask, trying to figure out what he means.

"The fact that I'm having a baby with someone else. Someone who isn't you."

The ache in my chest is now a stabbing pain. I realize we need to talk about this, but I don't know if I can. Even when I think about it in my head, I try to push it away to avoid the pain.

"Drew, I don't think this is the right time."

"We can't keep putting it off," he says. "Avoiding it is only going to make you feel worse. I'm here for you, Sara. Talk to me. Tell me how you're feeling."

"You want the truth?" I look him in the eye. "I'm angry. Furious! And sometimes I hate you. And I hate Molly. I don't want to feel this way, but I do."

"You have every right to," he says, gently rubbing my hand. "What else are you feeling?"

"Like I'm losing control. Like I don't have a say in anything. Like you're making decisions with Molly without even considering me. And like she's your priority now instead of me."

The thoughts I'd bottled up are spilling from my mouth so fast I can barely keep up. I didn't plan to say all that, but now that I have, I feel lighter, like a weight's been lifted off me.

"Are you jealous?" Drew asks softly. "Of Molly?"

I pause before answering. "I don't like admitting it, but yes. Of course I'm jealous. This baby was supposed to be mine. Ours. It's what we've been talking about, dreaming about, planning for. And now you're doing all that with Molly."

"I'm sorry," Drew says. "I really am. I wish I could change things."

"But you can't. She's having your baby, and I just have to sit here and watch you two share something that you and I may never have."

"Sara, don't say that. You and I can still try."

"When?" I snap. "In a year? Two years? Three? By then, it could be too late. I'm not getting any younger, and neither are you. Are you really going to want a baby in your fifties?"

"It wouldn't be that long. But I do want some time with my son before we start trying again. It wouldn't be fair to him to have to compete for my time with another child."

"But it's okay if I have to compete for your time?" I ask, only to realize how immature that sounds.

"Sara, I'll always make time for you. You know that. It just won't be as much time as before."

"Yes, I know you need time with the baby, and I want you to have it. I just don't know where that leaves me. Am I going to be alone here while you're over with Molly and the baby?"

"You'd come with me." He pauses. "Wouldn't you?"

"Yes, but not every time, especially if you're there every day, or more than that."

"Sara, I get the feeling this is less about the baby and more about Molly. Is the issue that you don't want to be around her? Or around me when I'm with her?"

I look down. "That's part of it. I'll admit this whole situation would be a lot easier if it were just me and you and the baby, and Molly wasn't in the picture."

"You wish she were gone," Drew says. "That she wasn't part of our lives."

"In a perfect world, yes, but we're not in that world. Molly isn't going anywhere. I have to accept that."

"But you're angry at her," Drew says.

I look at him. "Why wouldn't I be? Our life was wonderful until she came along and ruined it."

"That's good, Sara. Let your feelings out. Say how you really feel."

"You want to know how I really feel?" I huff. "I want to kill her, and not just because she slept with you and is having your baby, but because of what she did to my kitchen! That was purely aimed at me. She was telling me that all the kindness I've shown her doesn't matter. That she can be as mean as she wants to me because she has all the power. She's the one having your baby, and she thinks that gives her the right to do whatever she wants."

"Good, Sara," Drew says, encouraging me. "Keep going. Get it out."

"She's a liar!" I shout, a wave of relief coming over me as I finally express the rage I've been holding back. "And a thief! She keeps taking my things. She doesn't even ask. She just goes in my room and takes them!" I throw my hands up.

"How does that make you feel?" Drew asks, sounding like a therapist.

"Like I want to strangle her!" I take a deep breath. "I shouldn't say that, but I do sometimes wish she'd go away and never come back."

"Anything else?" Drew asks.

"I think I'm done." I fall back on the couch, exhausted from my rant. I don't usually do that. In fact, I don't think I ever have. I usually hold everything inside.

Drew picks up his phone and looks at it. "I got another text about an apartment Molly and I looked at." He sets his phone down.

"You should text them back. Let them know you're no longer looking."

"I will." He turns to me. "But first, I need to ask if you're okay."

"I'm not, but I will be. It'll just take time."

"Is there anything else you want to talk about?"

"Not now. I think I'm all talked out."

He leans over and kisses my cheek. "You surprised me. I think that's the most you've ever opened up to me."

"That's not true," I say, rolling my eyes.

"Going back to Molly, I don't want you to keep missing work so I'm going to work at home next week, and the following week if I need to."

"How can you do that when you have clients to meet with?"

"I'll do the meetings online. I'll need to get my things from the office. I could go tonight or get up early and go tomorrow."

"Why don't you go now? Get it over with."

"You'll be okay with Molly?"

"Yes. Why wouldn't I be?"

He smiles a little. "You just said you wanted to kill her. I'm not sure I should be leaving you alone with her after that."

I swat his arm. "Drew, don't joke about that. You know I didn't mean it."

He stands up. "I'll run to the office and get my computer and whatever files I need. It shouldn't take long."

While he's gone, I go to the kitchen and try to figure out what to make for dinner. I really need to go to the store, but I'm not leaving Molly here by herself. And it's not just because of her health, but because I don't trust her in my home. Just as I'm thinking that, I hear her behind me.

"Hey, Sara."

I whip around to face her, my heart racing because she startled me, but also because I don't feel safe around her. I realize that sounds ridiculous since she couldn't do much to me in her condition, but I'm still wary of her.

"What are you doing out of bed?" I ask.

"I was wondering if you have some crackers. My stomach is upset. I thought crackers might help."

"Help yourself." I fold my arms across my chest. "You already know we have them and where we keep them."

"I don't," she says, playing innocent. I must say, she's an excellent actor. "That's why I'm asking. I know you don't like me going through your cupboards, so I wasn't even going to try to look for them."

I laugh at the ridiculousness of her performance. "Are you really continuing this?"

She gives me a confused look. "Continuing what?"

"This innocent act." I glare at her. "I know what you did. Tearing apart my kitchen. Making a mess of the refrigerator. Why did you do it? I've been nothing but kind to you. I even—"

"What are you talking about? I didn't touch your kitchen."

"Molly, I am not playing this game with you where you pretend to be innocent. I know you did it."

"Did what? What happened?"

"You know what happened!" I say. "You emptied every cabinet and drawer and then put everything back in places they don't belong, knowing it would upset me! And as if that weren't enough, you made a mess of the refrigerator! The question is why? What were you hoping to accomplish? Were you trying to make me angry? Or waste my time having to fix the mess you made? Just tell me what your goal was so I can at least try to understand why you would do such a thing."

"Sara, it wasn't me. I swear."

"Really?" I huff. "Then who was it? Did some stranger break into my home, rearrange all my cupboards and drawers, and then leave? Is that what you expect me to believe?"

"I don't know who did it, but it wasn't me. When did it happen?"

"Sometime last night. I didn't have breakfast this

morning so I didn't discover it until later, when I went to make a sandwich for lunch."

"What about Drew? He had breakfast. Wouldn't he have noticed this and told you?"

She has a point. Why didn't Drew say anything? He definitely would've noticed things were out of place, so why didn't he mention it? Was it because he didn't want to upset me? Was he hoping I'd find out while he was out with Molly so he wouldn't have to deal with my anger? Or maybe he didn't want me yelling at Molly for what she did and having to intervene. Drew can't handle conflict so it's possible he didn't tell me simply for his own selfish need to avoid my reaction.

"How do you know he had breakfast?" I ask, wondering if Molly's lying to me. I don't recall Drew eating this morning. I assumed he skipped breakfast because he was in a hurry to search for apartments.

"I guess I don't know for sure if he did," Molly says, "but he definitely had orange juice. I saw him drinking it."

I didn't, which means Molly could be making it up.

"What about you?" I ask. "Did you have breakfast?"

"Not here. Drew got me something on our way to the first apartment. We just went through a drive-thru."

"But Drew didn't eat?"

"No, he said he wasn't hungry, which is why I thought he'd already eaten."

"Just admit that you did it," I say, frustrated with her. "I know you did, so why lie about it?"

"I'm not lying," she says, raising her voice. "I didn't do it." She points to herself. "Look at me. Look how short I am. How could I reach the top shelves in the cupboards? It's not possible."

"You could've used the stepladder." I point to it, folded up and neatly stored in the narrow space between the refrigerator and the wine cabinet.

"First of all, I didn't even know that was there," Molly says. "And second, I would never get up on a ladder when I'm this pregnant."

It's possible that's true. I can't imagine her climbing a ladder and reaching up to the cabinets with her huge belly sticking out. It'd get in the way, and it affects her balance, making her more likely to fall. So then how did she do it? How did she rearrange the shelves she wasn't able to reach?

"I didn't do it, Sara," she says. "I was asleep. I didn't get up once last night."

"Then how do you explain it? There are only three of us living here. Drew and I obviously didn't do it, which only leaves one other person."

"How do you know it wasn't Drew? You said it happened last night. Where was Drew? Did he sleep in your room or on the couch?"

"On the couch, but—"

"Then he would've known who did it. Did he say it was me?"

"No, he..." I clear my throat. "He claims I did it, which makes absolutely no sense. I don't know why he would even say such a thing."

Molly shrugs. "To confuse you? Take the blame off himself? Think about it, Sara. Drew had access to the kitchen all night with nobody watching him. You don't think it's possible he did it?"

"He would never do something like that. He has no reason to."

"Unless he wanted to make you angry."

"And why would he want that?" I ask. "He's trying to win me back. Get me to forgive him for the affair. He wouldn't purposely do something to make me angry at him."

"Did he tell you that?" Molly goes over to the table next to the kitchen and sits down.

"Tell me what?"

"That he's trying to win you back?" She leans back in the chair and moves her hand in circles over her stomach. "Because that's not what he told me."

She's baiting me. Trying to turn me against my husband. But I'm not letting her do it.

30

"I'M NOT TALKING ABOUT DREW," I say to Molly, joining her at the table. "Despite what you told me, I know you want him for yourself so you can live out this fantasy where the two of you and the baby are one big happy family. But Drew doesn't want that. He's committed to me, and committed to our marriage. So whatever it is you were about to say, I don't want to hear it."

She arches a brow. "Even if you might be in danger?"

I sigh. "Molly, you need to stop this. You are not going to make me afraid of my husband. I don't care what you say. I've known Drew much longer than you, and I can tell you that he is not a violent man. So making up stories about him in your attempt to get me to leave him is a waste of time."

"That's not what I'm doing." She reaches across the table and puts her hand over mine. "I didn't make it up. I'm telling you, Sara, he wants you gone. Out of his life. And if you don't leave on your own, he might—" She stops abruptly and glances away.

"Might what? Kill me?" I yank my hand back from hers. "Stop saying that. I mean it. I don't want to hear you ever say that again."

"What about how he complains about you? He did it again this morning. He said you're too controlling. That you're always telling him what to do. He said he feels trapped and that—"

"Enough!" I bolt up from my chair. "I'm not listening to this. It's all lies meant to convince me to divorce Drew so you can have him for yourself."

"No! That's not what I'm doing."

"Yes, Molly, it *is* what you're doing, and yet you continue to say these things as if I'm not on to you. As if I can't see what you're doing."

"What if I could prove it?" she says.

"Prove what?"

"That he's thinking of hurting you."

"And how would you do that?" I ask, challenging her.

"He has a gun. When I asked you if he had one, it was because I wanted to know if he was hiding it from you, and he was. You said he didn't have one, but he does. It's in a closet in his office. He keeps it in a suitcase, the one he had at the hotel. You can go to his office and see for yourself that I'm right."

"I already did," I calmly say. "Drew showed it to me when I went to his office yesterday."

That's a lie, but I need to convince her I trust Drew and don't believe what she's saying about him. It's like Drew said, we need to show Molly we're committed to staying together so she doesn't have this fantasy of someday being with him.

"I made some comment about guns," I say,

continuing the made-up story, "just to see what he'd say, and he told me he had something to confess. Something he knew I wouldn't like but that he didn't feel right not telling me. That's when he showed me the gun."

She looks down at the table. "I don't get it. He didn't want you to know he had it. That's why he hid it at his office."

"He keeps it there because of what happened. And also because he knows I don't want it at home."

"Because of what happened?" Molly says. "What do you mean?"

"Drew told me he was held at gunpoint last year while walking to his car after work. Luckily, the man ran off, but Drew didn't feel safe after that so he bought the gun."

"When did he say he got it?"

"It was a year ago, so probably sometime last winter."

Molly shakes her head. "He's lying. He bought it last May. I know because he asked me what kind to get."

"And why would he ask you that?" I say, not believing her.

"Because I know about guns. A few years ago, I dated this guy who worked at a gun store. He taught me all about guns. I even learned how to shoot."

"Assuming that's true, why would Drew ask you this? How did this topic even come up?"

"When he invited me up to his hotel room, I said something about how he better not be some psychopath who plans to kill me. I was joking, of course, but you never know, right?" she says with a laugh. "Anyway, I told him I'd shoot any guy who tried to hurt me, and then I told him about the guy I used to date and how he taught me about guns."

Why am I listening to this? It's just another one of her crazy stories. Drew told me the real story, which actually makes sense. He got the gun to protect himself. I may not like that he has it, but I understand why he does. Fear can make you do things you wouldn't normally do, and Drew was clearly terrified after that man nearly killed him.

"That's when Drew asked me about the gun," Molly says. "He wanted to know what kind to get and where to buy it."

"And did he say why he wanted one?" I ask, wanting to see what lie she'll come up with next.

"He just said he wanted to buy a gun. But he also made that comment about wanting to shoot you, so..." Her voice trails off.

"That's a very interesting story," I say, "but I'm going to believe Drew's version."

"Believe what you want. Just remember that he lied to you. About me. About the affair. About having a gun."

When she says these things, I find myself doubting Drew when I should be doubting Molly. I can't keep listening to her. I told myself I wouldn't let her get to me like this, and here I am, letting her do it.

"I think we've talked enough about this," I say. "I'll get those crackers you wanted and then maybe you could go rest in your room."

I go over to the cabinet we use as a pantry and take out the box of crackers. I bring it to her, setting it on the table.

"I'm not a bad person, Sara," Molly says. "Whatever Drew told you about me isn't true."

"We aren't talking about Drew," I say. "If you want to talk, let's discuss something else."

"Can I ask where he went?" she says, opening the box of crackers.

"He went to the office to get his things. He'll be working from home next week. He said the doctor doesn't want you being alone in case something happens."

"He's lying." She takes some crackers from the box and pops one in her mouth.

"Who's lying? Drew?"

"It never happened. We never—" She shrugs. "Forget it. You won't believe me, so I'm not even going to say it."

I'm curious what she was going to tell me, but decide not to ask. I'm sure it was another fabricated story to make Drew look bad.

"I wish I could talk to someone," Molly says, eating another cracker. "Someone who would actually listen to me and tell me what to do."

"What to do about what?" I ask.

"What's happening. I don't want to do it anymore."

"I don't understand. What don't you want to do?"

Her eyes meet up with mine. "I can't tell you. Even if I did, you'd say I was lying."

I keep quiet. I have no idea what she's talking about, but I'm sure it's something I don't want to hear.

Her shoulders slump. "I miss my mom. She'd know what to do. She was really smart."

"I'm sorry she's no longer here for you," I say in a

comforting tone. "But you could still talk to her. Does she have a grave you could visit?"

Molly shakes her head, not saying anything. Her mother must've been cremated, assuming she actually died. I still find it odd that nobody Molly worked with knew that her mother was terminally ill, but it's possible she didn't want them to know.

"I have to go," Molly says, getting up so fast she almost knocked her chair over.

"Are you okay?" I follow her as she goes through the living room. "Is it your stomach? I could get you some ginger ale."

She hurries down the hall, goes into her room, and shuts the door. She must be feeling sick. That's the only reason she'd hurry off like that.

"Sara?" Drew calls out.

I return to the living room and see Drew with his laptop bag and the navy suitcase that was in his office closet. The one that had the gun in it.

"Why do you have that?" I say, pointing to the suitcase.

He sets it down, along with his laptop bag, and comes over to me. "Sara, I know you don't want it here, but I couldn't leave it at the office. Not when it could be weeks before I go back there."

"No." I stare at the suitcase. "I don't want a gun in our home. I won't allow it. You know how I feel about this, Drew. You can't keep it here."

"Sara, it's only for a week or two. You won't even know it's here."

"Are you serious?" I look at him. "It's all I'll be able to think about! I'll have nightmares about being shot in my own home!"

"Honey, you're overreacting. I'll hide it in the back of our closet. You won't even see it. It will remain in the suitcase the entire time. We can even lock the suitcase if that makes you feel better."

"It doesn't. Drew, I want it gone. I mean it."

"I'm sorry, honey, but I'm not backing down on this. It's only for a short time, and I have nowhere else to put it."

"Why couldn't it stay at your office? No one looks in your closet."

"They might. I store files there. If someone needed one, it's quite possible they'd go in that closet to look for it."

"Yes, but they wouldn't look under the shelves, see a suitcase, and open it."

"Why wouldn't they? You did, which means someone else might. I'm not willing to risk it. I'm keeping it here. I'm not going to argue about it." He gets the suitcase and brings it down the hall to our room.

There's a gun in our bedroom. The thought of that sends a chill down me, especially after hearing Molly say that Drew wants me gone. Obviously, it isn't true. She was trying to scare me. Make me think Drew was dangerous. So why am I panicking, thinking she might be right?

I can't do this. I'm letting Molly get into my head. Into my thoughts. She doesn't even know Drew. She spent a few nights with him. I've been with him for years.

"Okay, it's put away," Drew says, coming up behind me. He touches my shoulder and I shudder and step away. "Sara, what's wrong?"

I turn to face him. "The gun! That's what's wrong!

I'm a nervous wreck having that thing in our home. In our bedroom. Just a few feet away from where I sleep!"

He rubs my arms. "Honey, you're shaking. Try to relax."

"I can't relax." I yank away from him. "I could be killed in my own home!"

"Only if someone used it, which isn't going to happen."

"Not according to Molly," I blurt out.

Drew furrows his brow. "What's that supposed to mean?"

I wasn't going to tell him what she said, but maybe I should. He already thinks she's trying to convince me to leave him, so this shouldn't come as a surprise.

"She said you joked about wanting to kill me." My eyes lock on Drew. "Is it true? Did you joke about wanting to kill me?"

"No! I would never do that!" He walks away, then turns back. "Why the hell are you still listening to her? And believing what she says?" He storms back to me. "She's a liar, Sara. She'll say anything to get what she wants. She wants you to think I'm dangerous so she's putting all these ideas in your head! If anyone's dangerous, it's Molly!"

"If that's true, then we shouldn't have a gun in the house!" I shout back at him.

We stare at each other, both of us breathing hard. Drew's face is red, and I'm sure mine is too. Our arguments don't usually get this heated. We shouldn't be talking when we're this upset. We'll say something we don't mean. Something we can't take back. But I have questions, and I need answers.

"How did she know?" I ask.

"Know what?" Drew says.

"Molly knew you had a gun in that suitcase in your office. How did she know that?"

"I told her," he says without hesitation.

"Why would you tell her that?"

"Because she asked."

None of this is making sense. His answers are only making me more confused.

"Why would Molly ask where you kept your gun?" I say.

"It was back when I was seeing her. She told me some story about a guy she dated who worked at a gun store. She asked if I had one, and I told her I did. That I had it at my office, and that's when she asked if she could see it."

"And you showed it to her? You took her to your office?"

"No, I brought it with me the next time I saw her."

"In the suitcase? You told me you'd never brought that suitcase to the hotel."

He pauses, then nods. "You're right. I'd forgotten I'd brought it there. But it was only that one time, when Molly wanted to see the gun."

"Why did you show it to her?"

"The first night I talked to her, I realized she knew a lot about guns. The different types. What they were worth. I was thinking of selling mine so I brought it to her so she could assess the value."

"You were going to sell it? I thought you wanted it."

"I did, but I felt bad having it and not telling you. But I knew if I told you, you'd tell me to get rid of it, so I was torn. I wanted it, but I didn't like hiding it from you."

"And yet you did," I say. "Is that because of Molly? Did she convince you to keep it?"

"No, I decided I wanted to be able to protect myself so you'd still have a husband if I ever got attacked again. I thought you'd want that too."

"Of course, but I still don't like that you have it, and I really don't like it being in our home."

"It's only temporary." He takes my hand. "I promise."

I don't care if it's only temporary. I don't want it here at all. We have a stranger living with us. A woman we barely know. She's told us almost nothing about her background, and what she *has* told us could all be a lie.

What if she's not who she says she is? What if she's dangerous?

A woman who could be lying to us and might be dangerous is in our home. And now we have a gun in our home. A gun she knows how to use.

31

"ROUGH NIGHT?" Marie says when she sees me at the coffee machine Monday morning.

"What?" I say, not comprehending what she said.

"I'm joking," she says with a smile. "You look like you didn't sleep much last night."

"I didn't." I take my coffee and walk over to Marie. "Molly is living with us again."

"I thought Drew was getting her an apartment."

"That was the plan, until Molly was put on bedrest." I tell Marie the story about Drew taking Molly to the hospital on Saturday, and how he's now home with her for the week.

"What a mess," Marie says with a sigh. "Your life is starting to sound like a soap opera."

I laugh, which I haven't done in days. "If only I liked soap operas, I'd be in heaven."

"At least you have a sense of humor about it."

"I really don't." I stare down at my coffee. "If I'm laughing, it's because I've lost my mind from all the stress."

"You haven't lost your mind," Marie says in an understanding tone. "You just have a lot to think about so you're feeling overwhelmed."

"It's more than that." I sip my coffee, then look at her. "It's being there."

"Being where?"

"At home. It doesn't feel like it used to. It feels dark and depressing and heavy. Sometimes I feel like I can't breathe."

"Is it really that bad?" Marie says with concern.

"It's worse. I'm always on edge. I can't relax. And now I can't sleep because Drew is keeping a gun in our bedroom."

Marie rears back. "A gun? Why does Drew have a gun?"

I quickly explain why, then say, "He knows I don't want it there, but he refuses to get rid of it. So now I have a gun in my bedroom and Drew's ex-lover across the hall. And I'm starting to wonder if Molly has some mental health issues. She tells me things that seem completely made up, but I think she really believes them."

"Like what?"

"I don't want to get into it. It'll just upset me more, and I won't be able to work."

"Are you sure you want to? Maybe you should take the day off."

"Then I'd have to go home, which is the last place I want to be right now."

"If you need a place to go, you could stay with me for a few days. You'll have to put up with the never-ending drama of my two teenage girls, but it's probably less drama than what's going on at your house at the moment, and that's saying a lot."

I smile. "Yes, I definitely have more drama."

"We have a guest room that's not being used. If you want to stay in it for a few days, just to get a break, you're welcome to."

"Thanks, Marie. That's nice of you to offer. I'll think about it."

"I need to grab some coffee and get to a meeting," she says, going past me to the coffee machine. "Let me know what you decide."

"I will." I leave the break room and go to my office. I sit down at my desk and take a deep breath. Being here, I already feel calmer, which is odd because work is usually a place I feel stressed. Now it's my home making me feel that way.

I'm tempted to take Marie up on her offer. It'd be nice to get a break from Molly and everything going on at home. But Drew wouldn't like it. He'd think I'm leaving because of him. He might even see it as a sign I want a divorce. He wouldn't believe me if I told him I just needed a break.

My phone rings. It's my mother calling. I've been avoiding her, not wanting to tell her what's going on.

"Hi, Mom," I say in a cheerful tone. "Is everything okay? You don't usually call when I'm at work."

"Everything's fine. I just haven't heard from you. I was getting worried."

"Sorry. I've been really busy trying to get some articles done."

"Honey, you need to relax and not work so much. You know, stress can make it harder to have a baby. I read that somewhere, or maybe I heard it on the news. I can't remember, but either way, they say that minimizing stress can make things easier."

"I'll keep that in mind," I say, tensing up. I love my mother dearly, but sometimes I can't take all her advice. She's constantly telling me what to do, which is why I haven't told her about Drew and Molly. I need to work through this myself before I tell her.

"How's Drew?" my mom asks. "Did you talk to him about when your dad and I could come for a visit?"

"No, but now's not a good time. Drew is really busy at work. Maybe you could come here in May, once tax season is over and Drew's had time to rest."

"May? Sara, that's months from now."

I don't have the time or energy to argue with her about this. I need to get her off the phone. "We can talk about it later. I have to get going. I'm late for a meeting."

"Okay, honey. Don't work too hard. Love you!"

"Love you too." I end the call, feeling anxious and like I need to walk around. I get up and pace my office, thinking about my mom and how she's going to react when I finally tell her what's going on. She'll be so disappointed with Drew, and probably with me, too, for not knowing he was having an affair.

My phone alerts me to a text. I pick it up and see a message from my mom. *Forgot to tell you that Margaret passed away last night. Her obituary is online if you'd like to read it.*

Margaret was our neighbor when I was growing up. She went into a nursing home a few years ago, but my mom would visit her now and then.

Going back to my desk, I wake up my computer and look up Margaret's name. Her obituary is at the top of the search results. As I'm reading it, I get an idea. I open a new search page and type in the name of Molly's mother. None of the results are a match. They're all younger women who aren't from the area. I add Boston to the search and the word 'obituary' but nothing comes up. Maybe I got the name wrong. Molly only told me it once. Maybe I misheard her.

"Hi, Sara," someone says, and when I look up, I see Emma, my assistant, at the door.

I smile at her. "Good morning. Did you just get in?"

"Yeah, I had an errand to run before work." She leans against the door frame. "I didn't know you were coming in today. I heard you had something going on at home. Some personal stuff."

"Who told you that?" I ask, thinking it had to be Marie, although that surprises me. She's never been one to gossip, and she knows I don't want the whole office knowing about Drew's affair.

"It wasn't anyone in particular," Emma says. "It was just some people talking in the break room last Friday. You'd already left for the day."

"What were they saying about me?"

"That you looked like you hadn't slept in days. And that old lady from accounting said she asked you something and you didn't even hear her. And someone else said they heard you talking to yourself at the copy machine."

"I wasn't talking to myself," I insist. But what if I was? I haven't been able to shut my mind off since Molly showed up. Was I saying my thoughts out loud and didn't realize it? If so, I need to get this under control. I can't have people at work thinking I'm crazy.

Emma shrugs. "Hey, I get it. When my boyfriend

ghosted me after two years of dating, I was so messed up I crossed the street without even looking. I totally forgot where I was. My point is, it's totally normal to act a little crazy when things aren't going well at home."

"Yes, well, you can tell everyone that I'm fine," I say with a tight smile. "I was just tired on Friday, but I got some extra sleep over the weekend."

"Yeah, okay," she says, eyeing me like she doesn't believe me. I do look pretty bad. I tried to conceal the dark circles under my eyes, but they're still visible. And when I was in the bathroom earlier, I noticed my skin looks sallow. I guess I'm not surprised people in the office are talking about me.

My phone rings, and I tense up when I see Drew's name on the screen, immediately assuming something's wrong.

"Hi, Drew," I say. "How are things going?"

"Sara, I hate to ask this, but could you come home for an hour or two?"

"Why? What's wrong?"

"Nothing. I just forgot something at the office and need to go get it. It won't take long. I promise."

I sigh. "Fine, but this can't keep happening. I can't keep missing work to deal with Molly."

"Yes, I know. I completely understand. I'll see you soon." He ends the call.

I pack up my laptop, then text Marie and Emma, telling them I need to leave but will be back after lunch. It's only nine, but I'm assuming Drew's trip to the office won't be as quick as he promised. I wouldn't be surprised if he was there for the rest of the day.

This isn't going to work. Drew isn't someone who can do his job at home. He can't focus there. He tried in the past and couldn't get anything done. He needs to be at the office. But if he thinks I'm going to step in and volunteer to stay home, it's not going to happen. Molly is his mess, and he needs to take care of her.

When I get to the apartment, I set up my laptop on the kitchen table. I'll try to get some work done while I'm here, but I doubt it'll happen.

"Drew, I'm home," I call out.

He doesn't answer, but I hear his voice coming from down the hall. I follow it to Molly's room, stopping before I reach the door.

"You need to stop this," Drew says in a harsh tone. "It never should've happened."

"But things are different now," Molly says.

"No. Nothing has changed! You're seeing what you want to see, not what's actually true."

"What if she divorced you?"

"She's not divorcing me. I've already told you this. And you know divorce isn't what I want."

Hearing Drew say that, I feel my anger toward him lessening. I feel my love for him coming back. He's told me many times in the past week that he's committed to our marriage, but I didn't believe him until now. Until I heard him tell Molly. Part of me thought he might choose her over me. Because of the baby. But that was my insecurity talking, telling me Drew no longer loved me because I hadn't given him a child.

"Sara's going to be home any minute now," Drew says. "If I find out you're telling her lies about me, I will no longer allow you to stay here. I'm serious, Molly. Stop trying to turn Sara against me. You're only making things worse for yourself."

"But what if—"

"We're done talking about this," Drew says. "I need to get to the office."

I quickly and quietly go back to the living room.

"Sara," Drew says, appearing from the hall. "When did you get home?"

"Just now. Why?"

"I didn't hear the door." He comes over and gives me a kiss. "Thank you again for doing this." He grabs his coat from the chair and his keys from the table. "I'll be back as soon as I can."

"How's Molly?" I ask.

"She's asleep. Or maybe she's up now. I don't know. I haven't been down there to check."

He's lying. He doesn't want me to know they talked or what he said to her. I wish he'd just tell me instead of hiding it from me.

"I'll go check on her," I say.

Drew gives me a peck on the cheek. "Bye, sweetheart. I love you."

After he leaves, I go down to the guest room and lightly knock on the door. "Molly, it's Sara. Can I come in?"

"Yeah," I hear her say.

When I open the door, I see Molly on the bed. She's sitting up and looking at her phone.

"How are you feeling?" I ask.

"I'm bored." She tosses her phone on the bed. "I can't take sitting here all day." She gazes at her stomach. "I wish he'd hurry up and come so I'd have something to do."

"He'll be here soon enough." I walk over to her. "How was everything with Drew this morning?"

She looks up at me. "Fine. I didn't really see him."

"He didn't talk to you?"

"No. Why?"

"I thought you two might talk."

She gazes at her stomach again, rubbing her hand over it. "I don't know why you're still with him. You could do so much better."

She's still trying to convince me to leave him, even after Drew just told her he doesn't want a divorce. I feel sorry for her. She's keeping her hopes up for something that's never going to be. Even if Drew and I did get a divorce, he still doesn't want to be with her, but she can't seem to accept that.

"Have you thought about it?" she asks.

"About what?"

"Leaving him." Her eyes rise to mine. "Before it's too late."

"Too late for what?"

She glances away.

"Molly, what did you mean?" I ask.

She moves so she's lying down and closes her eyes. "I'm going to try to sleep. Could you close the door on your way out?"

Why won't she answer me? Why would it be too late? What did she mean?

I'm sure it's just another one of her tactics to make me leave Drew. She wants to confuse me. Make me question myself for staying with him.

She's relentless. She refuses to give up on Drew, and I'm an obstacle to getting what she wants. She needs me to leave. But if I don't, how far would she go to get rid of me?

32

An hour later, Drew returns to the apartment. While he was gone, I spent more time searching online for anything I could find about Molly and her mom but nothing came up. It's odd someone Molly's age wouldn't have some kind of online presence.

"You can go back to work," Drew says, coming over to me at the table. "I've got everything I need now."

"Yes, I'll get going." I shut the laptop. "I was just looking up something."

"Anything interesting?" he asks, sitting across from me.

"I was looking for the obituary for Molly's mother, but I couldn't find it."

"Not everyone has an obituary."

"I suppose. I just find it odd that I can't find anything about her mother online. I can't find anything about Molly either."

"I'm sure it's there. You just have to look harder. It's a common name. A lot of other people with that name will come up before Molly. She hasn't done anything to earn a place at the top of the search results." He cocks his head to the side. "Why are you looking up Molly?"

"Because I'm still not sure I believe her story. Maybe we should hire someone to do a background check on her."

"We can, but I'm not sure it's necessary."

"Drew, she's having your child. We need to know if she has a criminal background or something else in her past we don't know about."

"Sara, you're the one who's always defending her, and now you think she's a criminal?"

"It's just..." I look away, then back at Drew. "Something she said to me while you were gone. It was strange. I don't know what she meant, but it didn't sit right with me."

"What did she say?"

"That I should leave you." I pause. "Before it's too late."

"Too late for what?"

"I don't know, and when I asked her, she wouldn't answer me." I lower my voice, although there's no way Molly could hear me from her room. "It sounded like a threat. Like if I didn't leave, she'd get rid of me herself." I lean toward Drew. "She wants a future with you. She keeps telling me she doesn't, but I know she does. And I'm in the way of that."

He sighs and leans back. "This is why I keep telling you to be careful around her."

"Yes, but what am I supposed to do? She's living here. I can't avoid her."

"Come on." He stands up. "I need to show you something."

I follow him into the bedroom and shut the door. "What is it? What do you need to show me?"

He goes into the closet and comes out with the suitcase and sets it on the bed.

"Drew, what are you doing?" I ask, my pulse racing.

"You need to know how to use this." He unzips the suitcase and takes out the gun case.

"No." I back away. "Drew, I do not want to see that."

"You need to. You at least need to know the basics of how to use it. Just in case."

"In case of what? Molly can't hurt me. She's nine months pregnant."

"Being pregnant doesn't mean she can't use a gun."

"Then why do we have it in our home?" I say, throwing my hands up. "What if she finds it?"

He takes a key from his pocket and holds it up. "I locked the case. She can't get to it without the key." He puts the key in the lock and opens the case.

Seeing the gun, I immediately tense up. "I'm not using that. I don't even want to touch it."

"Even if it could save your life?" He holds the gun out to me. "Sara, I realize there's probably zero chance that Molly would actually try to kill you, but if there's any part of you that thinks she might, wouldn't you feel better knowing you had a way to protect yourself?" He takes my hand, turns it palm-side up, and places the gun on it.

"It's heavy," I say, staring at the gun. My hand is trembling and I feel breathless because my heart's beating so fast.

"Try holding it," Drew says. "Aim it at the closet."

I look at him. "Is it loaded?"

"No, and the safety is on."

I carefully position the gun in my hand and aim it at the closet door. "I don't like this."

"Why? You're doing great."

I shake my head. "I would never shoot someone. I couldn't do it."

"You could if you had to. Even if you didn't actually shoot it, just holding it and aiming it at whoever's about to attack you could be enough to get them to back down."

"I don't think it'll come to that," I say, lowering the gun. "Molly's on bedrest. She's not going to attack me."

"You're right. She probably won't, but I still feel better now that you've done this." He nods at the gun. "You can put it back now."

I gently set it down in the case, then back away from it.

"I'm proud of you, Sara," Drew says, closing the case and locking it. "You overcame your fear."

"Not really," I mutter as I watch him put the gun case back in the suitcase.

"Later, I'll show you how to load it and take the safety off," Drew says.

"No. I'm done. I don't need to know anything more about guns."

"I was the same way until I was nearly killed."

"Yes, well, let's hope that doesn't happen to me."

He puts the suitcase back in the closet while I sit on the bed, trying to calm my racing heart.

"You okay?" Drew asks, sitting beside me.

"No. I didn't care for that."

He puts his arm around me. "It's all put away. You can relax now."

"I don't feel like going back to work."

"You should go. You keep saying you're falling behind."

"I know, but I can't focus. Every time I try to work on an article, my mind goes to you or Molly or the baby."

"Maybe you just need to be there longer."

"Where? The office?"

"Yes, you've spent more time here the past week than at the office. Once you get back into the routine of being there every day, you'll be better able to focus on work."

"That might be true, but I still don't feel like going back there today. I'm really tired. Maybe I should stay here and get some sleep."

"Then you'll be even more stressed about falling behind." Drew stands up. "Let's go. We'll finish our day, and then tonight, we can relax and maybe watch a movie."

We go back to the kitchen table and I pack up my laptop.

Drew walks me to the door and gives me a kiss. "I'll see you tonight."

On my way to the office, I think back to my life before Molly arrived. Everything was so much simpler when it was just Drew and me. Now we have Molly to think about, and the baby. And Drew and I have to figure out how to repair our marriage.

I'd give anything to go back to our old life, but it's over. I'll never have that life again. And it's all Drew's fault. When I think about that, I get so angry I don't even want to be around him.

"Problems at home?" Marie asks when I'm back at

work. She was coming out of her office as I was passing it in the hall.

I stop and turn to face her. "Drew had to run to the office so I stayed with Molly until he got home."

"You look upset." She frowns. "Did you and Drew have a fight?"

"No, I was just thinking about what he did and it made me angry."

"If you need some time away from him, the invitation is still there."

I pause to consider it. It might be good to get a night away from all the drama at home. "Maybe just for a night."

Marie smiles. "Sure! Just come over after work."

"I'll have to go home and pack an overnight bag." I bite my lip. "Actually, I probably shouldn't do this. Drew will think it means something."

"Let him. The man is putting you through hell. Let him go through his own personal hell for a night. Let him think he's losing you. It'll be good for him."

"I'm not so sure about that."

"Sara, it's one night. You're not moving out."

"Let me give it some more thought."

As the day continues, I go back and forth about whether to stay at Marie's house. Part of me would love to go home and cuddle on the couch with Drew while we watch a movie. But it would only make me miss the past. The life we no longer have because of Drew. Instead of watching the movie, I'd be thinking about Molly being just down the hall, and then I'd think about why she's there, and my thoughts would loop back to the affair.

Sometimes I worry I'll never be able to forgive Drew

for this, or love him the way I used to. Do I really want to be married to a man who cheated on me and lied? Can we really move past this?

By five, I decide I'm going to stay at Marie's house tonight. I need a break from Drew and Molly. I need a break from this whole situation. I don't even want to go home to pack a bag. I'm sure Marie has some clothes I could borrow.

I call Drew. He picks up on the first ring. "Hey, honey! How's work going?"

"I finished an article."

"That's great! What time are you leaving? I just started dinner and—"

"I'm not coming home."

"You're working late?"

"No, I'm leaving, but I'm not coming home."

"I don't understand."

"I need a break, Drew. Just for a night. I'm going to stay at Marie's house."

"Why? What is staying there going to do?"

"I don't know, but I think I need it. I need to be away from the apartment. It doesn't feel like ours anymore. And whenever I'm there, I feel stressed. I need a break."

"Sara, I know you're struggling right now, but running away isn't the answer."

"I'm not running away. It's only for a night. I need this, Drew. I really do."

He sighs. "Okay, but does it have to be tonight? I kind of had something planned."

"What is it?"

"It was supposed to be a surprise, but I guess I have to tell you now. I'm making a nice dinner, and I got that cake you love from your favorite bakery. I also got you flowers, and I might've got you a gift."

"How did you do all that when you weren't able to leave the apartment?"

"I made some stops on my way home from the office. I kept everything in the car so you wouldn't see."

"Why are you doing this? And why tonight?"

"I wanted to do something special for you. I feel like Molly's been getting all my attention, which isn't fair to you. It isn't right. So tonight is all about you. Molly's already had dinner and is going to sleep soon. She won't bother us. It'll just be the two of us."

"Drew, it's really sweet of you to do this, but I already told Marie I'd stay with her."

"You can stay with her tomorrow. Please, Sara. I really want to do this for you. I've been planning it for weeks."

"Weeks?"

"I meant days," he says with a laugh. "Sorry, I'm talking while stirring the sauce. I don't want to burn it."

I look out at the hall and see Marie going by. "Okay, let me go talk to Marie. I'll text you when I'm leaving." I end the call and hurry out to the hall. "Marie!"

She stops and turns back. "Yes?"

I walk over to her. "I changed my mind. I'm not going to stay with you tonight."

She sighs. "Drew talked you out of it?"

"No. Well, kind of. He planned a special evening with flowers and my favorite cake, and he's making a nice dinner. I didn't want to tell him no after he went to all that work. Could I stay with you tomorrow night?"

"Of course, but I doubt it'll happen. It sounds like Drew's working hard to win you back."

I smile. "It's sweet of him to be doing all this."

"It is, but don't let it make you forget what he did. He shouldn't expect you to forgive him just because he made you dinner and bought flowers."

"I know. It'll take more than that for me to forgive him."

"Get out of here," she says with a smile. "You've got dinner waiting."

On my way home, I feel my mood lift and a huge grin take over my face. I'm really happy Drew planned this special night for me. He hasn't done anything like this in years. It's too bad it took having an affair for him to finally do it.

I'm not going to focus on that. I'm going to focus on the good things about Drew. The things that made me fall in love with him. He put a lot of work into this night, and I just want to enjoy it. And enjoy being with my husband again.

It's going to be a great night. I just know it!

33

When I walk into the apartment, I expect to see Drew in the kitchen. But he's not there. And I don't see any pots on the stove. Maybe he already cleaned up, but then where is the food, and why don't I smell it?

"Drew?" I call out.

He doesn't answer. Did he go somewhere? He couldn't have, not with Molly here. Maybe he's in the bedroom and didn't hear me.

I take off my coat and hang it in the closet, then I go to the kitchen and look in the oven. There's nothing inside it. Where is this dinner Drew claimed he was making? And where are the flowers he got me? Looking around, I don't see them anywhere. I also don't see the cake he claims to have bought.

What is going on? Where's Drew, and why did he say he was making dinner when he clearly is not? Does he have something else planned? Is he taking me out? But he can't. We need to keep watch over Molly.

"Drew?" I call out again, but all I hear is silence. I go down the hall and see that both bedroom doors are closed. Drew must be in our room. Maybe he's changing his clothes.

When I open the door, I suck in a breath when I see Molly, standing next to my bed. My muscles tense and my heart beats faster. Why is Molly in my room?

"Hi, Sara." She smiles at me.

"What are you doing in here?" I step into the room, remaining close to the door.

"I was waiting for you. I'm so glad that you're home." She says it in a fake cheerful tone that sounds nothing like her usual voice.

"Molly, I don't know why you're in here, but you need to go. You're supposed to be in bed."

"That whole bedrest thing was made up," she says with a laugh. "I never went to the hospital. Never saw a doctor."

What is she talking about? Of course she went to the hospital. Drew took her there. Does she not remember going?

Something is wrong with her. Her eyes are glazed over and the smile she's giving me isn't friendly or sweet. It's strange, almost maniacal. Did she take something? Some kind of drug? Or am I finally seeing the crazy side of her Drew warned me about?

"Molly, you need to go to your room," I say forcefully. "Now."

"I'm sorry, Sara, but that's not going to happen." The hand that was behind her back appears. My heart nearly stops when I see she's holding a gun.

"Molly, what... what are you doing?" I say, my voice trembling. "Put the gun down."

"I can't do that, Sara." She slowly walks toward me, the gun aimed at my face.

"Why... why are you doing this?"

She stops a few feet in front of me. "I tried to get you to leave him, but you wouldn't do it."

"I will. I promise! I'll do whatever you say! Just put the gun down."

Where the hell is Drew? Did Molly do something to him? Oh, God, what if she killed him? Maybe he went into her room to check on her and she shot him. He could be in there right now, on the floor, bleeding to death. Or dead!

"Molly, please," I beg, my eyes darting back and forth from the gun to her face. "Don't do this. You can have Drew. I'll leave him."

"It's too late, Sara."

"Too late for what?" I say, panicking. "What did you do to him?"

She just laughs.

"Molly, tell me what you did!" I demand. "Where is Drew?"

"Right here." His deep voice startles me. I whip around and see Drew behind me at the door.

"Drew! Thank God!" I rush toward him, but he puts his hands up, stopping me.

"Turn around, Sara," he says in a calm, even tone.

"What?" I say, confused by his reaction. Why is he so calm? Why isn't he panicking like I am? Does he not see what's going on here?

"Drew, Molly has your gun!" I yell. "She—"

"I know," he says, a slight grin on his face. "I gave it to her."

"What do you..." I pause as I realize what's happening.

Drew and Molly. They're still together. They've been

pretending this whole time. Pretending to have no interest in each other so that I wouldn't suspect anything. So that I wouldn't find out their plan.

Their plan to kill me.

"I'm sorry, Sara," Drew says, blocking the door so I can't escape. "I didn't want it to come to this."

34

DREW

I NEVER WANTED my marriage to end this way. I'd planned to be with Sara forever. When we met, she seemed like the perfect wife. She had all the qualities I was looking for. Pretty, but not too pretty. Loves children. Enjoys cleaning, laundry, and other tasks around the home. Knows how to cook. Keeps herself fit and trim. Presents herself well in social situations. I could go on, but you get the point.

Sara was the ideal wife. She had traditional values and knew her place in the marriage. She was like my mother that way, which is just what I wanted.

My mother is a wonderful woman. She's always taken care of everything at home so that my father was free to do as he pleased. He could work late. Go out for drinks with his friends. Golf all weekend. Whatever he did, my mother never complained, even when his activities involved other women. Instead of shaming him for it or demanding he stop, she kept quiet and looked the other way. Because that's what a good wife does. She understands that men have needs that can't always be met within the marriage. As long as her husband continues to provide for his family, she should be grateful and treat him with kindness and respect.

When I met Sara, I thought she'd be that kind of wife. The good kind. And she was, for a while. She kept our apartment spotless. Had dinner ready when I got home. Took care of our errands. Made all our travel plans. Didn't bother me when I was watching sports. I know she wasn't always happy with me, but she kept quiet to avoid arguments.

Sara was exactly what I wanted. A low-maintenance wife who would do most anything to please her husband. But then things started to change. When we moved to Boston, she developed this obsessive trait that I hadn't noticed in her before. It began with finding our apartment. She became obsessed with finding the perfect place. When we finally did, she obsessed over what furniture to buy and what to hang on the walls. Then there was her obsession with organizing. Everything we owned had to have its own place, and if I didn't put it back in that place, Sara would have a fit.

I distinctly remember the time I put my toothbrush on the bathroom counter instead of the holder Sara had bought. She went off on me as if I'd committed a crime. I told myself it was because she was under a lot of stress. She had just started her job at the website and was feeling overwhelmed with everything she needed to learn. I decided that was the reason for her outburst about the toothbrush. I was sure it wouldn't happen again.

But then it did. She continued to throw a fit every time I didn't put something where she wanted it. And then the schedules began. Schedules for when lights were to be turned on and off. Schedules for when the sheets and towels had to be changed. She had a schedule for everything. Luckily, most of them were for her, not me. She used them to stay on top of her housework so that she wouldn't fall behind.

Looking back, the night of the toothbrush incident is when I first realized Sara was not the perfect wife. I decided I no longer loved her. Honestly, I'm not sure I ever did. But I loved what she could do for me. She had value, but that value was quickly fading as her obsessive side took over and I felt like she was trying to control me.

I could've divorced her, but I didn't want to start over with someone else, so I decided to try to make it work. After all, Sara wasn't all bad. She was still a devoted wife, and I knew she'd be an excellent mother. Sara adores children. I knew once we had them, she'd devote every minute to their care and I'd be free to do as I pleased, without Sara questioning me.

Unfortunately, having children wasn't as easy as we thought. We tried for months, which turned into years. We finally decided to consult with a fertility specialist, but all of them had a waiting list. Last week would've been our first appointment, but it was cancelled, and Sara didn't reschedule. It's almost as if she knew what was coming.

I certainly didn't. When I found out Molly was pregnant, I was shocked. I've been cheating on Sara for years without any problems. I'm always careful to protect myself, but the night Molly got pregnant, I let my guard down. I got swept up in the moment and forgot to use protection. When it was over, I realized what I'd done but told myself there was no possible way she'd get pregnant after one time.

Turns out I was wrong.

I've known for about a month. That's when Molly reappeared in my life. It's also when I realized she was more disturbed than I thought — even more than she was last May.

I'm not sure what the correct term is for Molly's condition, but it involves being unable to tell reality from fiction. She makes up stories about herself and believes they're real. For instance, when I first met Molly, she said she was an actor from New York in town for an audition. The next time I saw her, she said she was a nanny in Connecticut and was in town to see her mother. At first, I thought it was some kind of fantasy, like she was creating a character for the night to spice things up. I played along and found myself liking it. It was new and different and made every encounter with her exciting.

Molly was unlike any woman I'd been with. I loved that she was wild and uninhibited. I loved that I could tell her anything and she didn't judge me for it. Like my feelings about my wife. I told Molly that Sara was rigid and controlling and had all these rules she expected me to follow. I told her I dreaded going home, and that I hated Sara and would fantasize about her dying in a car crash or getting hit by a bus. Most people would be horrified to hear that, but Molly smiled. She said I should do it. That I should get rid of my wife. She said life's too short to be unhappy.

I thought she was kidding. I wasn't seriously going to kill my wife. But then I went home later and couldn't get the thought out of my head. What if I did it? What if I killed Sara? How would I do it? And could I do it without getting caught?

When I saw Molly again, I told her I wanted to get a gun. I didn't say why, but she knew. How could she not? I had just talked about killing my wife.

Molly knew all about guns. She told me exactly what to buy and where to get it. Listening to her talk about this aroused me in a way I can't describe. We barely made it up to the room. That was the night Molly got pregnant.

As we were getting dressed to leave, she told me she was a flight attendant and had to fly to Phoenix in the morning. I was confused. We'd already had sex, so why was she making up a new character? That's when I realized she wasn't pretending to be someone else. She actually thought she was that person.

After that, I decided I never wanted to see her again. I didn't go back to that hotel for over a month. I told Sara I wanted to go out of town for our anniversary in June because I had to get out of Boston. Throughout the entire summer, I found myself looking for Molly everywhere I went. I thought for sure she'd find me, even though I'd given her a fake name and told her I lived in Maryland.

By September, I finally started to relax. I convinced myself Molly was out of my life for good. But then, months later, she showed up again. I'd worked late that day. It was after ten when I left the office. I went out to my car and there she was, holding a gun at me. That story I told Sara about being held at gunpoint? It wasn't some random guy. It was Molly. She looked insane. Her hair was a mess, her eyes were lined with thick black eyeliner, and she had on this red lipstick that had smeared onto her cheeks.

When I asked her what she was doing, she said she

was there to tell me about the baby and that I was the father. I didn't believe her, but I wasn't going to argue with her when she had a gun aimed at me. She said she'd kill me if I didn't agree to marry her. I reminded her that I was already married, but Molly didn't seem to care. She demanded I marry her or she'd kill me right then and there. So I agreed to it. I told her we'd get married, but not right away. I needed to get things in order. I needed to get divorced, which takes time.

Molly didn't want to wait. She told me to kill Sara, and to do it as soon as I got home. I explained to her that killing Sara meant I'd go to prison for life. I wouldn't be around to be her husband or the baby's father. I asked Molly to give me time to think of a solution in which Sara was dead, but I didn't end up in prison. Molly reluctantly agreed, then demanded I give her money to cover her expenses until we could be together. She finally let me leave, but said she'd be back in a week to discuss my plan to get rid of Sara.

The next day, I decided I had to kill Molly. I'd use the gun I'd bought last May. I'd ask her to meet me in a remote location late at night, saying I wanted to talk, and then I'd shoot her so she'd no longer be a problem.

I was ready to do it until I saw a man walking down the street with his son and realized I couldn't kill Molly, because I'd also be killing my son. The son I've wanted for years. I'd have to wait and kill Molly after my son was born. There was no way I was letting his psychopath mother raise him. But what if I got caught? I wouldn't be around for my child.

I felt trapped. I didn't know what to do. I had to get rid of Molly, but I couldn't risk going to prison. And what about Sara? Ever since I talked about killing her,

I've fantasized about doing it, playing out different scenarios in my head. But how could I kill her and get away with it? I decided I couldn't do it myself. The police always suspect the husband. I'd need to find someone else.

Molly. The answer came to me in the middle of the night. And it was brilliant! Molly would kill Sara. She wanted Sara dead, and she was crazy enough to do it. Molly would be charged with murder and go to prison for life. I'd be rid of Molly and Sara, and have my son all to myself.

It was the perfect plan. There was just one problem. Molly wouldn't agree to the plan if it meant she might end up in prison. She wanted to be around for her son. I had to find a way to convince Molly she could kill Sara and not be locked away for the rest of her life.

By the time I met with Molly again, I'd figured it out. I'd set it up to make it look like Sara was so jealous of Molly for having my baby that it drove her to try to kill her. But before Sara could shoot Molly, I'd walk in, startle Sara, and she'd drop the gun. Molly would grab it and shoot Sara, saving both our lives. Molly and I would tell the police it was self-defense, and Molly wouldn't be charged.

That's what I told Molly, but what would really happen is I'd tell the police Molly murdered my wife. I'd describe how Molly had this fantasy of marrying me, and when I told her I wasn't leaving my wife, Molly became enraged and killed Sara.

Before all this could happen, I had to get everything set up. These things would take time. I told Molly to be patient and that I'd let her know when it was time to tell Sara about her.

I should've known Molly wouldn't listen. When she showed up at my apartment, I wanted to strangle her. She was deviating from the plan. She was supposed to stay hidden until the timing was right.

When I got her alone, Molly told me she didn't have a choice but to show up when she did. The elderly woman she'd been living with passed away and her house had been sold. Molly had to get out of there, but she had nowhere to go. Instead of telling me this so I could find her alternate housing, she tracked down Sara, who offered to let Molly live with us.

When Sara found out about Molly, I had to speed up the plan. I couldn't trust what either of them would do. I told Molly I wanted Sara dead within the week so that she and I could begin our life together. Molly said it wasn't enough time. That I didn't have the evidence to prove it was self-defense. She worried she'd go to prison. I assured her that wouldn't happen, then took the steps to prove it. I recorded Sara saying she hated Molly and wanted to kill her. I showed that Sara was losing her mind by doing odd things like rearranging the kitchen in the middle of the night, or not remembering the suitcase she bought, which was actually purchased by me. I brought the evidence to Molly and convinced her the police would see the shooting as Molly simply defending herself from my clearly deranged wife.

I was ready to do it. I thought Molly was too, but then she started having second thoughts. She started to like Sara and wasn't sure she should kill her. I was infuriated with Molly. And with Sara. Why was my wife being nice to the woman I had an affair with? That wasn't something I expected, and I couldn't let it continue. I tried to convince Sara that Molly was a con artist and dangerous and that we had to get her out of our apartment. Then I did things with Molly to make Sara jealous.

I eventually got Sara to admit that she hated Molly, and yet she still wanted to help her, which made absolutely no sense. But I couldn't worry about it. I needed to focus on Molly and remind her why we were doing this. I described the future that awaited us once Sara was gone. A future in which she and I were married and had a beautiful home where we would raise our son. I asked Molly to describe the type of house she wanted and how she wanted to decorate it, so she'd feel like it was actually going to happen. I had her describe our wedding and the type of dress she would wear. I used her delusional mind to my advantage, letting her live in this fantasy so she'd do what had to be done to get it.

It worked. Molly went back to seeing Sara as the enemy. An obstacle to getting what she wanted. She couldn't wait to get rid of her.

The plan was back on track, which brings us to now. It's finally happening. In a few short moments, it'll all be over.

35

SARA

"He's lying," Molly says. "He's wanted this since I met him." I turn back and see her looking at Drew. "He hates you. He hates being married to you. He complains about you constantly. He wants to get rid of you."

"Then divorce me," I say, whipping back to Drew. "You... you don't have to kill me. We'll get divorced and you can be with Molly."

"Divorce means giving you half my ownership in the firm," he says. "You know how many years it took for me to make partner? All that work, and you think I'll just give you half?"

"Take it! I don't want it!" I lock my eyes on his. "Drew, please, you can't do this. You're my husband. You love me."

"I don't love you," Drew scoffs. "What Molly said is true. I hate you! I hate that you're always trying to control me. That you demand everything be your way. That you have this sick obsession with organizing every damn thing we own!" He smirks. "I'm the one who rearranged the kitchen. And I loved every second of it. But even better was seeing how upset it made you."

"Drew, I'm sorry, but—"

"No!" he shouts. "It's my turn to talk!" He narrows his eyes. "No one should have to live this way. I tried, Sara. I really did. I tried to get along with you despite your need to control everything. But then I met Molly, and I finally felt free. I'd forgotten what that was like. But now that I know, I see how awful my life was with you."

"Then we'll get divorced!" I rush to say. "We'll—"

"Divorce wouldn't end this. You'd just go do this to another man. And another after him. Someone has to stop you, Sara."

He's completely lost his mind. While it's true I'm a bit obsessive about having an organized house, that's not a reason to kill me! And if he thought I was being controlling, why didn't he just talk to me? He always acts like everything's fine. I had no idea he felt this way. Why did he say he loved me and wanted to save our marriage if the truth was he hated me? Was he trying to mess with my mind before he killed me?

Seeing this side of Drew, I realize he's just as crazy as Molly. No wonder they were drawn to each other. They're both insane!

How did I not know this about him? How did I go this long without seeing this violent and unhinged side of Drew?

"I know you're angry at me," I say to him. "But you don't have to kill me."

Drew's eyes dart to Molly. "Do it. I'm sick of listening to her."

"No!" I turn to Molly. "Don't do it! You'll go to prison! You'll never see your baby!"

"It was self-defense," she says. "Right, Drew?"

I look back at him. "What is she talking about?"

"You were jealous of Molly," Drew says. "You hated that she was having my baby." He takes out his phone, and moments later I hear my voice coming from the speakers. It's the conversation Drew and I had about Molly, when Drew asked if I was jealous of her. He kept pushing me to talk, to express how I felt about Molly. He got me to say what he wanted so he could use it against me.

"You want to know how I really feel?" I hear myself say on the recording. "I want to kill her."

Drew shuts off the recording and smiles at me. "You admitted you wanted to kill Molly. And I was here to watch it happen. You went to shoot her, but I knocked the gun from your hand. Molly picked it up and shot you. She had no choice. She had to save herself, and save our baby."

"No one would believe that," I snap. "People know I would never do that."

"I was here. I saw you do it. And so did Molly. We both witnessed what happened. And your fingerprints are on the gun."

That's why Drew insisted I hold the gun yesterday. He wanted my prints to be on it.

I feel like I'm going to be sick. Drew has been betraying me for months. Maybe longer. Plotting against me. Wanting me dead.

"How long have you been planning this?" I ask.

"What's it been?" Drew asks Molly. "About a month?"

"That sounds right," she says.

I turn back to Molly and see the gun still aimed at me.

"She showed up outside my office building," Drew says, "and told me about the baby. Asked if I wanted to be involved. Obviously, I did, and we've been seeing each other ever since."

He must've been with her all those nights and weekends he claimed he was working late. He was planning a future with her while planning to kill me.

"You were never homeless," I say to Molly. "That whole story was a lie."

"But it worked." She laughs.

"Sara has a good heart," Drew says. "Unfortunately, it can be used against her."

Molly frowns, her eyes on me. "I think it's sweet. She was so nice to me, a total stranger. Even after she found out who I was, she was still nice to me. I never had anyone care about me like that." Molly's eyes go to Drew. "Even you."

"Enough talking," he snaps. "Hurry up and shoot her!"

"Molly, no!" I yell. "Don't listen to him! You don't have to do this!"

She tightens her grip on the gun. Her finger moves over the trigger.

She's really going to do it. Molly's going to kill me! And Drew's going to watch her do it!

My life is about to end, and nobody will know the truth about what really happened. My parents. My friends. People at work. They'll all believe my jealousy of Molly drove me to try to kill her. Drew and Molly will tell the police that it was me who caused this. That Molly had no choice but to shoot me.

"What the hell are you waiting for?" Drew shouts at Molly.

"She's standing too close to you," Molly says. "She needs to move or you risk getting shot."

Drew shoves me to the side so I'm standing against the wall. He remains at the door, blocking it.

"That's perfect," Molly says, grinning as she aims the gun at me.

"Molly, I'm begging you! Don't—" I stop when I see the gun jerk to the right. It fires, and my eyes dart over to Drew. There's a red dot on his shirt that's growing larger by the second. I look down at myself and see nothing.

Molly didn't shoot me. She shot Drew!

Looking back at him, I see his eyes widen as he stares down at his chest, his expression one of utter disbelief.

"What the hell?" he screams at Molly. "You shot me, you idiot!"

"You were never going to be with me," she calmly says. "All you wanted was the baby."

"That's not true!" Drew drops to his knees, clutching his chest.

My instinct is to help him. To call the police. Call an ambulance. But something's holding me back. I see him there, about to die, and yet I can't seem to make myself do anything.

What does that say about me? Does it mean I'm a horrible person? Or am I just so sickened by what he's done that I don't think he deserves to live?

"We had it all planned out," Drew says to Molly. "The house. Where we'd live."

"You were lying," she says, watching as he collapses onto his back. "You didn't mean any of it. You only said it so I'd go along with your plan to kill Sara." She steps closer to Drew, still holding the gun. "I talked to that lawyer you hired. She told me you were trying to get full custody. That you were going to take the baby from me."

"No," Drew mutters, his eyes struggling to stay open, his breaths slowing down. "You misunderstood. That's not—"

"Stop lying!" Molly shouts. "You never wanted *me*. You only wanted the baby. You were going to take him from me!"

"He never should've done that," I say to Molly. "A child should be with his mother."

Molly glances at me, then back at Drew. "Sara's a good person. Unlike you, she actually cares about me. She doesn't deserve to die."

Molly's not going to shoot me? I thought I was next. She's right there, a few feet away, holding the gun. All she'd have to do is aim it at me and shoot.

"Bye, Drew," Molly mutters, a tear going down her cheek. She loved him, or she thought she did. Maybe she loved the version of him she thought he was, just like I did. We both loved a version of a man who didn't exist.

Drew's eyes are shut, and I don't hear him breathing anymore. His shirt is covered in blood, soaked in it.

"Molly, please put down the gun," I say, my voice shaking.

She lowers it to her side but doesn't set it down. "I want you to take the baby."

"What do you mean?" I ask, trying to process what she said. My mind's still trying to comprehend the fact that Drew is dead, and that Molly isn't going to kill me. Or maybe she will. I'm still not certain I'm safe.

"When I go to prison." Molly glances at her stomach. "I don't want him going into foster care." She looks at me. "Please take him, Sara. You'll be a good mom. Better than me."

"Molly, I'm sure you'll be a wonderful mother," I say, trying to reassure her.

She shakes her head. "I won't. I don't know how. My own mom was horrible to me. She taught me how to abuse a kid, not how to take care of one."

"I don't understand. You told me your mother was—"

"Ow!" Molly cringes and leans forward.

"What is it? What's wrong?"

"It hurts. A lot." She drops the gun, and I shudder as I hear the hard metal clank against the floor. "Do something," Molly groans, gripping her stomach.

"I'll call for an ambulance!" I step over Drew and race to the kitchen where I left my phone. I call the emergency number, and a woman answers.

"What is your emergency?" the woman asks.

"There's a pregnant woman here in a lot of pain. She's due in a few weeks, or she might be having the baby now. I don't know. I need help."

She asks for my location, and I rattle off the apartment number and street address.

"I'm going to get someone there," she says. "But stay on the phone with me. I need to—"

"Wait! There's something else."

"Yes? What is it?"

"I need you to send the police."

"Why do you need the police?"

I pause to figure out how to say this. Do I go with the truth, or a version that might protect Molly from going to prison?

"My husband," I blurt out. "He's dead."

"How? Can you tell me what happened?"

I need to make a decision. A decision that will determine how I want the future to go. One that I feel is right. For me, the baby, and for Molly.

"The woman having the baby," I say. "Her name is Molly. And she... she killed my husband."

36

ONE YEAR LATER - SARA

"Come to Mommy," I say to Will as he crawls toward me, eyes wide, a big grin on his chubby face. I pick him up and kiss his cheek. "You did such a good job!"

He giggles and claps his hands as drool dribbles down his chin. I reach over to the basket and grab a clean cloth to wipe up the drool. This is why it pays to be organized. When you need something, it's there. You don't have to go searching for it.

Will is teething, so he's constantly drooling. Knowing this, I've set up baskets in every room filled with soft cotton cloths so I can quickly and easily deal with the drool. Having a baby has greatly enhanced my organization skills. There are so many supplies to manage and keep in their proper place. Every room in the house has exactly what I need, neatly stored in labeled containers.

If Drew were still alive, he'd complain about my system. He'd say it's too rigid or too hard to maintain. It just shows that we were never a good match. When I met Drew, I thought he would be perfect for me because of his profession. I assumed an accountant would appreciate my attention to detail and adherence to order. But Drew wasn't that type of accountant, which I didn't know until we were already married. There's so much I didn't know about Drew. For instance, after his death I discovered he'd been with not just Molly, but many other women. All women he'd met at the hotel bar.

The truth about Drew came out a few weeks after his funeral. A man who used to hang out at the bar with Drew contacted me and asked if we could meet for coffee. He said he knew things about my husband but wasn't sure if telling me would make me feel worse or better, so he let me decide. I told him I wanted to know everything and to not hold back.

The man said Drew would meet women at the bar, give them a fake name, and say he was from out of town. Drew told this man that being someone else for a night was exciting and freeing, which was how he described being with Molly.

I'll never know why Drew chose someone like me, with my rules and structure, if his desire was to be with someone who was the opposite of that. Perhaps he found comfort in my orderly ways, a calm amidst the chaos he had with his affairs. But over time, it seems he craved the chaos of his other life more than the certainty he got at home.

It's hard to say what was going on in Drew's head. Sometimes I wonder if he had some type of personality disorder that caused him to act one way at home and another way outside of it. How else do I explain why he acted as though he wanted a future with me, and yet hated me and wanted to kill me? It's as though he had different versions of himself living inside his head.

Molly's the same way. After her arrest, I found out she'd been wanted by the police on multiple fraud charges. Apparently, she has a long history of making up stories about herself and living them out as though they were true. She'd use these stories to convince people to give her money or a place to stay. Part of her knows what she's saying isn't true, but the part of her that believes it is what makes the stories so convincing.

For example, I found out that before I met her she had been living with an elderly woman for free in exchange for taking care of her. When the woman died, her house was sold and Molly had to move out. She didn't have anywhere to go, so she showed up at the cafe, pretending to be homeless so I'd take her in. But in her mind, part of her actually believed she had been living in the park. She also believed the elderly woman she lived with was her mother. The story Molly told me about caring for her mother before she died was about that elderly woman, not Molly's actual mother.

I talked to a psychologist friend about this and he said this type of belief system can develop after a deeply traumatic childhood. To escape the pain of the past, the person dissociates from reality and creates an imaginary life for themselves. A life that erases all memories of the past.

Knowing that made me curious about Molly's actual past, specifically her mother. I hired a private investigator who discovered Molly's mother is not dead, but living in Oklahoma with her husband, Molly's stepfather. The investigator found police records in which Molly accused her stepfather of abusing her, but her mother denied it and he was never charged. The investigator tracked down one of Molly's childhood friends who told him Molly left town after high school and never went back. She said her parents were dead to her and that she never wanted to see them again.

If I ask Molly about her mother, she still refers to the elderly woman. It's as though she has no memory of her actual mother. As for the other things Molly told me, they were also made up. She never worked as a nanny and never lived in New York. But to this day, if you ask her about it, she'll talk about the stories as if they were true.

It's because of this that Molly's lawyer considered using the insanity defense in her trial, but then decided not to after a psychologist met with Molly and found her delusions weren't enough to diagnose her as being insane. He said she's simply letting her mind rewrite the past in a way she wishes it had happened. She did the same for her future. She imagined a future in which she was living with Drew and they were raising their son together. But as Molly figured out, Drew never intended to be with her. The moment he learned she was pregnant, he began coming up with his plan to use Molly to kill me so she'd be locked away, I'd be dead, and he'd get the baby.

His plan almost worked. Molly told me she had every intention of killing me but was hoping it wouldn't come to that since she actually liked me. So she tried to convince me to get a divorce. That's why she kept telling me Drew was dangerous. I thought she was lying, but she was actually telling the truth. Drew *was* dangerous, but so was Molly, especially since Drew told her she had to kill me before their life together could begin. Molly said that every time Drew was alone with her, he'd talk about their wedding and the house they'd live in with a big yard where their son could run and play. It was everything Molly wanted to hear. The life she always wanted.

But then she got the call. The call from Drew's lawyer telling her that Drew had no plans to marry her and was going to take full custody of their son. The lawyer went on to say that Drew would tell the court she was an unfit mother and that he had evidence to prove it. By the end of that short, five-minute call, Molly knew that everything Drew had told her was a lie. She was devastated. She was crying before the lawyer could even finish the call.

I know this because it wasn't the lawyer who called her. Drew's actual lawyer would never do that. She was working behind the scenes, preparing a case against Molly, who wasn't supposed to find out what Drew was planning. But I felt Molly had a right to know. So I called her and pretended to be Drew's lawyer. Drew would say I betrayed him, but I felt it was necessary. It isn't right to take a child from his mother.

That's actually not the real reason I made the call, but it was certainly in the back of my mind. The real reason I told Molly what Drew was up to was because I thought it would make her get over her fantasy of being with him. I thought if she knew Drew only wanted custody of the baby, and not her, she'd finally stop trying to get me to divorce him. Of course, this was before I knew of Drew's plans for me.

On that horrible day when I thought Molly was going to kill me, I assumed that call I'd made as Drew's lawyer had been a waste of time. It clearly had no impact on Molly if she was still willing to murder me for Drew. I assumed she'd gone to Drew, confronted him about his plans to take the baby, and he convinced her it wasn't true.

But that's not what happened. Molly told me later that she'd changed the plan for killing me after she got that call. She decided to play along with what Drew told her to do until the very last moment, when she'd turn the gun on him instead of me.

Without knowing it at the time, I ended up saving my own life. That fake phone call woke Molly up to see that Drew's vision of their future was never going to happen. And finding out he saw her as an unfit mother had her thinking it might be true. She wanted her son to have the best possible life, and she decided he would have that life with me.

Molly had the baby on the day she shot Drew. She signed over full custody to me. I took the baby home while Molly was taken to jail. It's been a year now, and she's never asked to see him and doesn't ask about him.

My phone rings. I smile when I see it's Marie calling. I no longer work for her, but we've remained friends. She's been a huge help as I adjust to being a single mother. With my own mother several hours away, she's unable to assist me in the daily challenges of caring for a young child. So Marie has stepped in and helped. She's the first person I call when my parenting skills are tested and I'm not sure what to do.

"Hi, Marie," I say. "I was just thinking about you. I was wondering if you'd like to meet for lunch this weekend."

"I'd love to, but I'm taking my oldest to her dance

competition in Worcester. We won't be home until Sunday night. But the following weekend could work."

"Let's plan on it, and if it doesn't work, just let me know."

Since leaving my job, I find I have to force myself to get out and socialize. Otherwise, I'd spend every minute at home with Will, which sounds like a dream, but I do sometimes miss adult conversation.

"How's that darling little boy of yours?" Marie asks. "Any new teeth?"

"No, but he's working on it," I say, dabbing more drool from his chin.

"How's everything else?" Marie says in a more serious tone. "Are you nervous about the trial?"

"A little, but I really just want to get it over with. I'm dreading having to relive that time in my life."

Molly's trial is next week. I have to testify and tell my side of the story, which isn't the actual story about Molly plotting to kill me. It's one in which Molly was obsessed with Drew, and when he told her he wasn't leaving me, she went into a rage and shot him. That's the story she told the police when they arrived on the scene, and I decided not to dispute it. If I had, she'd have spent the majority of her life in prison. I didn't feel that was right. The more I've learned about Molly, the more compassion I have for her and what she's been through. She definitely should be punished for what she did, but life in prison seems far too harsh.

The revised version of the story makes what Molly did a crime of passion, meaning she acted in the moment. It wasn't premeditated. She's been charged with voluntary manslaughter, which carries a much lighter punishment than first-degree murder. Add in her fraud charges and her lawyer said she could get up to twenty years in prison, but it's likely she'll serve less than that. She'll be released in time to see Will become a young man and maybe get married and have children. Or she might decide she doesn't want to be involved in his life. It's too soon to say.

Will fusses and wiggles in my arms, wanting to get down. "Marie, I need to go, but let's touch base next week about lunch."

"Sounds good. Give Will a hug from me."

"I will. Bye, Marie." I end the call and carry Will out of his bedroom and down to his playroom.

Two months after Drew died, I moved out of the apartment and into a beautiful home with a large back yard. I saw the house online the day before I met Molly. I absolutely loved it from the photos and was going to contact the agent but wanted to talk to Drew first. Then Molly arrived and I forgot all about it. After Drew's funeral, I checked to see if the house was still for sale. It was, so I went to see it. I made an offer that day, which is not like me at all. I usually need months to decide on a purchase that big, but this time I didn't. I knew this was the right house, and the money I got when Drew died was more than enough to pay for it.

"What should we play with today?" I say to Will as I set him down on the carpeted floor of the playroom.

"Ball!" he yells, his eyes lit up as he points to the yellow basket.

"Okay! Go get it!" I say, smiling at him.

He toddles toward the basket, then stumbles and falls and decides to crawl the rest of the way. Sometimes, I wish Drew were alive to see his son. Will looks exactly like him. I hope that's the only way they're alike. I would never want Will to turn out like his father.

I'll make sure that doesn't happen. Will is already showing signs that he's much more like me than Drew or Molly. Like now, as I watch him take a ball from the yellow basket, he's careful not to tip the basket over, knowing Mommy doesn't like a mess. And when he's done playing with the ball, he knows to put it back in the yellow basket. Not the red one. Not the green one. But the yellow one, where the balls are stored.

If Drew were able to see Will following in my footsteps, he'd be furious. He'd want Will to be messy and to have no schedules or rules. But Drew is gone, and I can raise his son as I please. I'll teach him to be good and kind and to value an organized home.

"All done!" Will says, holding up the ball.

"Already?" I watch as he nods. "Okay."

He toddles over to the yellow basket and sets the ball in it. He never leaves his toys out. He always puts them away exactly where they belong.

It fills my heart with joy to see Will becoming more and more like me.

He may have Drew's genes, but he's definitely my son.

Printed in Dunstable, United Kingdom

77344714R00173